WINNER – Switchyard Ale Refreshing Book Award
WINNER – Warburton Prize for a Book of Medium Length
SHORTLISTED – Transatlantic Writers' Circle Puffin Prize

Praise for *How I Became a Famous Novelist:*

"I want to climb onto the roof of every bookstore in the country, throwing copies of *How I Became a Famous Novelist* at people and screaming 'READ THIS BOOK!' through a megapowered bullhorn."
—Ted Easkey, Warburton Prize–winning author of *A Fire in the Entrails*

"If you've ever read a book by James Patterson, John Grisham, Tom Clancy, Nora Roberts, or Dan Brown, then read this book."
—*Boston News-Intelligencer*

"With [*How I Became a Famous Novelist*], Hely enters into battle not just with the lords of the best-seller list, but with Twain, Melville, and the great ghosts of American letters; when he emerges after 322 pages, he's got a fat lip, two black eyes, and he's bleeding from the head, but he's still grinning, as if to say, 'is that all you got?' "
—*Sarasota Post*

"You wish to do more with this book than read it. You must eat it, consume it, make it a part of your physical form, as it is already consuming your mind space. It must have physical space too. It demands it." —Susanne Freidegger, author of *Myopia Dystopia*

"America's Cervantes has appeared."
—Sarah Bidgood, MSNBC's "Back of Book"

"Steve Hely is a like a giggling leprechaun, running through a bookstore lighting fire to everything in sight. And you find yourself rooting for him." —*Silverlake Review* (Book of the Week)

"I know that a novel is truly excellent if I feel obliged to set aside a long history of seething bitterness and call my ex-wife to tell her about it. After finishing this book, I prepared a gimlet for myself and dialed the hated digits. 'Marguerite? It's Ro. You must read *How I Became a Famous Novelist* by Steve Hely.' It was the first time we'd spoken in eight years."
—Ronald Campbell, editor, *Campbell's Review of Books*

HOW
I
BECAME
A
FAMOUS
NOVELIST

HOW I BECAME A FAMOUS NOVELIST

STEVE HELY

Black Cat
a paperback original imprint of Grove/Atlantic, Inc.
New York

Published simultaneously in Canada
Printed in the United States of America

FIRST EDITION

ISBN-13: 978-0-8021-7060-6

Black Cat
a paperback original imprint of Grove/Atlantic, Inc.
841 Broadway
New York, NY 10003

Distributed by Publishers Group West

www.groveatlantic.com

09 10 11 12   10 9 8 7 6 5 4 3 2 1

HOW
I
BECAME
A
FAMOUS
NOVELIST

PART I

RAGS TO RICHES

1

In strewn banners that lay like streamers from a longago parade the sun's fading seraphim rays gleamed onto the hood of the old Ford and ribboned the steel with the meek orange of a June tomato straining at the vine. From the back seat, door open, her nimble fingers moved along the guitar like a weaver's on a loom. Stitching a song. The cloth she made was a cry of aching American chords, dreamlike warbles built to travel miles of lonesome road. They faded into the twilight, and Silas leaned back on the asphalt, as if to watch them drift into the Arkansas mist.

Away from them, across the field of low-cut durum wheat, they saw Evangeline's frame, outlined pale in shadow against the highway sky, as it trembled.

That's the way it is with a song, isn't it? she said. The way it quivers in your heart. Quivers like the wing of a little bird.

In a story too. He spoke it softly in a voice that let her hear how close they were. That's the way it is with a story. Turns your heart into a bird.

—from *The Tornado Ashes Club,* by Pete Tarslaw (me)

You have to understand how bad things were for me back then.

I'd leave my radio alarm set to full volume at the far end of the AM dial, so every morning at seven-thirty I'd wake up to static mixed with a rabid minister screeching in Haitian Creole, because for sheer bracing power that sound cannot be bested. When the alarm went off I'd have no choice but to eject myself from my bed, panting, infuriated, flailing everywhere. I'd have to pee really bad.

There'd be either one or two beer bottles filled with urine next to my bed. I used to drink five or six beers before going to sleep, but I'm much too lazy to get up in the night to go to the bathroom. My roommate Hobart, who was a med student, only once brought up the public health implications of this arrangement. My feeling was, if he wanted to do something about it, terrific.

Sometimes I'd wake up wearing my jeans. I wore jeans daily because jeans can double as a napkin, and sometimes I fell asleep without bothering to take them off. So, often when I woke up I'd be covered in a film of sick feverish sweat. This was a blessing in a way, because it forced me to take a daily shower, which otherwise I might've done without.

Walking into the kitchen, I'd shove my hand into a crumpled bag of kettle-cooked sour cream and chives potato chips. Two fistfuls made breakfast. This seemed only a few steps removed from a healthy plate of hash browns like a farmer eats. Next I'd open a 20 oz. Mountain Dew. Coffee-making is a process for which I'd had no patience ever since one time when we ran out of filters and I thought I could use an old shirt. You can't use an old shirt. Bad results for floor, coffee, shirt, and the jeans I was wearing at the time.

This was a good system anyway because it involved no dishes. In the novel *Cockroaches Convene,* there's that great scene where Proudfoot puts his dirty dishes in the back of a pickup truck and drives through a car wash. Sometimes I wished I had a pickup truck so I could do that.

The Mountain Dew acquired an extra kick because I'd multitask by drinking it in the shower. Traces of soap and Herbal Essences would get into the bottle. This is called "bonus spice."

After dressing I'd get in my Camry, with which I had an abusive and codependent relationship. I'd pull out of the driveway, bashing up the fender a little on the wooden beams that held up the garage. It deserved that. But the car knew I really loved it.

In the car I'd listen to Donnie Vebber. He's this borderline fascist talk radio host who advocates, among other things, rounding up illegal immigrants and then deporting them to Iran and we'll see how the Islamopigs like it when they're selling their burritos and pushing their twelve kids in shopping carts around the streets of Tehran. Another plan of his is a nuclear first strike against China. I don't agree with this, I should point out. I listened to Donnie Vebber in the hopes that he'd rouse some scintilla of emotion or outrage in me. But I numbed to it fast. Then and now I thought about politics with the indifference a grizzled city coroner has toward the body of a murdered prostitute.

I'd drive south out of Boston down I-93, past those oil tanks by the harbor, until I got to the place where all the clams and mussels were dying of unknown bacterial wasting disease. The tidal marshes gave off a car-permeating stink. Then I'd follow Old Town Road past St. Agnes High, where I'd wait in front of the rectory and watch the half-Asian girl with the monstrous rack and her friend Sad-Eyes as they pulled cigarettes out of improbable folds in their uniforms. They'd smoke and I'd switch the radio to classic rock, except in November through January when the classic rock station turned to all-Christmas songs.

On Tuesdays the girls had chapel or something so I'd just go straight to work.

The Alexander Hamilton Building had little in common with its namesake, unless he was a brick man who squatted next to a bog. Hamilton was at one end of Founders Office Park, where in buildings named after Washington and Jefferson people managed mail-order sporting goods businesses, investigated insurance fraud, planned trips to Maui and so forth.

In the lobby of the Hamilton Building there was a koi pond. I loved the koi pond. I was jealous of those fish. Fat, lumpy, blissful. Their time was theirs, to do as they wished: open and close their mouths, float, suck the algae off rocks. Perhaps I would have used my freedom differently. But the koi were living much the way I wished to.

Exiting the elevator on the third floor, I would pass Lisa at her desk. She was a mountainous black woman who served as receptionist for a team of small-claims lawyers. At first I thought she was a cheery, lovely presence. On account of my undernourished physique, she frequently offered to take me home and "put some meat on those bones." This seemed cute and charming, and I'd grin and say "any time!"

But then she started adding that when she got me home she was also going to give me a bath. "I'll scrub you good. Scrub that dirt out of your hair." There were more and more details about the bath each time—which parts of me she was going to wash, and how, and with what kind of soap. I took to scurrying past while pretending to read the newspaper.

Thinking back on it now, this is about the only affectionate human contact I had around this time, and I guess I really appreciated it. On this particular day, Lisa was on the phone, but she stared at me and made a vigorous scrubbing motion. I hurried along, eyes on the rug.

This was a Friday. It wasn't going to be too bad. I was carrying Hobart's copy of last Sunday's *New York Times,* and there'd be ample time for going on the Internet, looking at pictures of pandas, YouTubes of Danish girls singing karaoke, cats on record players, kids in Indiana launching themselves from homemade catapults. (Remember, this was a few years ago— the Internet was much less sophisticated.)

My only assignment was Mr. Hoshi Tanaka. I had to write him a business school essay.

The company I worked for was called EssayAides. On its sleek brochures, EssayAides stated their goal of "connecting minds and expanding educational opportunities around the globe. Our 200+ associates, trained at the finest American colleges and universities, provide the highest level of admissions consulting."

What that meant "on the ground," as Jon Sturges was fond of saying, was that a wealthy kid would send us some gibberish words. We'd turn those into a polished application essay for college or grad school.

This raises ethical issues, if you care to bother yourself with them. I'd worked at the company for three years. It's not my fault the world is a nexus of corrupt arrangements through which the privileged channel power and resources in complex, self-serving loops. I needed to pay for Mountain Dew.

Many of the clients were rich American kids. They'd be applying to Middlebury or Pomona or wherever, and they'd send you something about how *Anchorman* or the golf team had changed their lives. I'd polish it up, change Will Ferrell to Toni Morrison, and golf to learning woodworking from a Darfur refugee.

I didn't *not* feel bad about this. But I took pride in my work. Sometimes we'd get some work from a current college student. I got one unspeakably dumb sophomore at Trinity an A– in "Post-Modern Novel" with a series of essays of which he should be quite proud, if he ever reads them.

Soon Jon Sturges, the entrepreneur behind all this, knew I had a gift. He promoted me to Senior Associate. Here I learned that the real money was coming in from Asia, where aspiring applicants would pay more and never raise the tiresome questions about "accuracy." I wrote the toughest essays myself and farmed out the rest of the work to part-timers among the starving and overeducated.

EssayAides had only one other full-time employee. As I sat down at my computer, she stood in my doorway.

"Hey."

Alice couldn't have weighed more than ninety pounds. Her voice should have sounded squeaky like a cartoon mouse. Instead it was disturbingly deep. She stood there for a really long time.

"What're you doing?"

"A Japanese guy applying to Wharton. You?"

"Just going over some things I farmed out. A lot of my team's been making them too smart. I had an essay for Colorado College that I sent to one of those Palo Alto guys, and he put in two quotes from Walter Benjamin."

"Yikes. Gotta cut that out." Jon was always warning us not to make the essays too smart or colleges would catch on.

Alice unfolded her arms and held out a hardcover book. On the cover was a pen-and-ink drawing of a flock of birds in flight. *Kindness to Birds* by Preston Brooks.

"I've been reading this."

"Oh. How is it?"

"*Breath*taking."

I knew this Preston Brooks. He was sort of the Mannheim Steamroller or the Velveeta cheese of novelists. But I just nodded, because I liked Alice. There was a lot weird about her. Her grandmother had died two years ago and left Alice all her clothes, mothbally '70s sweaters with big poofy necks. That was all Alice wore, as some kind of tribute. But back then I wore napkin pants and ratty running sneakers and my hair had mysterious crusts, so as far as that goes Alice was friggin' Donna Karan. Alice graduated from some woman's college in Nova Scotia or something, and how Jon Sturges found her I don't know.

That the two of us came into the office at all was, macro-economically, pointless, because no one called or came in. Jon Sturges just liked having some humans in an office so his company felt like a legitimate enterprise. He paid us more to sit there for an approximation of regular business hours.

My office was barren except for a framed poster of a Roman aqueduct. Jon Sturges based his business philosophy on this book called *Caesar, CEO: Business Secrets of the Ancient Romans.* He constantly made analogies to ancient Rome, in the flawed belief that knowing about one smart-guy thing made him not an idiot. He referred to our rival company, Academic Edge, as "Carthage." They did seem to threaten our empire; we'd been getting fewer and fewer Hoshi Tanakas this season. The application-essay "consulting" business was getting more and more competitive. But Jon Sturges had other businesses in similar moral gray areas. He couldn't really focus on one thing for more than like an hour at a time. "An empire has to expand," he said. He said lots of inappropriately grand things.

On my computer I opened up Hoshi Tanaka's essay. The topic was "How do you expect an MBA from Wharton to help you achieve your career goals, and why now?"

Hoshi had replied:

Wharton School of Business is held in the first category. At this time in my career, it is passing to the next step to attend business school for study. As to what I can provide, experience.

Warren Buffet has this word: "partnership." This is realistic. The many cases of blemishing companies were cases when this did not partnership. For one year

I have worked at sales managing. Here, I dampened with the Japanese method of business: loyalty, namely self-sacrifice, namely adherence to the group, namely entrusted effort. This maintains the strong corporation, the flood of all sections is very skillful. Yet also I learned "partnership." This is seen in the part of a car. They experience partnership or the car failures.

But "globalization" means changings in turbulence. The company and the leader where the entire market is part of success always maintain the necessity of adjust to the environment. As for the business school, "actual state," and the serious problems which face the entrepreneur are engaged in the setting of science.

This is as in a car's machinery. A new leader is prepared. This is my sincere hope.

Now began the part of the day where I would stare out the window and think about how I got here.

It began with my mom: she was vicious about limits on the TV. This was back when moms could still pull that off. There probably would've been nothing she could do if I was born ten years later. But we didn't even have cable.

Books, on the other hand, were allowed. Books are not as good as TV, but they were the best I could do, so I read a lot. By the time I was twelve I'd read the entire Nick Boyle oeuvre, from *Talon of the Warshrike* to *Fateful Lightning Loosed*. I'd go to the library and pick up any book that had a sword, a gun, or a powerboat on the cover. This led to an interesting informal education, like the time I read *The Centurion's Concubine*. I knew what a centurion was, and I assumed a concubine was a type of sword.

With no TV to fill it, my spongy brain absorbed everything. Once Mom took a bite of pecan pie and said it was really good. So I asked her if it made "her tiny muscle of passion quiver with inflamed anticipation." This was a line from *The Centurion's Concubine* that didn't apply.

But all this reading taught me how to churn out sentences. Before long, Mom was paying me to write thank-you notes for her, a dollar a pop. And they were good, too—"I was touched to my very core with gratitude," etc.

Thusly I cruised through high school.

In senior year, an English teacher who was called Weird Beard recommended his alma mater, Granby College, "sort of a small college Ivy." The brochure he gave me showed a flaxen-haired woman in a skirt, half sitting and half lying next to a field hockey stick while listening to a guy with glasses reading from a book. The moral was clear: guys with glasses who read books could do well here. So that's where I ended up.

Suddenly I found myself transported to a secular paradise. A lush green valley where no one expected anything of anyone. I could do whatever I wanted, which it turned out was not very much plus drinking. I played Flipcup and Beirut and Knock 'em Toads. Off trays I ate cheese fries and ageless pizza in the Commons while girls scurried through in their last night's clothes and fliers demanded I free Tibet and take guitar lessons. I slept on futons and went for pancakes and pounded the Plexiglas at hockey games and parsed *The Simpsons* and lost bets and threw Frisbees. I went to seafood dinners with people's uncomfortable dads.

The stoner who couldn't shut up about Radiohead, the guy who tried to pull off smoking a corncob pipe and loaned me his dog-eared copy of *Atlas Shrugged,* the premed who would fall asleep with a highlighter in his mouth, the dude already with a huge gut who quoted *Rudy* and ordered wings—I loved them all. I knew the taste of Busch Light as the sun came up after a drive to the beach.

But best of all was my girlfriend. The fetching Polly Pawson first slept with me because it was easier than walking back to her room. We'd have low-energy make out sessions that devolved into naps. She wore faded sweatshirts and track pants over her dainty figure, and her flops of hair smelled like raspberry shampoo.

The actual classes of course were pointless. I signed on as an English major, but the professors were dreary pale gnomes who intoned about "text and countertext" and "fiction as the continuance of a shared illusion." Instead of loving perfectly good books like *Moby-Dick,* where a fucking *whale* eats everybody, these fuckers insisted on pretending to like excruciating books like *Boring Middlemarch* and *Jack-Off Ulysses.* They were a bloodless and humorless race who spent their hours rooting around in eighteenth-century sonnets and old *New Yorker* stories looking for coded gay sex. But I got their lingo down. I could rattle off papers on *"Moby-Dick:* A Vivisection of Capitalism" or whatever in a couple hours and get an A–.

Polly had her own ingenious strategy to get herself out of papers.

THE PAWSON METHOD. Rub bits of crushed-up flowers or peppers under your eyes. Your eyes will get red and puffed-up. Go to your professor at his office hours. He'll (or she'll, but Polly was especially good on males) be stunned to see you because nobody ever goes to office hours. He'll be so excited he'll start prattling about the Northern European Renaissance or whatnot. Look distracted. Stare out the window, look around the office, pick up a book or something. Then sob—once, not loud. Hold your face in your hands until he stops talking. He'll ask you what's wrong. Say "I . . . I need to go home for a while." GIVE NO DETAILS. The professor, remember, is just an awkward grad student, grown up. If he had people skills he'd be doing something cooler than lecturing hung-over twenty-year-olds about the Northern European Renaissance. He'll be ashamed that he prattled on. Say, "I don't think I can take the exam right now." Remember that these academics are trained to be on the lookout for depression, schizophrenia, etc. He'll envision nightmare scenarios where you kill yourself and after an investigation and a lawsuit he doesn't get tenure. He'll agree to anything. Stand up and give him a hug. Hug him for a few seconds too long, to reinforce the awkwardness.

Polly was brilliant.

If I could've stayed in college forever, everything would've been fine. Sometimes, on dull afternoons, I'd duck down to the Talbot Reading Room, a wood-paneled chamber in the library, full of voluptuous leather chairs. I'd take out *Stackpool of Granby College*, a nineteenth-century boy's book set at my very institution. It tells the story of Stackpool, who after a few missteps wins the big game for the Granby eleven in between innocent hijinks and courting visits to the daughter of a local farmer. Here's Stackpool's assessment of College Days:

> Bless the blissful idyll! Bless the companionable pipe, and the low arm-chair, by now well-broken for comfort. Bless evenings among that hearty fellowship, reading the old volumes and filling the head with wonders. Bless days free to wander in the scholar's revelry, before the cares and labors of the world press down upon the brow. Bless those days before the summons of manhood must be answered, and one may linger for a fading hour as a carefree youth.

Exactly. I'd fall asleep and dream of Polly.

Stackpool ended his college career carried off the field in triumph. I was not so lucky.

I should have known. The signs were everywhere. I even saw a test prep book in her room once. She claimed it was her roommate's. And I guess I just wanted to believe her.

Polly Pawson was cheating on me. With the LSAT. The whole time she was secretly working on her law school applications. Those times when she told me she was taking a second nap—a second nap! Think of how I loved her!—she was working.

She hid her law school acceptances from me until graduation day. And then she broke up with me. I pleaded. I told her about my plans for us (conning a wealthy dowager) and she retorted that they weren't "realistic." It was awful. There were hysterics and there would've been worse hysterics if I hadn't been so hung over. I swore at her before vomiting on the granite steps of Prendil Hall.

So I was shoved, bloodied, into adulthood.

My friend Lucy told me to get a job like hers. She became an assistant at Ortolan Press in Manhattan. But I knew they'd find some twisted assignment like making me edit textbooks. The last thing I needed was for the universe to impose a *Twilight Zone* ironic twist.

Anyway, that summer I decided to stop reading, because of the worst book I ever read.

The Worst Book I Ever Read

During the Dark Period, right after graduation, I loafed around the Granby campus, sleeping on a friend's futon, working at a sandwich place called Stackers. If you ate at Stackers that summer you should know that I rarely washed my hands.

Worried about my condition, my mom paid me a visit. She gave me a copy of *The Chronicles of Esteban,* which her lesbian sister had told her was inspiring. It said "a touching, uplifting narrative of love, pain and healing" right on the cover. Sounded like just what I needed.

Wrong. Here's the plot of *The Chronicles of Esteban.* As his ten-year-old daughter lies in a hospital bed, dying of leukemia, Douglas entertains her by telling a story of his own invention. It's about a shipwrecked sailor from the Spanish Armada, Esteban, who's stranded in Ireland.

The daughter gets sicker and sicker. Meanwhile Douglas continues the story, in which Esteban gets sick. Esteban is helped along by kindly spirits and fishermen full of folk sayings. He searches Ireland for a mystical spring that's been blessed by either Saint Patrick or some leprechauns, depending on who he asks. All of Douglas's characters talk in a ludicrous brogue, but they all agree that there's a spring somewhere with healing powers.

Here's the last paragraph of *The Chronicles of Esteban*. Douglas is talking to his daughter:

"There, beside the cool and clear and dark, the placid waters, Esteban raised his hand. Trembling. He grasped at the thin mist as though he might capture it in his palm like a butterfly." Douglas paused. And he knew, in the silence, that the strained, timid breathing that had been to him like a second heartbeat, that faint and fickle dream of love and life, was gone. The moonlight illuminated the unforgiving steel of the respirator and cast its pale light across the bed. But Douglas wouldn't look, knew he couldn't look, not until he finished his tale. And so he continued, summoning everything within him. Memories and hands and remembered laughter he called upon now, to keep his voice steady. So he could finish his story, into the still air. "Esteban bowed before the waters, the sacred waters he had seen in visions. The waters that promised to heal. To restore. To give. He dipped his face, closing his eyes as his lips touched. And he drank."

I read that last section while I was adding bacon to a Stackers Meat Combo. In furious disbelief, I almost dropped the book into the vat of spicy southwest sauce.

"Oh, for fuck's sake!" I shouted, alarming several customers.

It wasn't that big of a deal at the time. I stopped reading. Whatever. The tide had already been turning me toward TV for a while.

* * *

At the end of the summer I found the EssayAides job on Monster.com. Jon Sturges was impressed by my Granby degree and my shallow but convincing erudition. In a practice test, I turned a Korean high schooler's dense babble into a tidy five paragraphs about how her pet snail taught her to love biology.

Now here was Hoshi Tanaka. A core of earnestness runs through all four paragraphs of Tanaka's work. You can tell he means what he says, whatever that may be.

Hoshi did manage to get across that he worked in the auto industry and this had taught him something or another. So I made up a story where Hoshi learned about how important cars were from an aging mechanic. The mechanic took him into the shop and showed him how all the pieces had to fit together just so. It was a nice moment, ending with a grease-stained hand-shake. This, I'd have Hoshi conclude, was a good metaphor for running a company.

This had all the elements of a tight business school essay. There was a vague metaphor, a sense of respect, a mentor fig-ure, evidence that the applicant didn't think it was all about money, and creative thinking (but not too creative). It sounded plausibly Japanese. Pleased with myself, I decided to knock off for lunch.

For lunch I favored Sree's USA Nepal Food Fun, located in a strip mall across a four-lane highway from the Hamilton. Trying to cross without being killed was the most invigorating part of my day. This was in January, too, so there was the ob-stacle of melting snowpiles to add to the challenge. The thrill made Sree's feel extra-relaxing, like sitting on the beach of a remote island surrounded by sharks.

Sree's was decorated with Nepalese posters for the movie *Ghostbusters*. Sree loved *Ghostbusters*, and he liked me. So, solid guy.

"Hello! Pete."

"Hi, Sree."

"Did you see Conan O'Brien show last night?"

"No."

Sree heaved with silent laughs. "Oh! He had a comedy who talked about women's thighs. Oh!"

This may not have been the conversation we had that day, but it's the kind of conversation we had. Actually, I think that day he was in the back, setting traps for an animal of some kind, so I ordered from his wife who was shaped like a squash. I got the Nepalese Fish Fry, which was fish sticks with some sort of pineapple sauce smeared on top, $3.99.

The only other regular was there. He was a lopsided old man with chapped lips who always wore a New England Patriots parka, ate a Curry Hamburger, and drank a Bud Light. When he finished his food, he would saunter over to me. He would tell me about his daughter, who lived in Arizona, and how when she was a little girl she could sing like Judy Garland. Then he would start alluding to terrible things he'd done as a Marine in Korea.

Hearing him out was the closest thing I did to charity, but today I didn't want to deal. So to keep him away, I'd brought Hobart's Sunday *New York Times* along with me. I ate hunched over the magazine. I stared at the ads for houses in the back, sprawling Gothic castles in places called Bass Harbor and Elm Neck, and wondered how I would get the requisite 3.5 million dollars. I flipped through an article about the next generation of kitchen designers.

Turning the page, I saw a full-page photograph that cap-
tivated me.

It was black-and-white, and this is what it showed: in front
of the shattered window of a discount electronics store, the
mystery novelist Pamela McLaughlin was squatting, clutching
a notebook. She was leaning over the chalk outline of a body.
Her tube top was pulled tight over her fulsome cleavage by the
weight of a pistol in her shoulder holster, and she stared grimly
at the camera. Next to the chalk outline lay a book. Unclear
what book, but you don't have to be the steel-willed and firm-
bodied, half-Vietnamese, half-Cuban crime reporter/freelance
investigator Trang Martinez to realize that's an important clue.

It was part of one of those photo essays they have sometimes. This one was called Best Sellers, and it was all portraits
of writers who were currently on the best-seller list.

The Pamela McLaughlin photo suggested an editorial
message, like "readers are America's real victims." You might
agree, if you read Pamela McLaughlin's latest, *Fashion Victims,*
wherein Trang penetrates the lingerie industry in a desperate
ploy to stop a serial killer who targets makers of bridal wear.
For one regrettable chapter, Trang poses as a pre-op transves-
tite to lure a depraved leather magnate into an unwitting con-
fession. The tagline on the paperback was *Blood is the new pink.*

I took a bite of fish, and with a mouthful of saccharine
sauce turned my attention to the opposite page: the sunglassed
eyes of Nick Boyle, my beloved author of action thrillers,
gleamed against the light. Nick Boyle was wearing a wind-
breaker, and a baseball hat that said "USS Hornet—CV-12."
Framed against the sky, ocean spraying behind him, he was at
the helm of a hulking World War II amphibious landing craft.

True Nick Boyle fans wouldn't call it a landing craft, of course. They'd identify it as an LCT Mk-5 or whatever, because you'll find his books baffling if you can't keep track of different pieces of military hardware.

Nick Boyle has the smushed-up face of a bullfrog. His cheek-skin could be stretched into a full yard of normal face. I counted twenty-six folds of faceflesh, and eight isolated bulges. But he was grimacing with vindictive American anger. And he pulled it off. He looked ready to start setting wrong things right with the business end of a 20mm machine gun.

The eyes of Nick Boyle, who'd given me so much weapons-related entertainment, accused me of civilian weakness. He looked at me with revulsion, knowing I was unworthy to stand beside him in the crush of battle. He looked at me as though the best thing I could do was get the hell out of his way, so he could launch armor-piercing shells and win freedom for pantywaists who didn't know what to do with it. Later, at some salty bar where war banners hung, he and his comrades would mutter grimly over bourbon and nod at each other's bloodstained shirts.

I took a sip of Nepalese nut soda and turned the page.

Next was Josh Holt Cready. He was done up like a Civil War tintype. Clever enough, although it looked like those old-timey photos lame families get at amusement parks. Josh Holt Cready was the precocious author of *Manassas,* a novel about a precocious author named Josh Holt Cready who retraces the steps of his ancestor who fought for the Union and died at Cold Harbor. Writing a novel about the Civil War is lazy. Brother against brother, battles in peach orchards and wheat fields, all those Biblical names, the poignant geography, Abe Lincoln and slavery hanging over everything. There's so much built-in pathos, it writes itself.

But being lazy myself, I couldn't fault Josh Holt Cready for cheating. So I didn't hate him. Not even when his book first hit the best-seller list. Or when awestruck profiles of the fresh-out-of-Yale prodigy started cropping up everywhere. I certainly didn't hate him when *Entertainment Weekly* ran a three-page feature and talked about him as though you were some kind of crazed nihilist if you failed to be floored by his brilliance. I didn't hate him when his smarmy wide eyes stared out at Ann Curry on the *Today* show while I tried to get through a bowl of Froot Loops. And I didn't hate him when he was briefly linked to Scarlett Johansson. Or when Sean Penn signed on to play Grant in the *Manassas* movie, to be directed by Tim Robbins.

In a burst of not-hatred I turned the page so fast I gave myself a paper cut.

There was Tim Drew, he of *The Darwin Enigma,* posed with his arms folded, in a natural history museum, in front of a Victorian phrenology model.

Turning the page again, I was confronted by a man of about sixty. In contrast to Nick Boyle, the skin on this face was stretched tight around the skull like a drumhead. Two thin lines of beard converged on his chin into a vulpine point. He was sitting on a park bench, shot in dreary overcast gray. Along his arms and legs, birds were perched. Different kinds and sizes of birds. One nestled in the lap of his corduroy pants.

The picture, like all those in the Best Sellers series, was identified only by the author's name and his current best-selling book: "Preston Brooks, *Kindness to Birds.*" This was just too much, the old bastard sitting there with birds on his arms. I smushed some fish rind on his face, threw him in the garbage, and said good-bye to Sree.

It's likely I never would've thought about Preston Brooks again if it wasn't for an e-mail that I read when I got back to my desk.

2

FROM: pollypizzazz@gmail.com
TO: undisclosed recipients
RE: announcing . . .

Hello all—

Sorry for the mass e-mail, but not sure when I'll see some of you, and wanted to give you the news. It's been a year and a half since I first met James. Back then I thought he was the only good thing about DC:) Last weekend we went up to the Shenandoah Valley, blankets, hot chocolate, lovely B&B. James played me a song on the piano (I know, almost too cheesy, right?) and—you know what's coming— WE'RE GETTING MARRIED! So weird even to type it, but I'm giddy.

Okay, so planning time, guys—wedding is a year from April. I know it's a long way off, but now you're committed! That's the only time we can get the whole James clan in from Australia. And it'll be cherry blossoms, Virginia spring—the works! Plus all of you are coming! OF COURSE you're all coming. Mark those calendars. Big drunk wedding, cheesy band, crazy relatives, the whole deal.

Anyways, drop me a line, let me know what's happening. I'm still doing diligence (and avoiding office politics!) at Mintz Cohen. Probably get a chance to see you New York folks a bit this spring, and also hoping to get back to Granby and show James all the places I puked. You guys ALL have to call and fill me in!

Cheers,

Polly P.

Polly Pawson
Associate
Mintz Cohen Condon Keane
Washington, D.C.

—E-mail sent to Pete Tarslaw

Now, I'm not saying I'm blameless in all this—far from it. But read that e-mail. Start with the address—I don't care if "pollypawson" and "ppawson" and "pawsonpolly" were all taken, "pollypizzazz" is unacceptable.

Imagine reading that e-mail like I did, after everything I just told you. And I think I won't seem quite so bad.

The news wasn't a surprise, really. She'd mentioned this "James" in our awkward and infrequent conversations. Losing Polly didn't bother me. That false-hearted overcapitalizing strumpet was welcome to marry whatever Pacific Rim lout would call her missus.

The problem was the wedding.

I could picture it. I'd be seated at a table with the disgusting sort of apprentice adults with whom Polly had now made common cause. Strapping men with dimpled chins in khakis and blue oxford shirts, with false casual laughs and slappable shoulders, who look like they're fresh from crewing the first boat and are now in the glorious rise as junior analysts at Bain. Men already accustomed to putting their BlackBerries and laptops through airport security as they fly back from Denver and Dallas.

If it sounds like I'm describing someone specific, by the way, I am—this dude named Chad Cooley who went to Granby with us, a guy we used to mock when we'd see him jogging, who was now Friendsters with Polly (this was before the Facebook Revolution). I'd stuff artichoke appetizers into my face as this vapid ant regurgitated magazine articles and spouted misremembered movie quotes and faulty sports analogies.

Also at the wedding would be women, talking about how beautiful Polly looked. Secretly of course they'd all be full of the primal jealousy that surges through women at weddings. Their crazy woman-brains would be telling them they'd better get cracking if they wanted to avoid a life of barren spinsterhood.

So there'd be that to deal with.

Worst of all, Polly's wedding would be filled with Australians. Men who forked snakes in the sun-baked desert, and popped the eyes out of dingos with old ANZAC rifles, and surfed between gaping shark mouths, all while downing 20oz. cans of Victoria Bitter. Men trained by gap years padding about Thailand and India in a drunken stupor, flipping off the local constabulary. These men, friends of the groom, would dare each other to feats of athletic drinking. One of them, the one called Bonky or Rhino, would collapse off his chair half conscious as his comrades hooted with raucous delight.

The desperate women, bridesmaids especially, would swoon over these marsupials, and wedding-weakened ladies would be treated to vigorous matings on the coatroom floor.

Back at my table, some well-meaning bald guy who's Polly's boss or something would turn to me and ask, "So Pete, what do you do?"

I'd answer, "I write fake application essays for foreign kids."

My neighbor would look at me with enough shame for two. Then, first chance he got, he'd wheel himself—for some reason I pictured this guy in a wheelchair—to the bar.

Rumors of the shattered ex-boyfriend whose pathetic presence was a blight on the reception would trickle through the hall. The aunts and cousins and the reverend would all hear about it. As I stumbled to the bathroom, Polly, glowing and radiant, would clutch the firm arm of her new husband, and point at me, and whisper to him about the sorry wretch she toyed with in her younger days. Then they'd kiss, full on the mouth, as the entire assembly applauded.

I'd end up carried home by my two remaining college friends, Lucy and Derek. They'd haul me back to the Marriott as I alternated between begging them to stop for pancakes and passing out.

Polly would win. The whole event, from the reading of First Corinthians 13 to the dainty little chocolate tarts with raspberry filling and the creepy old guy who dances with the little kids, it wouldn't just be a wedding. It would be a celebration of how Polly defeated me.

That's how I thought about it at the time.

Now, you might suggest that I could've just declined Polly's invitation. But that would be admitting defeat. I'm lazy, but I'm no quitter. I wouldn't let her have the satisfaction of telling her friends, "I wish Pete had come," and later sending me a little note about how "unfortunate" it was that I "couldn't make it."

Again, I'm not proud of feeling this way. I'm just trying to let you know where my head was at.

After work, on the way back to Somerville, I stopped at a liquor store and picked up a case of Upstream Ale. I don't even like Upstream Ale. It tastes spiky like it's brewed from a mixture of club soda and creamed corn.

But the label features a grinning cartoon salmon. He's flinging himself into the air from a rocky stream. He's smiling like he loves the challenge. That was the spirit I needed.

A few hours later I was sitting on the couch in my apartment, watching TV with seven empty bottles of Upstream Ale in front of me, eating some smoked almonds I'd found in the bowels of our kitchen cabinets.

Next to me was my roommate, Hobart. He was eating instant mashed potatoes right out of the pot. This was the only thing he ever ate.

Hobart had hair that looked like a nest made by an incompetent bird. He seemed not to know how to shave quite right, so tufts of fur were always lingering on his face.

But lifewise, he seemed to have me beat. Hobart was a grad student at Harvard, studying for a joint MD/double PhD in chemistry and economics. The only books on his shelves were volumes of medical reference and a thin guidebook called *The Gentleman's Code: Etiquette for the 21st Century Man.* This was produced by "MacAllister Distillers, Crafters of Fine Spirits Since 1818." Hobart had gotten it for free with a bottle of whiskey he bought one night after a pained conversation with his girlfriend back home in upstate New York. At least half of his conversations with this woman were followed by hours of piercing sobs. This was his major flaw as a roommate. On the plus side, he was rarely home. When he wasn't studying, he was a research assistant at Lascar Pharmaceuticals, where they made medicines to control attention deficit disorder.

Hobart and I sat on a secondhand beige couch that sagged and slumped like an old lady's bosom. We watched our TV, which had had a green tint ever since an incident three months ago when I threw my shoe at a commercial for a Zach Braff movie and scored a solid hit.

I'd like the reader here to really get a sense of how pathetic our apartment was. It's important, storywise. Just know that there was a scratchy gray carpet splotched with Rorschach stains, random bolts and things sticking out of the walls, and deep fault lines in the plaster. There were no posters. I've never had a poster I wasn't later embarrassed by, so why bother? Some US Postal Service crates held my old paperbacks. A review copy of *Peking,* a novel Lucy had sent me, had been on the coffee table for months. We used it as a coaster.

I opened another beer.

Hobart had only one vice, and he was indulging it now. It was a show on CBS called *Summer Camp.* If you never saw it, it was a reality show—basically a *Survivor* rip-off—where there'd be four teams of "campers" and they'd compete in canoeing and making s'mores with, like, Mario Batali as the guest judge. But the unbelievably unsettling and creepy "twist" was that each team consisted of half adults and half six- to eight-year-old children.

Now, obviously, if I start writing about how weird this program is, how it's a sign of the complete post-postmodern collapse of Western civilization, I could fill a whole book, so I'll just point out one crazy thing, which is that the kids—because they were all screwed-up precocious showbiz kids whose brains are so warped they know how to smile on cue and so forth, are always much smarter than the actual adults.

Hobart watched this show every Friday, without fail. What dark recess of his brain compelled him to do this, I don't know, but I didn't complain. Tonight a six-year-old named Brooke was in a screaming match with a divorced accountant over this berry-picking challenge they'd been teamed up on.

This took my mind off Polly's wedding.

The show went to commercials, and Hobart clicked around from police videos to European soccer.

In a way, I guess all the events that followed were the result of a channel flip. Because Hobart clicked again and paused, because he saw the comforting figure of Tinsley Honig.

Hobart and I agreed that Tinsley was our favorite television-news-magazine journalist. Several times Hobart and I had watched her auburn tresses float about her porcelain-doll face as she interviewed a nun who makes prizewinning saltwater taffy, or an autistic kid who's an expert on the Founding Fathers, or teacher who turned an inner-city classroom around by teaching the kids Scrabble.

On this night, Tinsley was sitting on a country porch, on a hand-crafted wooden bench next to an older man, stout as a beer keg, with a thin beard like an evil count. The camera shot from a distance, so as to take in the gables of the enormous house and the piney mountains in the distance. The house was the kind of glorious country house that people in catalogs live in, where the woman modeling the Sea Pine Rangely Knit pullover brings iced tea to the man modeling the Cropped Linen Washables.

Tinsley had on her trademark Listening Face, cocked fifteen degrees to the left, one slender finger on her chin. The stout man was talking. He spoke as though for medical reasons he had to keep his lips as tightly sealed as possible. His voice sounded like crinkling tissue paper.

"Some say the novel is dead. Well, some say the Devil is dead. I don't think so," he said. "Writing is a cudgel I wield to chase away the brigands who would burn down the precious things of the human heart. Today we have too much of the image, video screens everywhere. Girls barely off the playground gyrating about like trollops at a Turkish bordello. But words still count. They still break hearts, and heal them."

"Don't change this!" I cried, with difficulty because at that moment I'd been seeing how long I could hold eight Upstream Ale bottle caps in my mouth. I recognized the man with the thin beard and the tissue-paper voice. It was terrible novelist Preston Brooks.

The screen cut to Tinsley and Preston walking by the reeds along the edge of a brook. Over the footage, Tinsley's voice-over was saying, "There are no teenage wizards, or codes hidden in paintings. But *Kindness to Birds,* a quiet story of love, family, and the power to believe, has touched readers across the country on its way to the best-seller list. I traveled to Preston Brooks's horse farm in West Virginia, to talk to a writer who says he's an old dog"—here her voice lilted upward—"who's learned a few new tricks."

Cobralike I shot out my arm and snatched the remote from Hobart.

"I was a foolish kid, a dumb kid, so I dropped out of school and joined the Air Force," Preston was saying. "There's a lot wrong with the military, more now than there was then. But they know what to do with a dumb kid. They sent me up to a radar post on the DEW line in Alaska. That was my job, for three years—*listening.* I didn't know it then, but it's the perfect training for a writer. In the Arctic, I listened to the elders of the Gwich'in people. They've lived there for thousands of years. They know a thing or two. We'd all be in better shape if my grandchildren listened to a Gwich'in elder for a while, instead of Lindsay Loohoo and Dee-Jay Stupid Face, or whatever these rappers are calling themselves now."

Preston held out his arm and stopped Tinsley short. He crouched, and scooped something off the ground. The camera went in close and showed a newt, or a salamander or something. Some kind of terrified lizard, trembling on Preston's palm.

After a moment's contemplation, Preston put it down. The newt was shaken for a second but then realized it got off easy and made a dash for the reeds.

"Uh, Pete?"

Hobart was staring at me.

"We'll miss Fireside Chat."

I'd like to believe I said something soothing, but I think what I did was sort of swat my hand. In any case, I missed what Tinsley asked next.

". . . Four Roses, Old Charter, Mud River, Jim Beam, Crooked Chinaman, Colonel's Daughter," Preston was saying. "I drank any kind of forgetting juice in a bottle. I kicked around from job to job. I was in a granite quarry for a while. On a lumberjack crew. One summer I tried to mine uranium. Spent awhile in a fish-gutting plant in Tacoma. Hell of a way to earn a dollar.

"Then one morning I woke up in an alley in Minot, North Dakota in the snow. I rooted around in a trash can, hoping to find an old jacket. And I found a tattered copy of *Of Mice and*

Men. Maybe from an angel's hand. Maybe just a lazy school-boy. But I read it. And John Steinbeck showed me there was stronger stuff than whiskey."

I leaped up and tossed the remote against the wall, where it smashed and the little batteries rolled out. First of all, it was obviously a lazy schoolboy. I am 100 percent certain a tattered copy of *Of Mice and Men* was not put there by an angel's hand.

Second, *Of Mice and Men*? That stupid ninety-page eighth-grade-English Hallmark Special bullshit about the re-tarded guy who loves rabbits? You want me to believe that kept you off whiskey?!

Hobart was looking at the broken remote. "Maybe we can change it manually."

The TV cut to Preston Brooks leading Tinsley into an airy, book-lined office with bay windows facing a still lake.

"I call this the dance hall," he said. "Because characters will appear, and introduce themselves and ask me to dance. The character always leads. I bow, accept, dance for a while."

Tinsley nodded sagely as though this were the wisest, truest thing anyone had ever said. Then she pointed at a vintage typewriter.

"And you always work on a typewriter."

"My daughters tell me to get a computer. But they also told me we'd have eight years of Jimmy Carter, and magnet cars. So what do they know? I hate the damn things. A typewriter was good enough for Faulkner, and it's good enough for me."

"Oh, come ON!" I shouted at the TV. Hobart was crouching over the broken remote.

Preston nuzzled his cheek against the tongue of a horse that leaned over a picket fence. "A horse can tolerate anything except a liar. A horse knows a liar. Readers can tell a liar, too. If I put one false word, one *lie,* down on the page, readers would buck me as fast as a horse bucks a fool."

Then Tinsley began explaining the plot of *Kindness to Birds.* It was something to do with a convicted prisoner named Gabriel, who finds redemption during Hurricane Katrina. The video accompaniment to this was Preston, playing washboard in a zydeco band. Apparently he'd spent time in Louisiana "helping hurricane victims, and listening to their stories, and learning the rhythm of their language."

Tinsley explained that Preston was head of the creative writing program at Shenandoah College. And we watched as he declaimed from his book in front of a packed college lecture hall.

"Is they chickory in that coffee?" she bellowed down, in a tired voice that still shook like a thunderclap, a calling-hounds voice.

"No, ma'am," Gabriel hollered back, steadying himself against the buckboard of the Tidecraft Firebird, swaying in the swamp water that swelled and fell like the breast of a mother asleep. "No chickory, but you sure a Cajun woman, asking for chickory coffee when you stuck on a patch-tar roof and more water coming up, they sayin. Now reach out your hand, Mez Deveroux."

And slowly her fingers, rich in texture as a knitted throw rug, fitted into Gabriel's palm, stained by motor oil and bacon grease. And they looked at each other, and felt that touch, the one from the other, until each helped the other and soothed the other and where the one began and the other ended was lost to both of them.

One could spend hours parsing that intricate latticework of literary sewage: the cartoon bayou dialect, the touches of "realist" detail, the labored folksy imagery, the vague notes of spirituality and transcendence muddied enough to make it palatable to anyone. I didn't bother. Instead I focused on Preston's audience.

Maybe you'd have to see this audience to understand my epiphany. And weird issues with Polly were in play—I'm not going to psychoanalyze myself. I'll just tell you what I saw.

In the rows of the lecture hall, listening to Preston, their backs arched forward and their eyes expectant, were rows of college girls. Young women in little sweaters and tight jeans, pliant and needy. Girls with names like Sara and Katie and Chrissy, no doubt, who had read *Chronicles of Esteban* and *Kindness to Birds* while curved on couches in their bras and pajama bottoms, giving themselves over to this magician of words. Corn-fed girls from small towns, where girls were still graceful and feminine. Pageant winners and soccer players and swoony pseudopoets. Girls who were smart-cute and wildly passionate, who'd traveled from Connecticut and California to Shenandoah College to submit themselves to Preston Brooks. Their faces yearned with nameless desire, pleading with Preston to guide them and fill them with hard truths.

That was when it all came together. That's why I always tell people Preston Brooks was my inspiration. Because right then, I figured him out. I realized what a magnificent, ridiculous bastard he was.

Down in the uranium mine, or at the fish-gutting plant, he'd realized that work is for chumps. And one day he got his hands on *Of Mice and Men*. He'd realized, "Hey, I could pull this off!"

He'd had a vision. He saw that life as a famous novelist would mean sitting around in a country mansion, playing with horses. So he strung together some mushy novels and pawned them off on thousands of book-buying saps. He'd moved out to West Virginia. This was a perfect defense, because what publisher in Manhattan would dare say a guy from West Virginia was inauthentic? In the publishing houses and news-show conference rooms they took him to be a backcountry sage. They bought him as a wise old uncle who could give something authentic. He spoke in platitudes dripping with writerly juices, and Tinsley Honig came out to pay homage at his feet as he churned out "realist" detail from a beat-up typewriter in exchange for fortune.

And, best of all, college women, women at their most nubile and desperate, would pay to come fawn over him. In late-afternoon office hours, they'd hold some crappy story in their trembling hands and he'd start issuing platitudes in his tissue-paper voice.

"In an age when zealots would blow us all to bits, I parry with something more explosive than a bomb," Preston declared to the hall. "Words. Words alone can mend the heart," Preston told them as he folded up his text. Katie's and Sara's lips quivered with ecstasy as he spoke.

The screen cut back to Preston and Tinsley walking again, now with the sun going down.

"Let me tell you a story. That's my trade, after all. I'm a teller of stories. This one happened in 1653, when England was going through a hell of a bad time." Tinsley leaned in to him and listened. "Churches were being torn down and destroyed. But in one place, a place called Staunton Harold, a man built a church. I've been there. I've seen the church, prayed there. There's a plaque on the wall. It says, 'In the year 1653, when throughout the nation all things sacred were either demolished or profaned, this church was built by Sir Robert Shirley, whose singular praise it is to have done the best of things in the worst of times, and to have hoped in the most calamitous.'"

If you're trying to picture this, imagine a sort of hammy, B-grade character actor pretending to be a solemn preacher. That was part of Preston's genius. I saw that now. He was an actor, and he'd written a pretty good role for himself. I wondered which church newsletter or book of anecdotes for ministers he'd gotten this little story from, but I gave him credit—it was good material.

Preston stopped, and Tinsley stopped next to him.

"To do the best of things in the worst of times, and to hope in the most calamitous. That's why I write."

The TV cut to an anchor in New York. She paused for an appropriate length, then half smiled and said, "Powerful stuff," before segueing into a profile of a cabdriver who got his leg crushed by a bus and now does stand-up comedy about it.

Hobart retreated to his room to check the *Summer Camp* message boards as I stomped around, aflame with beer and epiphany. Preston Brooks is a genius, I decided. He's the greatest con artist in the world.

It's hard to describe how you feel when you discover something like that. I guess the closest metaphor is that it's like solving an irritatingly stupid brainteaser that has stumped you for a long time.

I thought about the pictures I'd seen at lunch, of Pamela McLaughlin and Nick Boyle and Josh Holt Cready. Of course! They were all con artists! They'd been staring out at me like a grifter stares at a shill! The costumes, the Civil War getups, the fake crime scenes, the armored vehicles—it was all part of the act! If you could write a book and act like you meant it, the reward was country estates and supple college girls.

I needed to talk to somebody. I took out my phone and dialed Lucy in New York.

"Pete? What's up?"

"Lucy, hey what's up, it's Pete." (I was kinda drunk by now.)

"Did you hear about Polly's wedding? Are you excited?" Lucy is one of those girls from the Midwest who think everything's terrific.

"Yeah, super news. Listen let's talk about some books."

"Oh, did you start *Peking*?"

"Not yet. Listen what's the deal with Preston Brooks?"

"The *Kindness to Birds* guy? You called me at eleven to ask about Preston Brooks?"

"Yeah you know, just talk to you."

"Um, we don't publish him or anything, but everybody's—"

"Listen, how much money do you think a guy like that makes?"

"Well, I can't really say; it sort of depends. There's—you know—paperback rights, and—"

"What would be the ballpark?"

"Well, I actually saw just today that the movie rights sold. It said *high six figures.*"

I put down my phone. I could hear Lucy's chirp come through. But I was busy picturing Polly's wedding.

I would walk in wearing a suit I'd paid someone to pick out for me. At the bar I would order something writerly, perhaps naming a Scotch they didn't have. My contemporaries, American men—who are philistines—might not recognize me, because my book's publicity had not yet penetrated the CNN/ *SportsCenter* loop in which they are trapped. But there would be no mistaking the reaction of the whispering women. The aunts and cousins would be braver, coming up to me, clutching my arm and telling me how they'd loved my novel, and wanting to know where I got my ideas, and how I'd gotten my start. The young women would crane their necks to hear me. Had I just mentioned "Elijah"? For surely by now they'd seen in the *Entertainment Weekly* profile that Elijah Wood was starring in the movie based on my book. Ron Howard was attached. James and his cloddish Australians would sulk and stare at their beers and punch each other in the arm. And Polly would be dragged away, again and again, by bridesmaids asking to be introduced to Peter Tarslaw. And as the evening wound down, I'd hold the prettiest one, the smart-cutest, enthralled as I issued quiet pronouncements about how "a writer makes it his duty to be midwife and doctor to an idea being birthed." And then I'd lead her away, kind of discreetly, but she'd privately delight in knowing that eyes were cagily seeing her leave to be favored by the writer Peter Tarslaw. And Polly herself would slap her flowers to the table in rage, upstaged at her own wedding. Defeated.

I decided to become a famous novelist.

THE NEW YORK TIMES BOOK REVIEW
Best Sellers

This Week	FICTION	Last Week	Weeks On List

1 **MINDSTRETCH**, by Pamela McLaughlin. (Warner, $24.95.) Trang Martinez suspects her Pilates instructor may also be a vicious serial killer. — Last Week: 1

2 **SAGEKNIGHTS OF DARKHORN**, by Gerry Banion. (Morrow, $26.95.) Astrid Soulblighter attempts to reclaim the throne from the wicked Scarkrig clan. The fifteenth volume of the "Bloodrealms" series. — 1 | 3

3 **THE BALTHAZAR TABLET**, by Tim Drew. (Doubleday, $24.95.) The murder of a cardinal leads a Yale professor and an underwear model to the Middle East, where they uncover clues to a conspiracy kept hidden by the Shriners. — 3 | 58

4 **GREAT FISH**, by Liz Martin. (Simon & Schuster, $23.95.) The Biblical story of Jonah, retold from the point of view of the whale. — 5 | 18

5 **NICK BOYLE'S SHOCK BLADE: LYNCHPIN**, by Simon Moskowitz. (Broadman & Holman, $24.99.) After a coup by Admiral Chao threatens to destroy the Internet, the ShockBlade team is forced to ally with their Chinese rivals. — 1

6 **KINDNESS TO BIRDS**, by Preston Brooks. (Penguin Press, $25.95.) On a journey across the Midwest, a downsized factory worker named Gabriel touches the lives of several people wounded by life. — 2 | 4

7 **A WHIFF OF GINGHAM AND PECORINO**, by Jennifer Austin-Meyers. (Osprey, $19.95.) On a hilltop villa in Sicily, an American divorcee finds new love with a local cheesemaker involved in a blood feud. — 6 | 11

8 **INDICT TO UNNERVE**, by Vic Chaster. (Putnam, $24.95.) A prosecutor is the target of an investigation spawned by the daughter of an international assassin he paralyzed in a golf accident. — 11 | 3

9 **EXPENSE THE BURBERRY**, by Eve Smoot. (Simon & Schuster, $23.95.) A young woman in Manhattan spends her days testing luxury goods and her nights partying and complaining. — 1

10 **SECRETS OF BEFORE-TIME**, by T. Addison Rich. (Morrow, $26.95.) In a post-nuclear future inhabited by intelligent cockroaches, Lt. Cccyxx discovers there was once a race of sentient humans. — 7 | 6

11 **THEY PLAY RED ROVER IN HEAVEN**, by Gary Reed. (Hyperion, $19.95.) A grouchy old man discovers the afterlife is a lot like the summer camp he tried to have closed. — 12 | 112

12 **THE LAVENDER WILLOW**, by Thomas Quinn. (Viking, $24.95.) On Nantucket, a beautiful nun who's given up on love finds herself attracted to a psychic who may be a dangerous arsonist. — 8 | 12

13 **MANASSAS**, by Josh Holt Cready. (ReganBooks/HarperCollins, $26.95.) Accompanied by the ghost of Ulysses Grant, a young writer goes in search of his ancestor, a gay Civil War soldier. — 14 | 28

14 **THE JANE AUSTEN WOMEN'S INVESTIGATORS CLUB**, by Loretta Nyer. (St. Martin's, $24.95.) Housewives inspired by the 19th century novelist probe a murder mystery in their quiet suburb. — 1

15 **ADJUST LEVELS FOR DEATH**, by Kent Clear. (Delacorte, $20.00) At the funeral of a music producer, the chief of a secret counter-terrorism team has to protect a sultry pop star who's marked for murder. — 9 | 14

This Week	NONFICTION	Last Week	Weeks On List

1 **CRACKED LIKE TEETH**, by Dexter Eagan. (Morrow, $25.95.) A memoir of petty crime, drunken brawls, and recovery, by a writer who was addicted to paint thinner by age nine. — 1

2 **EMPANADAS IN WORCESTER**, by James Wirzbicki. (Farar, Straus & Giroux, $27.50.) Traveling from Khartoum to Madras to Rhode Island, a commentator for CNN suggests globalization means a stranger but friendlier world in the 21st century. — 26

3 **WRONG: THE LIBERAL PLAN TO HIJACK YOUR LIFE AND PERVERT YOUR KIDS**, by Katie Crispin. (ReganBooks/HarperCollins, $25.95.) The host of TV's "Smashmouth" takes aim at "Hollywood mind-molesters," "media jihadis," public school teachers, and others. — 1

4 **NEEDS IMPROVEMENT IN ALL AREAS**, by Margot Kilby with Sean Boyland. (Regan Books/Harper-Collins, $29.95.) An attack on President George W. Bush, written by his former kindergarten teacher. — 3 | 4

5 **JOCKSTRAPS AIN'T FOR EATING**, by J. D. Preggerson. (St. Martin's, $29.95.) The former Mississippi coach offers advice and anecdotes about football and life. — 7 | 2

6 **BONDS SEALED IN FREEDOM**, by Lawrence Dubbin. (Knopf, $30.) An account of the signing of the Declaration of Independence, focusing on the friendship of Washington, Jefferson, and a little-known Philadelphia orphan. — 5 | 19

7 **MOAN LOUD AND ACT LIKE YOU MEAN IT: A PORN STAR'S GUIDE TO LIFE**, by Natasha Tates. (Fireside/Simon & Schuster, $21.95.) A tell-all memoir by the actress known as the "Queen Bee with Double-Ds." — 4 | 31

8 **JENNA VS. CHELSEA**, by David Fenner and Josh Decherd. (ReganBooks/HarperCollins, $21.95.) Drawing on current trends, two political consultants handicap the 2032 presidential election. — 1

9 **ON—HOLES**, by Lewis I. Talbert. (University of Chicago Press, $19.95.) An ethicist offers intellectual speculation on whether society has a place for the "recurrently obnoxious." — 9 | 18

10 **CUMIN, THE SPICE THAT SAVED THE WORLD**, by Arthur Grunberg. (Walker & Company, $19.95.) How a rarely used seasoning occupies a central place in Western history. — 12 | 9

11 **CAP'N JAY & US**, by Matt McKenna. (Osprey, $22.95.) A newspaper columnist and his daughter learn lessons from a mischievous squirrel. — 8 | 40

12 **GUESS**, by Hayden Callister. (Little, Brown, $25.95.) An economist analyzes the importance of random choices in everything from investments to choosing sushi to professional bull-riding. — 1

13 **ABANDON THE CREAMSICKLES**, by William Su-choi Cappo. (Little, Brown, $24.95.) Humorous essays on family and childhood, by the author of "Which Dog Means I'm Fired?" — 10 | 12

14 **WHAT'S SPOKEN OF BEYOND**, by Elsa Shane with Tom Deering. (Dutton, $24.95.) A self-described "paratransient" relates conversations she's had with the dead. — 15 | 6

15 **EAGLE'S FLIGHT**, by Alan Jost. (Penguin Press, $25.95.) An account of the training and mission of an elite commando team sent to rescue Winston Churchill's bulldog from the Nazis during World War II. — 11 | 4

Rankings reflect sales at almost 4,000 bookstores plus wholesalers serving 50,000 other retailers, statistically weighted to represent all such outlets nationwide. An asterisk (*) indicates that a book's sales are barely distinguishable from those of the book above. A dagger (†) indicates that some bookstores report receiving bulk orders. Expanded rankings are available at The New York Times on the Web: mytimes.com/books.

3

A writer's job is to tell the truth.

—Ernest Hemingway

A writer strives to express a universal truth.

—William Faulkner

If you want to write, and have your writing mean something to someone, above all it must be true.

—Preston Brooks

What a crock of horseshit. Since when has anybody wanted to hear the truth? People hate the truth. It's literally their least favorite thing in the entire universe. People will believe thousands of different lies in succession rather than confront a single scintilla of truth. People like love that crosses the years, funny workplaces, goofy dads who save Christmas, laser battles, whiny hags who marry charming Italians, and stylish detectives. But try telling somebody a single true thing about human experience and they'll turn on the TV or adjust their Netflix queue while you starve to death in the rain. People don't trot down to Barnes & Noble to pay $24.95 for the truth.

I'm willing to give Faulkner and Hemingway a pass. But when Preston "My Writing Is a Cudgel" Brooks declaims about truth, he's lying.

Rule 1: Abandon truth.

That was my first rule for my novel. By six o'clock on Saturday evening, I'd outlined *The Tornado Ashes Club*. Here's how I did it.

The morning after I decided to be a famous novelist, my head was throbbing more than is ideal. But the image of Preston Brooks and his college harem hung before me like a torchlight guiding a mountain climber. And the image of Polly Pawson and her degenerate Australian wedding party prodded me from behind, like Sherpas with pointy sticks.

A first step was itemizing my goals.

GOALS AS A NOVELIST:

1. **FAME**—Realistic amount. Enough to open new avenues of sexual opportunity. Personal assistant to read my mail, grocery shop, and so on.
2. **FINANCIAL COMFORT**—Never have a job again. Retire. Spend rest of life lying around, pursuing hobbies (boating? skeet shooting?).
3. **STATELY HOME BY OCEAN (OR SCENIC LAKE)**—Spacious library, bay windows, wet bar. HD TV, discreetly placed. Comfortable couch.
4. **HUMILIATE POLLY AT HER WEDDING.**

Next, rules. A Googling of "rules for writing" unveiled the truth fallacy. Another Brooks quote, frequently cited online: "As a rule, a writer would be better off hauling tar or stunning calves in a slaughterhouse. Real writing, honest writing, will tear your guts out."

By this point, I was just in awe of the guy. He'd use any wild deceit to hide his fraud. Writers couldn't be trusted. I'd have to discover the real rules for successful novel crafting on my own.

I had novelists I admired, but they don't offer much inspiration.

Consider Whit Kerner. He wrote *The Forbidden Chronicle of the World,* a terrific, funny book about a conspiracy of harridans who secretly run the universe. Current rumor among the few who cared was that Whit Kerner had done so much heroin his hands had fallen off and he was trapped in a cabin, unable to dial a phone, somewhere in British Columbia. So he had achieved none of my three goals.

The summer before college, *Cockroaches Convene* blew my mind. I read along as Proudfoot tramped through the cemeteries, and then I went back and read it all again. But Jim Dinwiddle, the man who invented all that, was found dead by Memphis police in a Dumpster in 1978, with a plastic bag taped around his head. Likewise, 0 for 3.

After the impossibly good *Well Bred,* Helen Eisenstadt morphed into a gnomish far-left scold, whose essays about "oilocracy" appeared in the shrillest of alternative newspapers. I don't know what became of Kim Szydlowski (*Quiet, You Bastard*) or T. T. Hauser (*Storm Drain*), but they were never on TV, so doubtless grim fates had met them, too.

The financial success of an author is inversely proportional to the literary worth of the book. Take the authors of the Bible. Those garment-rending saps ate cockroach dung in caves in the Gaza desert and scrawled tortured epiphanies on papyrus before being stoned to death or dying in plagues. Or Herman Melville, who barely staved off debts by assessing tariffs on crates of imported wool in New York Harbor for twenty years. Meanwhile Pamela McLaughlin, whose books can be read and forgotten in the time it takes for ordered Chinese food to arrive, flies in a private helicopter to the Caribbean island she owns. She named it—and this is not a joke, I read it in *Vanity Fair*—"Bellissima Haven."

Rule 2: Write a popular book. Do not waste energy making it a good book.

I decided to head to the big bookstores in downtown Boston. There the behavior of book buyers could best be studied. Grabbing Hobart's two-week-old *New York Times Book Review* from my room, I headed downstairs.

While waiting for the subway, I saw a woman with cat's-eye glasses reading Dexter Eagan's *Cracked Like Teeth*, which is what cat's-eye-glasses-wearing women were reading back then. Sadly a memoir wasn't an option for me, because my youth had been tragically happy. Mom never had the foresight to hit me or set me to petty thieving or to enlist us in a survivalist cult. I wasn't even from the South, which would've bought a few dozen pages. Lying wouldn't work; these days memoir police seem to emerge and make sure you truly had it bad. And the bar for bad is high—reviewers have no patience for standard-issue alcoholics and battered wives anymore.

I spent the train ride scouring my memory for an angle. Once a wasp had flown up my pants and stung me several times. Sometimes when I was a kid "Funny Mom" would appear, singing Patsy Cline and wanting hugs, and I later learned this was drunk Mom. One February vacation I'd spent at a vegan farm in Vermont, cross-country skiing with my lesbian Aunt Evelyn and her friends. They'd made me write a prayer to the Earth on

degradable sorghum paper and leave it in a crevice in a boul-
der. Still, pretty thin cheese.

Rule 3: Include nothing from my own life.

My experiences were dull. If I'd led an interesting life, I'd
be a smuggler or a ranch hand or an investigative reporter
penetrating deep within the sinister world of Tokyo's
yakuza.

Emerging from the T at Downtown Crossing, I strode
down Washington Street and into Borders Books & Music.

Placed like an altar for entering customers to pass was a table
arranged with neat stacks: BEST-SELLING AUTHORS. Preston was
there, and Pamela, and Nick Boyle. Most fascinating was Gerry
Banion's *Sageknights of Darkhorn*. The cover art was like the
geometry-class doodle of an unsocialized ten-year-old: a square-
bodied king wielding a crude sword with his stumpy arms from
the back of a horse that appeared palsied. Both man and beast
were lumpier than is natural—the king's left leg had a bonus
knee.

I ran my finger along the smooth covers. These weren't
novels you creased with rereading, and pressed into the hands
of trusted friends, and carried around in beaten backpacks.
These were tidy candy-package novels you wrapped up and gave
as presents, which moved from store shelves to home shelves
to used-book sales unread, as money flowed authorward. That
was the cash pie of which I wanted a slice.

In the second-floor café I ordered a coffee served in a cup
as big as a dog's head, opened the *Book Review* to the Best
Sellers list, and got to work. By the time I was done shoveling
in sugar, I had another rule.

Rule 4: Must include a murder.

Sixty percent of that week's best-selling novels involved killings. Glancing around the bookstore, I estimated that fifty thousand fictional characters are murdered every year. Not including a murder in your book is like insisting on playing tennis with a wooden racket. Noble perhaps in some stubborn way, but why handicap yourself?

Many types of best sellers had to be eliminated from contention. Thrillers, mysteries, fantasy, and sci-fi all require intricate construction and research. I had no intention of spending my nights on ride-alongs with homicide cops, or mapping magical empires and populating them with orcs.

Writing an updated version of some public domain story seemed like a worry-free route to literary success. A ready-made plot would keep my mental effort to a minimum. It would just be gussying up the SparkNotes, really. In my notebook I wrote down a few ideas: *Oliver Twist* in exclusive San Diego gated community? *Huckleberry Finn* with a hovercraft? *Hamlet* but he loves sudoku? *Iliad* among Hawaiian surfer chicks? But these all seemed tough to maintain past the first hundred pages.

Most of my scattered impressions gleaned from the best-seller list gelled all at once, in a flash, when I gazed up and saw the Crazy Muffin Ripper.

Rule 5: Must include a club, secrets / mysterious missions, shy characters, characters whose lives are changed suddenly, surprising love affairs, women who've given up on love but turn out to be beautiful (MUFFIN RIPPER RULE).

The only other customer at the coffee bar was an electric-haired woman of about fifty. If I had to guess I'd say that she maybe worked in an art supply store? Probably in the back. She was tearing apart a cranberry-raisin muffin with frantic violence. Crumbs were strewn across her open copy of *The Jane Austen Women's Investigators Club*.

And this woman, I decided, who sits at a bookstore and assaults muffins and reads, was my target audience.

Of course such a woman would be enthralled by the idea of a club. All lonely people wish they were in a cool club. I certainly do—we'd have neat jackets and nicknames. That's why readers are the top club-formers of America.

Of course she'd like secrets and mysterious missions. For loners, the next best thing to belonging to a club is guarding a dark secret or a mission, which makes shyness a heroic necessity. Perhaps she had a dark secret of her own—a house full of cat bodies stacked like firewood.

Of course she'd like sudden love stories. The Muffin Ripper wasn't spending Thursdays fending off dudes at José McIntyre's Margarita Night. For a love story to be plausible to her, it had to arrive suddenly, and the man needed to be bundled with another dose of dark secrets, to explain what took him so long. The best-seller list is always peopled with divorcées and wounded women who, on storm-tossed islands or the hills of Italy, find to their surprise that olive-toned men want to make careful Cambrian love to them.

If that's what she wanted, I'd give it to her.

Tipping my cup to the woman who'd set my mind ablaze, twitching with creativity and caffeine, I folded up my book review and headed for the aisles.

I wasn't so arrogant as to think my own first effort would stay on the best-seller list. Not for more than a week or two. I had a more realistic objective: getting hired as the writing professor at a prestigious college. Williams, or Princeton, some-place kinda away from it all seemed nice. I'd read enough cam-pus novels to expect sexual frolicking and light work.

But becoming a professor called for a particular kind of book, a "literary" book. These books can be identified in two ways. One: at the end of a work of literary fiction, you're supposed to feel weirdly sad, and perhaps cry, but not for any clear reason.

Rule 6: Evoke confusing sadness at the end.

Two: the word "lyrical" appears on the back cover of literary fiction.

Rule 7: Prose should be lyrical.

Since the definition of "lyrical" is "resembling bad poetry," I could crank it out. Just for practice, in my head I tried describ-ing what the Muffin Ripper was doing, right then. *"Back arch-ing like a perched swallowtail, her hand hovered with quivering gentility as she picked up a dropped raisin off the sheet-white floor. She raised it to her lips slowly, like a sacrament, as the dust of wheat flour drifted down her chin."* Good enough.

Now that I'd started cracking the Code of the Novel, in-sights seemed to burst out at me off the shelves like firecrack-ers. Walking through the audiobooks, I realized that here was an entire market ordinary novelists didn't plan for. There was a whole bunch of people who listened to books in their cars.

Rule 8: Novel must have scenes on highways, making driving seem poetic and magical.

Next, I bumped into the cookbooks, an overwhelming wall where in one eyeful were pictures of pastas and steaming meat stews and mac and cheese next to piles of gravy-smothered biscuits. I decided to get some lunch. The human brain is easily lured by food. And people are fat these days and think about food all the time.

Rule 9: At dull points include descriptions of delicious meals.

Rounding the corner, I knocked some oversized volumes on *The Art of Pork* to the floor. Nearby a bookstore employee looked up from his reshelving with a flat expression. Bookstores are filled, customers and employees alike, with people who hate their jobs.

Rule 10: Main character is miraculously liberated from a lousy job.

I walked away as he picked up the books.

Rule 11: Include scenes in as many reader-filled towns as possible.

On my way out I passed "Local Interest," right by the register. Here were books of old photographs of Boston, a collection of poetry by and about the Red Sox, a history of Newbury Street, and a few Boston-related novels, like *Murdah by Chowdah* and *Bud Light, Freckles and Hair Gel: A Southie Love Story*.

I realized this was shelf space rife for exploiting. My novel should be "Local Interest" across the nation. I'd inject the names of popular bars in Ann Arbor and Austin and Portland and have our hero stop in for a beer or some chili fries. Impressed by my authenticity, locals would write up my novel for their local independent press. And I'd get free meals from grateful owners while on my book tour.

Time for a Chacarero! These tasty Chilean sandwiches are served from a stand near Filene's, and at lunchtime the line stretches around a corner, following the track of the wafting smoke from the grilled steak and spiced chicken. It was one of those creepily warm winter days, and though this was a Saturday, the line was still full of discharged office dwellers with crossed arms and dangling ID badges.

I gave my protagonist a job. He should be like these harried types who eat lunch on the fly. Corporate, but in some vague capacity since I don't know how real businesses work. "Human Relations" seemed safe. But he should also be totally awesome. A dexterous athlete and a soulful lover, with the wisdom of a mystic and the abs of a rock climber. He should have a set of unusual skills, like underwater caving. The schoolchildren who made J. K. Rowling a billionaire were the ultimate proof of.

Rule 12: Give readers versions of themselves, infused with extra awesomeness.

Awesome heroes stuck in mediocre lives are compelling, because they suggest that having a mediocre life may not be your fault.

In a way this was all just a subset of a rule all authors should memorize.

Rule 13: Target key demographics.

Ideally my protagonist would be somehow "multicultural." Unusual racial backgrounds garner at least pretend interest from all readers. But as a standard-issue white male, I didn't have much to offer. There was one black guy I knew well—my college roommate, Derek. But no one wants to read about a black guy who went to Exeter and wore a bathing suit and a Star Wars T-shirt and spent all his time playing World of Warcraft. There's only one interesting story about Derek.

The One Interesting Story About Derek

In junior year, he resolved to lose his virginity. He took a bus to Mount Holyoke, vowing not to return until he had achieved his goal. After a week spent sleeping in trees and dodging the campus police, he acquired a kind of folk-legend status, and a "not unpretty" woman in his words took pity on him to the approval and acclaim of all.

The point being, my protagonist would have to be a white guy.

I named him Silas Quilter. Silas had literary connotations that made readers feel smart. Quilter was the author's last name on a book about rare coins I'd seen on the bargain shelf. Vague—lots of ethnic groups could get behind it.

By the time I got my sandwich, I'd earned it—earned the savory flatbread, seasoned beef, Muenster cheese, tomatoes, roasted red peppers, and green beans, all awash in spicy sauce and guacamole. I gave thanks to the Chilean people with each flavorful bite as I walked into the nearby Barnes & Noble.

Rule 14: Involve music.

Playing over the speakers was gentle adult rock with a folksy twang, a banjo in the background. This is what the NPR-listening, book-reading crowd likes best, tunes given a veneer of hipness with some "authentic" element, but without the embarrassing emotions of country or the irritating cacophony of world music. So that's what I'd include. It would sound good on the soundtrack when they turned my novel into a movie.

In the travel guides section, I picked up four Pathfinders books: *Corsica, Sardinia & the Balearic Islands, Northern Peru, Hilltowns of Tunisia,* and *Coastal Slovenia.*

Rule 15: Must have obscure exotic locations.

Americans trust knowledge acquired abroad. The Mediterranean, in particular, has a potent sun-dried magic for them, as evidenced by their love of Andrea Bocelli and the Olive Garden. Even kids like Chef Boyardee. But as with any pornography, readers need increasingly weird and kinky thrills. Tuscany and the French Riviera don't arouse anymore. I'd never been anywhere more exotic than Epcot Center, but how many readers would know I was fudging about the teeming markets of Sartène or the smell of *carapulca* in Trujillo?

Rule 16: Include plant names.

I also bought *Field Guide to American Trees, Plants, and Shrubs.* Sometime around 1970, writers decided it was crucial to include specific plant names. Take this example, from Cready's *Manassas:* "Bivouacked amongst the mockernut hickory and the sourwood as the sun melted over the Rappahannock, Ezekiel still smelled the distant hints of trampled chickweed, torn up by the cavalry when old Jeb Stuart rode by last April."

It was three-fifteen. I'd broken the craft of the novel down into sixteen easy-to-follow rules. I decided to go home and watch TV.

But on the subway a fear gripped me: the fear of falling short. Arriving at the Pawson wedding as a renowned author would be glorious. But the specter of ending up a failed novelist, that most pathetic of creatures, made me tremble. I imagined telling wedding guests the title of my novel, and receiving a dim look and "I'll have to look for it" as they jumped away into a conversation about the shrimp Gruyère puffs. I imagined Polly and Lucy and Derek sending cheery e-mails ("loved it, duder" . . . "so vivid! now you're in publishing after all!" . . . "can't believe you're a PUBLISHED AUTHOR!") while texting each other to commiserate and worry about my sanity. I imagined the bearded Brooks himself coming across my efforts by chance, and letting out a hearty laugh as he glanced at my puny attempt to enter his charlatan's Valhalla.

Perhaps in composing my rules, I'd held back too much.

Like a soldier on the eve of battle my instinct was to stuff my pockets with extra ammunition. Consider the Chacarero. With just grilled steak and Muenster cheese, it would achieve a certain modest success as a sandwich. But they didn't stop there. Added were tomatoes, and roasted peppers. More than enough. Yet still, they added green beans—green beans, on a sandwich!—and *two* kinds of sauce. It's the excess that sold it. That's what kept the lines around the corner. Hold nothing back. That's how you get your novel on the sacred table.

I took out the folded-up best-seller list from my pocket, this time looking at nonfiction. Anything people liked. I started writing. *World War II. Football. America. The afterlife. Wise lessons learned. Food again. Sex.*

I needed more. Maybe readers weren't a diverse enough pool. What did people watch on TV? *Crime. People accused of*

crimes they didn't commit. Pursuits. Las Vegas. Natural disasters—
earthquakes, tornadoes, etc. Families. Gentle humor.

My eyes darted around the subway car. A girl across from me was spread out along the bench, sketching the river as we rode across the bridge. *Art.* Next to her was an elderly couple. What do old people like? *Old people.* I went back and crossed off *Sex,* and wrote in *Telling stories.* At Charles/MGH two middle-aged women got on clutching Old Navy bags. *Bargains.*

What kind of characters do people want? *Hoboes.* Hoboes had been popular since cartoons were invented. Lately they'd been enjoying an ironically appreciated renaissance. *Bounty hunters.* Always compelling.

I remembered something I'd read about a huge percentage of books being given as gifts. *Christmas.*

My mind was now churning so furiously that I missed my stop. I got off at the next one and walked a mile home, staring down at the pavement, trying to slide all the pieces into place. By the time I walked in my door, I had it.

4

Outline

After a murder at the Las Vegas hotel where he
works, Silas Quilter is accused of a crime he
didn't commit and forced to turn to the only person
he has left—his grandmother. She makes him a
bargain—she'll help him stay ahead of the law if
he'll help her on a mysterious mission to bring
a soul to the afterlife. Together they embark on
a quest along America's highways, drawn along
the way by the haunting sounds of a beautiful
country singer. As they dodge bounty hunters,
we hear the tale that brought them together, a
story of lost love that begins in the hobo camps
of the Depression and on mud-stained college
football fields, crisscrossing through the fury
of World War II France to the islands of the Mediterranean and the kitchens and vineyards of Peru,
a saga whose heartbreaking but uplifting end can
only come in the swirl of a tornado, sweeping
across the milkweed and the bluestem of the prairie on a Christmas morning.

A stunning literary debut, told with lyrical
prose, gentle humor, and an artist's eye, *The
Tornado Ashes Club* is a novel for anyone who's
had love or lost it, learned a wise lesson or a
dark secret, or felt the magic of the story that
is America.

—Outline for *The Tornado Ashes Club*
by Pete Tarslaw

My problem was that I didn't know how to write a novel. I knew writers drank whiskey and sat around in bars, so I took a notebook and went down to The Colonial Boy, a pub with a half-assed Revolutionary theme on Mass. Ave.

I chose this place because I knew no one would be there, so I wouldn't overhear any actual conversation that might confuse me as I tried to put down lyrical prose. I ordered a Jameson from the indifferent bartendress and took a seat in a booth under a print of the Boston Massacre, which was across from a photo of Carlton Fisk.

My basic plan for the whole thing: Silas and his grandmother are driving around the country avoiding bounty hunters. Along the road, they pick up a beautiful country singer, Genevieve (solid literary name). Genevieve and Silas fall in love. As the three of them drive around, the grandmother tells Silas the story of her long-ago lover, a man named Luke (biblical but still sounds cool). Whenever I wanted I could cut to Luke's awesome adventures in World War II, in France or Peru or Sardinia. That would keep readers from getting bored.

IDEAS

- Grandmother should talk like one of those wise old ladies who's amused by everything. She should have lots of stories of hardship. Made her own soap? Had to slaughter favorite chicken?

- Use words to describe old ladies that make them sound beautiful (graceful, regal, etc.).
- Silas should be the kind of guy who notices the beauty of light filtering through a beer bottle.
- Silas and Grandmother should come across Genevieve when she's playing to a rowdy pool-hall audience that doesn't appreciate her subtle lyricism.
- To get thirties and World War II details right, add old movies to Netflix queue.
- Luke in World War II: he hides in a haystack. He sleeps with a farmer's daughter in Holland. He sees something that takes his mind off the war (nuns? children playing?). He has a chance to kill a German, but he doesn't because the guy looks homesick. Luke throws his gun in the ocean (symbolic).
- Luke was a high school football star, but he also read poetry to Grandmother under the stadium.
- It turns out that Grandmother promised Luke that, when he died, she'd throw his ashes into a tornado. So they chase tornadoes.

POSSIBLE METAPHORS / MOVING SCENES

- Woman who says stuff that turns out to have extra meaning when it's revealed she's in a wheelchair.
- They pull over by a prison and see the prisoners working on the farm. One of the prisoners tips his hat.
- Gambling / taking a chance (on love? ironically named horse? "he's scared, like us, but that's the kind of horse that runs his heart out, like he's got nothing to lose").

- Overheard conversations at truck stops (blue collar earnestness).
- Everybody singing along to the same song (Patsy Cline?) on the radio. It reminds them all of different stuff (first kiss, night before he shipped out, etc.).
- They pass some kids going to the prom. Genevieve says she never had a prom, so Silas dances with her in a cornfield.

This was all terrific, but I didn't know how to get started. Do you just start writing sentences? That seemed a bit rash.

By now the whiskey was making me sleepy. I got up to order some boneless buffalo tenders.

At one end of the bar was a rough stack of old newspapers. There was a week-old sports section with two cigarette burns over Tom Brady's eyes and a *Want Ad* folded open to guitar amps. But beneath that I found a catalog for the Metro Boston Learning Center. I flipped through and there it was, between "Winning the Airfare Game" and "You and Your Wok": "Writing Your Novel: From Idea to Publishing."

Everybody has a book in them—even you! Gain insight from a published author into how to get your idea out of your head and onto the page. Learn techniques, styles, and tips on everything from creating characters, building suspense, and making your work marketable to how to beat writer's block. Meets Mondays at 8 P.M.

The next day at work I was in a better mood than usual. I lingered with the koi just long enough to watch my favorite, Lumpy, eat a piece of a Maple Frosted Donut I'd picked up at

Dunkin'. Lisa looked busy with files as I approached, but when I passed she said potatoes were going to grow behind my ears if I didn't get a good scrubbing soon.

Alice's sweater that day was emblazoned with an outline of Rudolph made out of rabbit hair or something, with a red bead for the nose. This despite that it was well after Christmas. She held out her hands like a scale.

"Okay. On one hand, we've got a very dumb young man from Manhattan. His essay is about how he learned about other cultures when the doorman at his building took him to a cockfight.

"On the other hand, we have a Russian girl. Her essay is about how she wants to attend Brown. She's under the mistaken impression Madonna went there. Jon Sturges says this is a priority assignment, because her dad is some kind of oil guy or something."

We flipped a coin, Alice went off to fix cockfights and I ended up with the oil baron's daughter. Not trusting her English, she'd written her essay in Russian and then used a computer translator:

> Madonna, by her is convincing feminitaj, has inspired her
> the artistic individuality, and her courageous states on the
> political problems, the women all over the dirt. Because
> of her example I wanted to visit university Brown.

It was simple enough to redo. I Wikipedia'd Brown and found that Kathryn S. Fuller, former president of the World Wildlife Fund, went there. I whipped up some froth about how "this inspiring woman offers a clear example of the kind of dynamic leadership I myself hope to provide someday, as my own nation, Russia, continues its uneasy transition to democracy and faces its own environmental challenges."

I was done by eleven. With the rest of my day I tried to draw a sketch of myself in the style that *The New Yorker* would print next to its gushing review. I imagined middle-aged women, drinking coffee, arguing passionately about Silas and Genevieve and the scene where Luke is given a ceremonial knife by his host in a hut on the coastal hills of Tunisia. I imagined myself giving an interview to Tinsley Honig as the Atlantic crashed beneath the deck of my tasteful mansion. Her blue eyes would drink it in. Then later, with the camera crew gone, I would make tender love to Tinsley in my bedroom with cathedral ceilings that overlooked the back of my estate, where one pool flowed into another pool in a miniwaterfall. The point was, while all this was going on, Polly would be in some D.C. apartment with her hair in curlers, nagging her unfortunate shrivel-testicled husband to put the kettle on.

But all this was roughly 300 pages away.

So that night I went to St. Joseph's School, where the stairs down to the basement reminded me of the taste of square pizza slices and cups of applesauce. I found the right room, 12B. A wave of nostalgia hit my nostrils as I smelled the industrial cleaning solvent janitors splash on linoleum floors.

The only other student present was a fat man in a T-shirt that read "Something's Cookin' In . . . Tennessee." He had gamely wedged himself into one of the twisted desk-chair combinations that were arranged in a circle beneath a battered map of "The United States In The Civil War." He sat there playing games on his cell phone.

The instructor was at the teacher's desk, fussing about with papers. For ease and accuracy I'll call her SpaghettiHair HamsterFace. She whisked around when she saw me. From two yards away she stank of cigarettes.

"I'm sorry—are you in this class?"

I was prepared for this. "Oh, I thought Janine talked to you."

"Janine? No." Then she waved her hands around like two hummingbirds. "Okay." And I took a seat.

Janine Figero was a name I'd gotten out of the back of the Metro Boston Learning Center catalog, where she was listed as "Head of Programs." I gambled on adult education classes being appallingly disorganized, I figured if I threw Janine's name around, no one would give me any trouble about joining midway without paying.

My classmates trickled in, until there were seven of us. A small and bespectacled lady, who looked like the kind of grandmother who writes long letters, sat down next to me and poured herself a cup of coffee from a thermos.

Then SpaghettiHair HamsterFace picked up a worn paperback off her desk. It was decorated in streaks of hideous blue and orange pastels, and the title read *Sun Tokens.* It looked cheaply bound.

"Okay, let's get started," she said angrily. She opened a Diet Coke and took an unladylike swig. "So we've been talking about creating that sense of vividness, scenes that really seem alive. Also, the internal, getting at the character's feelings and thoughts and putting that in words. Those of you who have been here before have heard me read from my stories drawn from my experience in New Mexico—here's a passage I think gets at some of the things we've been talking about."

Just as she was about to get started, Alice walked in.

This was a delightful surprise. My coworker had a Mead composition book pressed to the Rudolph poof on her ancient sweater. She didn't see me at first. HamsterFace gave her a dark look for lateness, and Alice scurried to a desk opposite mine. As she sat down she saw me and I smiled at her—the only thing to do, really. Alice's eyes bulged like a comedian of the silent film era as HamsterFace opened *Sun Tokens* and started declaiming:

"*Lovemaking for me, on the porch of the bungalow,*" she read, "*was frenzy, teeth and biting and hair meshed against teeth, blind clenches against skin, mashing jammed knees and elbows, scratching and pulls, fingers stretching in mouths and crunching against the sandalwood boards, stickyhot tangles of toes entwined in flesh. Urges ancient and animal bubbled out like tar through the cracks in our humanity. We rammed at each other like bison bursting forth in a dawnspring. . . .*"

One of many amazing things about all this was how many students were taking notes.

Alice was staring at me with an investigative look, as though I were a word search.

Hamsterface continued for a few minutes, reading as though she were almost bored with her own brilliance.

"*Our couplings were a lie, but they were an honest lie. And that was enough.*"

She closed the book and set it down behind her.

"Thoughts?"

Nobody said anything. Then the grandmother next to me slurped some coffee and declared, "Very vivid. I did have a question. When the speaker, the narrator, refers to her lover as"—she glanced down at her notes—"'baboon-thighed.' What does she mean by that? Is that a compliment?"

Hamsterface pulled on the Diet Coke. "Yes, but it's *nuanced*. That nuance is a good thing to work on in your dialogue."

Some people noted this.

"All right, so, reading. The assignment was *epiphanies*. Did people find that difficult?"

The grandmother gave emphatic nods. Alice stared down at her pencil and avoided my gaze.

"So let's go around the room, and everybody can read a passage from their epiphany scene."

First at bat was a put-together woman in a pantsuit who'd been discreetly checking her BlackBerry all night. She read from her financial thriller: *Amelia, stunned, swiveled in her chair and faced Tom. 'Confitrade may manage online investment portfolios in the convertible bond market, but they're not making their money from growth assessment, Tom. They're making it from cocaine!'*

A young man with a complexion like wet plaster who weighed maybe eighty pounds read from his first-person account of a lovelorn dolphin: *Eniok stayed in the corner of the pool as he heard the Man make man-noise at Ongtak. He could do nothing. He thought only of being free in the Deep Place, where the fish didn't smell of man-stink. And he decided to escape.*

As we kept going around, through confusing mysteries and adverb-choked accounts of love, I could see Alice growing nervous. I saw her look around, as though she might make a break for it. Finally we came to the guy in the "Something's Cookin'

in . . . Tennessee" T-shirt. He explained that he'd been working on something that "wasn't sci-fi, precisely, but a sort of sci-
historical fiction, alterna-fiction version of the Pocahontas
legend." His reading concluded with this sentence: *His moans
from the pain delivered by the energy tendrils were muted by the
plastic sheathing on his biosuit.*

   Then we were at Alice.

   God bless her, she went for it.

   *Like a struggling woman sailor trying to keep her head afloat
in a wildly raging tide, Xenia tried to keep mind and body apart,
tried to keep her senses keen and aware, feeling the delights of each
new touch from the Captain's hands, now two staves of lustfire.
And though she was a novice in the arts of sea-bound lovemaking,
she didn't shy away, no trembling virgin her. Indeed, she felt herself moved as if by an unseen hand, into him, with a vigor and
animal wildness that would have stunned a Mongolian tiger. His
thrusting member rumpled her petticoats around her yearning
thighs.*

   No one seemed fazed by this. With a neutral expression I
stared at the ground as Hamsterface mentioned something
about "good imagery."

   And then we were done. Alice tore out through the door
without looking at me, and everyone else filed out.

As I walked home, I assessed what I'd learned—about writing,
not about Alice.

   The main thing was confidence. My classmates didn't get
it. They all had some rich personal vision they were struggling
to get into words. They were trying to work out all sorts of issues

and ideas and personal traumas. They were strangling themselves trying to fit it all in.

But that wasn't the game. That wasn't the Preston Brooks con. The key was just to *seem* significant. To distract the eye. If you tried to fit in actual emotion, or stuff you cared about, you'd just bog your novel down. Writing was like a magic trick. But instead of focusing on the illusion, the showmanship, the people in the class were wasting their time trying to work actual magic. Except for Alice, who seemed to have a genuine gift for soft-core pornography.

These people were all working too hard.

5

- Against the crisp canopy of the desert air, the sound of a gunshot travels for miles.

- In the desert air, you can hear the sound of a gunshot for miles.

- When Silas heard the sound, his first thought was, *I've never heard a gunshot before.*

- A gunshot doesn't pop or bang, it vibrates through you, setting everything off its track.

- That low hum, electricity throbbing slowly through a deserted office hall, was like a womb to Silas, but like every womb, it had to be shattered.

- In Las Vegas, that city of extravagant dreams and garish spectacle, no one paid any attention to a quiet, pensive man.

- You never recognize it, not at first, and only later do you realize it was the sound that changed your life.

- A gunshot sounds like a bird, plummeting dead to the ground.

- In Las Vegas, that city of garish spectacle, a gunshot falls lost into the cacophony like a scream at a hockey rink.

—discarded first sentences for
The Tornado Ashes Club
by Pete Tarslaw

For the rest of the week, a great fog of awkwardness hung over the offices of EssayAides. Alice and I stayed in our respective offices and avoided each other. She would get to work before me and not leave until I was gone. Sometimes I'd hear her footsteps in the hall, rising to a furious speed as she zipped past my office. Or I'd hear her making tea in the kitchen. For fun I'd loudly start to pound down the hall. She'd frantically try to finish or make the decision to abort, leaving mug abandoned in the microwave and sugar and tea strewn along the counter.

There weren't many essays to work on that week. Business always slackened by midwinter, but this year seemed especially dry. Luckily Jon Sturges never bothered checking in. He was probably off defrauding nursing homes or something.

So with this time I got cracking on *The Tornado Ashes Club*.

Writing a novel—actually picking the words and filling in paragraphs—is a tremendous pain in the ass. Now that TV's so good and the Internet is an endless forest of distraction, it's damn near impossible. That should be taken into account when ranking the all-time greats. Somebody like Charles Dickens, for example, who had nothing better to do except eat mutton and attend public hangings, should get very little credit.

The first sentence took me nearly a whole day, but I was happy with the result: *A gunshot sounds like nothing so much as a book slamming closed.*

I put Silas to work in a Las Vegas hotel and casino called The Elysian Fields. Coming up with that took a long time. I wanted to make it a satire of Vegas casinos, because I knew reviewers and book types, who hate popular things, would find such a skewering delicious. But it's hard to satirize Vegas casinos, which already have indoor canals with singing gondoliers and mock Eiffel towers and Star Trek restaurants. So I made the place Heaven-themed, slapping on the irony like mustard on a sandwich.

I got Silas's boss murdered: gunshot, Silas is working late because he's a pushover, hears the noise, in trying to help puts his prints all over everything. I got Grandma sitting in an Adirondack chair, watching the moon rise over Buzzard's Bay, and reminiscing. High school in a Pennsylvania coal town. Falling in love with strapping young Luke, who reads her Catullus. The mine shuts down and Luke heads out for hobo adventures.

The hardest thing about writing was picking which words to use. I thesaurused until every *walked* was an *ambled* and every *bright* was *luminescent*. But by Thursday I had twenty-six pages.

As a reward to myself, at around four I turned out the light in my office and pretended to leave, loudly closing the door to the EssayAides suite. In the hallway, I waited.

Sure enough, about ten minutes later Alice, thinking she was safe, came out in a checkerboard sweater.

"Oh hey, Alice! I was just leaving, but I realized I forgot my phone. Stick around, I'll walk down with you."

"That's—uh, okay I'm kind of—"

"No problem, I'll just be a sec."

I dashed in; then Alice and I headed down the hallway.

"So . . . how'd you hear about our writing class?"

"Oh, I saw a flier. Thought I'd check it out. 'Cause, you know, I dabble."

"Me too, me too, dabbling. Definitely just dabbling. Different stuff. I try and make my writing, you know, as ridiculous as possible. Just for fun."

"Right, yeah, ridiculous, definitely," I said, and we got on the elevator. Silence for a minute, I let her feel secure.

"So how are things going with Lady Xenia? Did she and the Captain hit it off?"

"What? Oh, that thing; yeah, that was just—just an exercise, nothing. . . ." Alice trailed off. We walked past the koi pond.

"You're not, uh—you're not coming next week, or anything, are you?"

"I dunno—I'd kind of like to hear what happens to Lady Xenia."

Alice made her silent comedy eyes of terror again, then said, "I wouldn't—you know I probably won't—" Then she turned and bolted for her car.

Anyway, that was the last conversation I ever had with Alice.

The next day she hid in her office. There were still no essays, so midmorning I crossed the highway, said hello to Sree, and settled down with a nut soda.

Most of my lunch I spent fleshing out some details for a fantasy I'd been running in my head. This would be after my

novel was generating some buzz, and I'd be on my book tour.
Behind the podium, at a bookstore in Richmond or wherever,
forty sets of female eyes would stare back at me as I opened my
crisp copy of *The Tornado Ashes Club*. Before I said a word, I'd
scan the room and find the prettiest woman there: a cute girl,
scarf tossed insouciantly over her shoulder. As I began, speak-
ing in a rolling, ponderous voice, I'd focus on her.

*There are sanctuaries in the human heart, deep and secret
chambers that we lock away. Even from ourselves. Sometimes, as
years pass, we forget they were ever there. They're lost to us then.
But sometimes the simplest of things—a faint melody heard and
remembered, the feel of your grandmother's soft hand, smelling of
baking, touching your cheek, a return to a place you dreamed of
as a child, a bend in a tree worn from climbing—can open those
chambers again. Suddenly your soul fills up, like warm cow's milk
filling a pail on a chill November morning.*

I jotted all this down.

When I was done reading, and the applause had died
down, and I'd signed copies, the cute girl would be waiting,
standing in a corner. She'd come up to me, awkwardly. She'd
say she *never* did this, but my book just meant so much to her.
You're my favorite novelist, she'd say. I thought Preston Brooks
was good, but you, you . . . Then she'd screw up her speech and
dissolve into blushing. I'd smile and invite her back to my hotel
for a drink.

Anything cut out of the novel I'd have saved for bar pat-
ter, over Dewar's and soda at the Ramada lounge. The piano
guy would sign off for the night, and I'd invite her up to my room.
Maybe on the pretense of "I'd love to get your thoughts on something I'm working on." She'd come. She'd sit on the bed, un-

sure even of what strange hypnosis was keeping her there. With a few deft redirects, I could turn her nervous tremblings into sexual availability. And the next morning I'd be on to Nashville or Trenton.

Then I thought about a reading in D.C., where Polly would sit in the back, her eyes awash in tears as admirers scrummed around me—

"Nice jacket bro. I think we're gonna have a good season next year, real solid midfield."

Thus interrupted I looked up to see Jon Sturges himself, founder and CEO of EssayAides, talking to the old man in the Patriots parka, giving him the kind of sideways handshake that white dudes who say "bro" give.

Jon Sturges had eyebrows thick as cigar stubs, beneath a bald spot that spread like a spider across his scalp. Although he was ten years older than me, he cornered and weaved like an athletic eighth-grader playing dodgeball. I walk with the lethargy of a gout-ridden spinster, so I was always impressed to watch him move.

Jon slapped Patriots Parka on the back. The old man looked thrilled as Jon pointed with both hands at me and glided over.

"Broseph! Bronaparte!"

He pulled up a chair and straddled it, tossed his yellow tie over his shoulder, and took a sip of my nut soda.

"Great that we can meet here like this, outside the office. Roman patrons used to meet their clients in the Forum, the marketplace. They weren't constrained by offices. They thrived on that bustle, that energy."

The only bustle at the moment was Sree, who was attacking his stove with an ice scraper.

"You've got to respect the Romans. That was the original business culture. They completely got it. All this"—Jon waved his hands at our present circumstances—"the Romans established all of this. We're just replicating their systems. The Romans were brilliant at infrastructure. That infrastructure—their word, from the Latin—that let them *shift* resources."

He took another sip out of my can, appeared stunned, and turned to call back to Sree.

"What are you working here? Some kind of nut flavor in here?"

"Yes," said Sree. "Nepalese nut soda." He smiled. "Pete, my daughter Martha is going to a roller-skating party this weekend." I nodded. Sree retreated to his kitchen.

"Good times," said Jon. Then he formed his fingers into a triangle under his chin. "So, admissions is in a soft cool. You've been doing a great job bro, no question, but I tell ya, I just can't make the math work anymore. I've got other enterprises I'm trying to get off the ground."

"I see."

"I'm sorry. I gotta let you guys go." Jon drained the last of my nut soda. "Alice sent me here, I just told her."

"So, wait—I don't have a job anymore?"

"Sorry dudely."

Here—I'm pretty proud of this, actually—my first thought was about Alice.

"How'd she take it?"

He crushed the can against the table as he shook his head. "Not well."

So now I was unemployed. At the counter Patriots Parka was picking at a chunk of Curry Cheeseburger that had wedged in the space between his dentures and his gums.

"So listen, Pete. When a Roman legionnaire retired after distinguished service, he would be given a plot of land. I can't give out land, bro. Real estate's a sucker's game. But that's something," he said, as he slid an envelope across the table.

I opened it and counted $320 in twenties.

The situation wasn't ideal. But Jon Sturges had employed me for three years, and now he'd given me an arbitrary amount of cash. I owed him something.

"Jon, I'm reminded of the emperor Augustus and his words to the Senate. You may know this speech. 'Fellow Romans,' he said, 'we bleed the same blood. Our hearts beat with the same fire. When I strike, we strike together. When I rest, we rest together. We are borne together by the same wind, always.'"

Those were lines I remembered from *The Centurion's Concubine*. The centurion says them to his woman. I committed them to memory all those years ago, because they had a powerful effect on the concubine. And they had a powerful effect on Jon, who stood up.

"When ancient Romans swore an oath, they would place one hand over their testicles," he said. "That's where our word *testimony* comes from. Bet you didn't know that, bro." He gripped his testicles tightly. "You've done great work for us, Pete. You're a gifted writer. And I swear to you, we'll work together again."

He then ungripped and stretched out his hand, sideways. With great reluctance I shook it.

Jon turned and walked toward the door, slapping the old man in the Patriots parka on the shoulder.

"We got Pittsburgh to worry about. That's it. Maybe Buffalo. Gonna be a hell of a season." The old man was baffled but charmed. Jon looked at the posters on the wall.

"Hey, cool posters. Is this *Ghostbusters*? Pete, you see these posters?" Jon yelled into the kitchen. "*Ghostbusters*, bro, *Ghostbusters*."

In a Nepalese fast food restaurant where the sanitary conditions were suspect and the food was near poisonous, alongside a highway laid across a bed of brackish marshes, I'd been fired from my job as a forger and plagiarist of application essays by a man whose "business" philosophy was based on gladiator fantasies and epic self-delusion.

That night, as I drank myself to sleep, I heard Hobart through the wall, talking to his girlfriend or his ex-girlfriend or whatever. I couldn't make out words, but his sounds grew more and more pleading, until they were followed, inevitably, by long, deep sobs like the moans of a wounded manatee.

6

The Secret Service agent turned, and surprised him with a smile. "Good luck, Mr. President." He walked out, closing the door behind him, and Mike "Mac" Tipton was alone in the Oval Office. *President Tipton.*

This was where it had all led, from Little League games in Ohio, through the Naval Academy and the combat missions in an F-16 over Kuwait, the lonely campaigning in shopping malls and on street corners, and the ugly haggling of eight years in Congress. And then the campaign, the nights of bad coffee and bad jokes, throat sore from speeches, stomach stuffed with a thousand chicken dinners, face burning with the heat of television lights. Then the longest night of them all, in November, as he watched the states on CNN turn green and he knew he'd entered history as the first independent president since Washington.

As the January morning sunlight streamed in through the windows, the music of the Inaugural Ball still rang in his ear. But Mac Tipton—President Tipton—was finally alone. Not even his blonde wife Lizabeth could understand how he felt as he looked at the telephone and knew that in under a minute he could reach the premier of China, the South Pole, or—God forbid—the Nuclear Launch Center.

Mac looked at the portraits of Theodore Roosevelt, John F. Kennedy, and Abraham Lincoln. "I know how you feel," he said aloud, as he looked into Lincoln's somber face and laughed.

Suddenly he was aware of two figures in the room. He wheeled. "How did you—"

Across the rug, two men in dark suits, both clutching titanium briefcases, faced him. One had dark eyes and a military bearing, and stayed rigid, but the taller man held up his hand.

"No need to worry, Mr. President. We're friends."

"But how did you get in here?"

The taller man smiled. "We're men with . . . access. This is Riggs. You can call me Hopkins. Our names are not important."

Tipton, baffled, wondered whether to call for security.

"Mr. President, this briefing isn't on any schedule. In fact, for all intents and purposes, no one knows we're here. But we need to discuss a matter of the utmost urgency," Hopkins said.

Riggs opened his briefcase and removed a thin file. "Sir, how much do you know about outer space?"

—page one of the unfinished novel
Angels in the Whirlwind
by Pete Tarslaw

Since all this went down, various critics and bloggers have asked why I didn't just write a trashy airport thriller instead of a literary novel. In fact, I tried exactly that. Here's what happened:

After I'd been fired, the novel project took on a real desperation. I'd sit in my boxers and stare at the blank screen. Above my desk I'd taped a picture of Preston Brooks shoeing a horse.

Writing a novel would be easy if it wasn't for the frills. Take, for example, the scene early in *The Tornado Ashes Club* where Luke parachutes into Normandy a month before D-Day. The local resistance fighters find him, and together they celebrate his arrival over a bottle of calvados in a Bayeux root cellar.

This scene took me *two days*. Lots of Internet research was required to find out pesky details like what they drink in Normandy, and the name of a town, and what kind of parachute they used in World War II. Plus, since this was a "literary" novel, I couldn't just say "they drank some calvados and it was terrific, everybody shook hands and got blitzed." I had to describe the

warming, burning apple brandy that first arrived in a vapor, wafting along his nostrils before the harsh pure wetness enlivened his tongue. Carried with it was a history of orchards and harvests and aging time in old oak barrels. Visions that transcended that dank and dangerous place, and the fear of death, stark and present now like a cat perched on a bookshelf. The amber liquid carried visions that transcended even the war. Luke smiled as he sipped. The bottle said 1928. Carried inside were tastes wrought before there was a war, tastes that would remain long after the tanks had gone to rust and the generals gone to flag-draped graves. Tastes that would linger epochs after soldiers turned to fathers and lovers and warped-fingered old dreamers of memory, inhabiting languid houses on tree-lined streets where children ran and sang and played. Not even the war could take away these small, good things, flavors remembered, and preserved, and stored away.

Exquisite material but it took a lot out of me. So I'd take long breaks. I'd go down to the store on the corner and tally the total number of pornographic magazines (eighteen varieties, eighty-four total magazines, with *Shaved Sluts* in especial abundance). I'd walk to the only newsstand in the Somerville area that sold Take Five bars, and I'd listen to the half-witted proprietor monologize about the Yankees and Israel (both enemies of his). I'd study the movement of squirrels, name them, and choose favorites based on temperament and style. I read the *Boston Globe* every day, from cover to cover, including "Mallard Fillmore" and the death notices and the names of all the racing greyhounds.

During one of these readings, I came across an article in the business section:

FOR AUTHOR DREW, BIG BOOKS
ARE BIG BUSINESS

He talks about branding, market saturation, and revenue margins. But Tim Drew didn't make his fortune cooking the books—he made it writing them. And his profit margins would humble those of most CEOs.

"I see myself as a content sourcer, delivering a content product just as Nissan supplies cars or Papa John's supplies pizzas," says Drew, a 54-year-old Harvard MBA who gave up a financial career for a literary one. "I establish and maintain reliable delivery streams of entertainment."

It isn't the typical image for a writer. But Tim Drew isn't your typical writer. He's a one-man empire. His latest thriller, *The Darwin Enigma,* earned him an estimated $25 million from paperback sales, international and movie rights, and franchising.

But Drew says the secret to his success is straightforward. "I'm an entrepreneur who makes literary product. And that product is easy to make. A Tim Drew book starts with a handsome and talented protagonist, like Dr. Drake Hartbeer in *The Darwin Enigma,* who slowly unravels a conspiracy. Then I tie the conspiracy in with something big. In *The Hieroglyph Nexus,* it was pyramids. In *Leviathan's Rage,* it was whales. In *Valley of the Bent Spear,* it was those stone spheres they found in Costa Rica. In *Darwin Enigma,* it's the human brain and Buddhism. You throw in a woman whose skills the protagonist needs, dark secrets, lots of action, and you've got a book."

The accompanying picture was Tim Drew poolside at his house on Kauai. He was wearing sandals and sipping a smoothie with the Pacific shimmering below.

The view made Preston Brooks's pad look like a decrepit shanty. This Tim Drew was worth studying. An inset photo showed some serious-suited types in a boardroom, gazing at a blowup of the cover for *The Darwin Enigma.*

In the course of describing this "new model of literary capitalism," the article also mentioned Pamela McLaughlin. Not only the mystery novels but *The Trang Martinez Guide to the Mysteries of Dating & Sex, The Trang Martinez Cookbook,* a Trang Martinez–themed empowerment seminar, and Pamela McLaughlin's line of wine coolers were all arms of a multimillion-dollar empire. Pamela didn't even write the books herself anymore; she farmed them out to a battalion of freelancers before slapping her name on the cover. "The results are hard to argue with; McLaughlin owns her own Caribbean island, which she accesses via her personal helicopter." The article mentioned that the manager of her personal hedge fund gives talks to business school students about the challenges of such an enormous portfolio.

This all made a tremendous impression on me, having just paid for an Egg McMuffin with quarters.

Maybe with a literary novel, I was aiming too small. Compared to these titans of the writing con, Preston Brooks was like a street-corner shortgamer in a patchy sportcoat hustling three-card monte.

What was most magnificent about Tim Drew was his unabashed commercialism. He didn't even bother thinking up pretentious quotes or pondering the beauty of the newts he found. He told you what he was selling, people bought it, and the *Boston Globe* business section gushed over his joyous capitalist spirit.

The Tornado Ashes Club now seemed all wrong for me. I imagined guests at the airport heading to Polly's wedding, passing a huge stack of Pete Tarslaw paperbacks at Hudson's. They'd hardly be surprised when I arrived at the nuptials in an Escalade —or one of those Lexus hybrids; keep it tasteful—and deposited some high-ordnance gift like a Sub-Zero fridge or a Bose stereo that would prove in the most material fashion my clear dominance and James's inadequacy as a mate. Ten years down the road, I could be BlackBerrying money managers from my villa on Lake Como as starving MFA students hacked out the latest "Pete Tarslaw Presents" novel.

In the living room, I dug up my copy of *The Darwin Enigma.* I'd read it over the course of eleven toilet sittings that followed the week after I ate some bad shrimp pad thai delivered by a dubious Thai place called Prik King and I, which has since closed and been replaced by a tanning salon, so my memory of the book was hazy. But although it had, according to the *Globe,* made Tim Drew into the world's forty-fourth largest economy, I recalled that its prose would embarrass an even modestly gifted fourth-grader. I opened to the first page:

> A frigid November wind blew off the Potomac, hitting the face of Dr. Drake Hartbeer like a fistful of icy broken glass. But Drake kept up his intense pace in sheer defiance of his screaming thighs, aching pecs and throbbing triceps. Defiance and intensity were scripted into Drake's DNA. After all, you didn't make it from the docks of

Seattle, where arguments were settled at knifepoint, without a big helping of both. Defiance had kept him alive through bare-knuckled scrapes along Puget Sound, where he learned to keep his eyes sharp and his fists clenched. Defiance had sent him surging across the football field, on his way to winning a scholarship to Princeton, where he bashed heads with the prep school boys on his way to the Ivy League championship.

But defiance wasn't enough. Drake also had intensity. It was intensity that had carried him beyond, through Yale Medical School, as he studied the intricate channels of the brain. It was intensity that had landed him at his current post—Head of Neuroscience at the National Institutes of Health. Not bad for a scrappy kid from a devoutly Irish Catholic family of longshoremen, where communion wine and whiskey were both familiar tastes by puberty.

Finishing his daily ten miles at a solid clip, Drake puzzled mentally over a challenging section of Bach's "Goldberg Variations." He enjoyed classical piano. Like his other passion, rock climbing, it diverted him from the torturous mazes of his research. But Bach was tricky, even for his nimble fingers.

Slowing to a trot, Drake bent down. Picking up a rock, he flung it over the river and watched it sail in a graceful arc almost to the far bank. Not a bad analogy for a neuron firing an impulse along an axon, he thought, thinking of the electrical pathways along which the brain sends information. He flexed his most well-developed muscle, his cerebrum.

Suddenly, his balance was disturbed. He saw his research assistant, F. Jansen Teat, trotting his bulky frame along the river path. "Dr. Hartbeer! Dr. Hartbeer!"

We learn that Drake—on the verge of a breakthrough discovery that will revolutionize our understanding of the brain—has been visited by two shadowy monks from a mysterious Tibetan Buddhist order. They reveal that the discovery he's about to make is nothing new. In fact, they've known about it for centuries. But to make it public would shatter humanity to the core.

The rest of the novel is Drake running around the world, piece by piece discovering that, for centuries, certain humans have had superevolved brains that allow them to bend space-time. Jesus and Buddha are two prominent examples, both of them blessed/cursed with genetically warped brains that allowed them to walk on water and such. But a devious secret society has conspired to keep this all hidden, lest superbrains undo the order of the world.

It turns out, in the book, that Charles Darwin discovered all this in the nineteenth century. It was just evolution's course. Darwin left clues around the globe before the secret society silenced him. One of the clues, for instance, is carved on the shell of a very old Galapagos turtle. Drake Hartbeer discovers there's one of these hyperbrain kids in Russia, and he and a beautiful Russian scientist race to save him. Over the course of this mad pursuit, Drake's abilities as a classical pianist and a rock climber both come into play (when he's wooing the Russian lady and when they have to scale the wall of Chartres cathedral).

But what I took away, from my brief review of *The Darwin Enigma,* was that this kind of writing is easy.

You invent the awesomest hero you can think of, pit him against dark, mysterious forces, and let a secret spill out as he crisscrosses the globe. You write about something that people know is important but that they don't really understand, and you make it seem diabolical. You don't bury your action under a lot of nuanced characters or artful prose. Then you buy yourself a pimped-out Escalade, triumph at your ex-girlfriend's wedding, and retire to Hawaii.

Here's the challenge I set for myself: with a baking timer and one of Hobart's Lascar Pharmaceuticals notepads in front of me, I sat at the kitchen table and resolved to spend one solid hour seeing if I could come up with an idea for an airport thriller.

LIST OF BESTSELLER IDEAS

- It's July 1776, and George Washington and Ben Franklin and all those guys are in Philadelphia. There's a murder, and the local authorities turn to the only man they think might be able to solve it: Thomas Jefferson. (*Ties in to the always popular Founding Fathers, plus murder.*)
- A Border Patrol officer in the Texas desert discovers that some al-Qaeda guys are sneaking across from Mexico. He tries to warn the folks in Washington, but they don't believe him. So it's up to him and a tough but beautiful lady rancher to stop the terrorists from hijacking a train, filling it with chemicals, and blowing up the Alamo. (*Might prompt a tie-in cover story in* Time: *"How Safe Is Our Border?"*)

- A Hollywood actor filming a jewel-heist movie has to stop thieves who try to purloin the real jewels that are being used as props. (*Maybe Clooney or somebody would play himself in the movie?*)
- A lowly but handsome US Department of Agriculture inspector discovers a vast conspiracy to sterilize American men through poison in food. (*Relatable: everybody eats food. Another possible* Time *story: "How Safe Is Our Food?"*)
- A lithe and athletic former gymnast/archaeologist in Central America stumbles across a long-lost city and translates some inscriptions that reveal a diabolical secret: the ancient Maya discovered how to make nuclear weapons. Pursued by deadly guerrillas and shadowy CIA agents, she has to race through the jungle to stop the technology from falling into the wrong hands. (*Anything Mexican/Central American would probably make for a popular Spanish language translation.*)
- A fetching young computer programmer discovers that a Japanese video game company has implanted a code in their game that makes kids kill their parents. (*Could market a tie-in video game.*)
- A handsome geologist and a beautiful former ballet dancer/penguin expert in Antarctica discover a sinister oil company plan to destroy the icy continent. (*Penguins are sellable.*)
- A CIA agent discovers the Chinese are secretly training an army of genetically engineered dragons.
- An American college guy on a Rhodes Scholarship discovers a code in Shakespeare's plays. The code leads to a secret about the Bible.

- A yoga instructor/marine biologist discovers that dolphins have a code in their DNA. (*Put there by aliens? The Catholic Church? Oil companies?*)
- A hip modern Londoner discovers she's under a zombie curse that's followed her family since her sixteenth-century pirate ancestors. She's helped by a reggae singer who also teaches her how to relax and let love happen.
- A New York City cop discovers that some Hasidic Jews have found a long-lost eleventh commandment that changes everything.
- Pharmaceutical companies are poisoning everyone's brains.

The last thing, I realized, wasn't my idea. It was something a homeless guy had shouted at me as he was stuffing newspapers into his shirt.

Let's say each of my ideas was worth $500,000 in royalties, plus $1 million in movie rights, and an additional $1 mill in franchise fees and such. That meant the paper in my hand was worth $32.5 million. I decided to cut that in half, to be conservative, but still.

Maybe it was thinking about the stern faces and strange symbols on dollar bills that gave me one last idea as the baking timer went off.

- A newly elected idealistic president discovers that the history of the United States has been guided by a cabal of aliens and a secret society of their human collaborators.

This was the one, I knew it. People love reading about presidents, and I could pack in the Monsters of Best-Selling Nonfiction: Washington, Lincoln, Jefferson, Teddy Roosevelt. A suitably epic title occurred to me: *Angels in the Whirlwind.*

The image of mammoth stacks of copies of *Angels in the Whirlwind* at Costco, of movie posters and readers' guides and tied-in *National Geographic* specials appeared so clearly that I couldn't wait to make it a physical reality. I rushed to my computer and started typing.

What I discovered that afternoon dramatically shifted my understanding of entertainment's economics.

Writing a thriller, a Hawaii beach-house personal-helicopter-level blockbuster, is damn near impossible. That's why Tim Drew can give away his secrets for free.

It's easy at first, describing your hero's monumental chin and iron-core integrity and so forth. But slowly you discover it's like a complicated math problem, or assembling a bookshelf. You have to keep track of dozens of tiny parts, which good guys will turn out to be bad guys, and which cars will get blown up by which helicopters. And you know your readers will have no patience. They're demanding entertainment, so every page has to be interesting and full of guns and veiled threats and snappy retorts. It's exhausting.

With literary fiction, on the other hand, you can just cover everything up with a coat of wordy spackle. Those readers are searching for wisdom, so they're easier to trick.

I put *Angels in the Whirlwind* aside. I still think it's a decent idea, and if anybody wants to pay me to finish it, call my agent.

But that afternoon I went back to *The Tornado Ashes Club*.

I Google'd CALVADOS and learned that "the region known as Calvados, home to the eponymous apple brandy, is bordered on the north by Baie de la Seine and on the east by the Seine River."

I looked up at Preston Brooks, shoeing his horse. I knew I could beat him.

7

Luke gazed around the stout knotted walnut table at his new comrades: azure-eyed Marcel, Guillaume of the quizzical smile, Lavroche with his cheeks seared by knife wounds. But as he raised his glass, and felt the subtle, awakening wafts that filled his nostrils, Luke felt himself transported as if by a zephyr. He felt himself float away to the orderly orchards, flowering avenues of apple blossoms that threaded the dew-glazed western bank of the Seine.

He allowed himself that, a flight around the distant blossoms, and let his eyes linger half closed for one more moment before opening them again.

Guillaume spoke.

"Mis-tair Luke," Guillaume said. "We are always in danger here. The Germans, they march about on our streets. They tramp through our fields. They have captured many of us. They have tortured many of us. And they have killed many of us.

"But for us," he said, "the fear, the danger—it is nothing. Because we are in our home. And we fight for our home."

He poured, let the amber run into Luke's glass, playing the bottle against the candlelight.

"You have come to us," Guillaume said, "from far from your home. But because you fight with us, because you drink with us, because you are our comrade, this, too, Normandy, will be your home."

Luke lifted his glass. Perched it just beneath his lips.

"Let us drink then, mon ami," he said. "Let us drink to home."

—excerpt from Chapter 3 of
The Tornado Ashes Club
by Pete Tarslaw

Picture this preview—which by now I'd fully formed in my head—and tell me you wouldn't go see this movie:

First, the logo for Miramax or Fox Searchlight.

Then the logo for my production company. Either: a turtle swims up and imprints his hand on the screen over no-capitals lettering that says turtlehand films. Or: thousands of CGI snowflakes fall, and then superfast zoom in on the intricate pattern. "Snowflake Films."

Then sonorous piano chords. A woman's voice, soft and distant like the sound of a dusty music box you open on your great-aunt's dresser: *There are memories burned in the human heart.*

The screen fills with a falling shape against a night sky, shot through one of those filters that make colors distinct. (Probably a young guy from a small stylish country like Iceland or Estonia would be directing. Or else some sharp-eyed kid who'd done a Regina Spektor video or something.) It would take a second to realize what the image was: a parachute. An American soldier (Luke, played by a slightly unshaven but all-American actor, the guy from *Prison Break* maybe. Or: Christian Bale) descending into an apple orchard along a French river.

There are secrets we hide from each other. Now we'd see Silas (Paul Giamatti–type but handsomer) alone in his office, with the lights of Vegas glistening through a window. A gunshot.

He turns his head. The camera follows him as he walks down the hall and finds an artfully posed dead body.

There are people we turn to. Luke, now an old man, lies in a hospital bed as Grandmother opens the window. Two larks flutter away in the streaming sunlight.

There are journeys we must take. Close-up on Silas and Grandmother, in their beat-up Ford Maverick. A shot from a helicopter that shows a herd of mule deer running in between oil derricks along the highway, as scrubby Texas mountains rise in the distance.

There are promises we keep. Luke walks up to the church door of a Slovenian hill town. Then we cut to Grandmother and Silas, holding an urn as a tornado (done with computers) surges along the prairie in front of them.

And loves we find, and make our own. Genevieve (ideally Scarlett Johansson, but whatever, sort of a smarter-looking version of Gretchen Mol) walks off the stage in a Western bar lit by Budweiser signs. She sits down at the bar. Silas slides her a whiskey over ice.

The tempo picks up. One of the country singer's songs plays (opportunity for licensing—maybe a sexed-up cover of an old Loretta Lynn tune). A quick montage: Luke fighting behind a crashed and burning airplane in the Tunisian desert; Vegas cops kicking in the door of Silas's apartment; Luke playing smashmouth football in a sweater and leather helmet. Silas and Genevieve dancing and laughing in the rain under an iron bridge that spans the Mississippi. Grandmother clutching Luke to her sweatered shoulder as he sobs. Luke sampling wine in a Peruvian vineyard as the workers celebrate and play their Andean panpipes.

Based on the acclaimed best-selling novel by Pete Tarslaw

would be Chyroned on the screen. Genevieve, Silas, and Grandmother stand on the hood of their Ford, grimacing in spiritual
revelation as a tornado prepares to envelop them.

THE TORNADO ASHES CLUB. I doubt I'd write the screenplay,
but maybe I'd take an uncredited cameo as a French resistance
fighter or tornado expert.

Picturing myself in the theater watching it, I almost teared
up. Yet it was impossibly far away.

FOUR ANECDOTES ABOUT WRITERS
TO ILLUSTRATE MY PROBLEM

1. The essayist Dalton Tierguard was once asked by an
   interviewer what he hated most about being a writer.
   Without a second's hesitation he answered, "Writing."
2. The nineteenth-century French writer Jean-Jacques
   Plachet so despaired of ever finishing his novel *Les
   Femmes Laides* that he loaded a hunting rifle and shot
   himself in the right foot. Thus immobilized at his desk,
   he was able to finish his masterpiece.
3. The stories for which Scottish writer Hamish Baird is
   known were all written during a six-year period, after
   which Baird took a job cleaning the sewers of Glasgow.
   He said his second career was a welcome relief from
   the misery of writing.
4. American novelist Amy Abbott McNicholas found
   writing so difficult that each morning she had her servant lock up all the chamber pots in the house, and
   keep them locked up until she was presented by her
   mistress with ten pages of prose. McNicholas died at
   forty-eight of a bladder infection.

When you think of the great writers, penning a novel seems terribly romantic. You think of F. Scott Fitzgerald, a Riviera breeze billowing his curtains and the sounds of the Cap d'Antibes street cut by the tapping of his typewriter, as he lacerates the rich and dreams of the past. Or Hemingway, in a hotel in Pamplona in the heat of the afternoon, as bullfighters take their siesta and drops of water bead on a bottle of kirsch. Or Joyce, squinting his Irish bead-eyes as he blends his classical training and his Gaelic imagination to summon up allusive rhythms and language dense and enfolding.

Even lesser novelists seem glamorous. Some scribbler burning twigs in a boardinghouse in the second arrondissement as he dips his quill pen into the ink. Or a slim and shoeless thirty-something, taking a year off from his job as an alternative-marketing consultant to sit in a park in Vancouver or Park Slope and type into his PowerBook a wry yet soulful take on the paradoxes of hypermodernity.

That is all delusion. Writing a novel is pathetic and boring. Anyone sensible hates it. It's all you can do to not play Snood all afternoon.

Understand that in my account here, I've cut a lot of the boring stuff out. It wasn't like writing essays, where I could bang one out and go to Sree's. This was three *hundred* pages. It's not that it was hard, exactly. It was more like shoveling snow or cleaning out the attic, tedious labor toward a very distant end.

Intractable literary problems kept presenting themselves. Example: one night Derek called me from The Colonial Boy, so I went to meet him, we drank Salt Lick bourbon with ginger ale, and the next morning my brain was in a vice and my poop was viscous. I wrote nothing.

A few days later there was a John Hughes marathon on WE, and to skip that would be downright un-American. Again, wrote nothing.

Another day while napping I had a dream about an old Nintendo game called *Kid Bubble* where you float around in Soap Land and bop monsters with your bubble while avoiding cactus spikes and sharp birds, so I spent most of the day finding and playing a downloadable version. Wrote nothing. Each morning I'd wake up and see Preston Brooks, shoeing his horse, staring down at me. Taunting me.

At the end of all this I had 112 pages of *The Tornado Ashes Club* groaning like a wounded deer in the road. The sooner I had a sharp rock in my hand to finish her off, the better.

But out of desperation came an ingenious solution.

First step: On a Friday about four weeks after I'd gotten fired, I waited for Hobart to come in. He arrived at about 11 P.M., haggard and pale.

"Hey, Hobart. You know, I went on eBay, and I got us something."

There, on the coffee table, next to *Peking,* was an unopened DVD set of the original version of *Summer Camp,* made for Danish television.

"It's supposed to be extra screwed up."

It was. Instead of the comforting warmth of the Asian-American hostess on the American version, this thick-necked Danish guy with salami fingers barked out orders. The translations on the subtitles weren't quite right either, so an eight-year old girl shrieking and crying at an adult in her cabin was translated as "You are far irritating!"

And in the American network version, they go out of their way to assure you there's no pedophile stuff going on. They're much more cavalier about this in the Danish edition.

Every night that week we watched an episode when Hobart got home. We did not speak.

Once I ordered a pizza without telling Hobart. When it arrived I paid but said it was for both of us. Hobart stared at it like a refugee child being offered chocolate. Non-instant-mashed-potato food was foreign to him, but he pounced on it until grease and cheese dribbled down his stubble.

The next week, I started making parries and thrusts of conversation. I asked him about his work at Lascar and his med school studies and what it was like to carve up a cadaver.

"You stop seeing it as a person," he said.

"That's interesting. I totally can see that." I paused while the Danish campers lustily sang competing campfire songs. "Man, I could never make it in med school. I've always had trouble concentrating. Probably has something to do with never knowing my dad."

I left that one hanging there.

When he got home a few nights later, I was wearing a button-up shirt and my finest dining-out pleateds. As he opened the door I was tonging ice into my two surviving Larry Bird commemorative glasses, our apartment's finest drinkware.

"Oh, hey Hobart."

"Hello."

"I thought, you know, Friday night and all, we should have a cocktail hour. Like gentlemen, you know?" I poured two glasses and offered him one. "It's MacAllister eighteen," I said, before a slow and gentlemanly sip. "Mmm, very *peaty*."

I handed him a Scotch.

*   *   *

Two hours later: Hobart was holding forth in a voice that quivered with anguish. Scotch slopped all over the carpet as he paced back and forth.

"She says she's 'coming into her own as a woman.' Into her *own*! That the distance is good for us! She said 'we're better as two separate entities that care about each other than as one unit.' Bullshit!"

"Man."

"It's bullshit! And she's always, she's mentioning all the time *Nevin*."

"Yikes."

"Some guy named Nevin who works at Washington Mutual. 'You'd like him.' She said that! I wouldn't like him! I friggin' . . . I hate him!"

"That's tough, man. But, you know, give it some time. It'll work out."

"It sucks!"

"Yeah man, I hear ya. I've been having a rough time, too. I lost my job."

"It sucks."

"Yeah. I mean, I've been working on my résumé, but I just have so much trouble concentrating."

"Concentrating. That's all I ever do is concentrating."

"It's just, you know, I don't know if I'm gonna make rent."

This seemed to hit, triggering Hobart's terror of disorder. He looked up at me. "Dude are you serious?" He seemed to grasp instantly how unnatural he sounded saying *dude*.

"Yeah." This was not true. Signing up for unemployment had been easy, made me feel like a real writer, and had me stable for a while.

"That's . . . God!"

"Yeah. If I could just figure out a way to *concentrate*."

Hobart's eyes showed determination as he struggled to stay seated upright. I saw my time to strike.

"Hey, you guys at Lascar are working on a drug for that kind of stuff, for like hyperactivity and stuff?" A pause. Then he spoke, slurred, as though reading off a chart on the wall.

"Reutical is a medication designed to reduce the symptoms of hyperactivity and ADD, improving focus and concentration in adolescent males."

"So it helps kids pay attention in school and stuff?" Heavy, thudding nods from Hobart.

"I mean, it probably has something to do with never knowing my dad. I've tried all different stuff that doctors gave me." This was not true. "But one of them said the only thing that might help was this Reutical thing. Do you think you could get me some?"

There was a long pause, as his whiskey-soaked neurons made ethical calculations.

"We're only in phase two trials." He said this as though it concluded the matter.

"So that's experiments, right?"

"Yeah, experiments."

"Sweet. I mean, I'll be an experiment."

Hobart laughed. "We're all friggin' experiments." Some rolling of the head about his neck like a statue teetering on a podium.

"You know it's great what you do. It's medicine, after all. To help people."

I fixed him with my eyes.

"Hobart, you're a good roommate. And a good friend. I knew you'd help me out on this. Because you're a gentleman." He looked at me. I knew I had maybe twelve seconds before he could say anything. So I dashed into the bathroom. I waited there. I heard him pour another glass. Then silence. I saw him passed out on the couch.

Early, very early the next morning, I left a note on his desk saying "Hobs, thanks so much for promising to get me that Reutical." Then I hid in my room.

For two days I didn't see Hobart. But I knew how his brain was working. He was thinking, "Pete can't make rent. He has trouble concentrating. It probably has something to do with never knowing his dad. It's medicine, to help people." But above all he was thinking, "I promised him. He called me a gentleman. I am a gentleman. I'm better than Nevin. I made Pete a gentleman's promise."

I walked into the living room one morning and found a clear plastic jar holding thirty gray oval pills.

Beneath were eight pages written in his meticulous hand. It was warnings and instructions, with tidy arrows of emphasis, a diagram explaining in basic terms Reutical's chemical structure, and charts. I skimmed it and got the main point, which was "don't take Reutical with alcohol." I gleaned the subtext, which was "please, Pete, don't screw me on this."

In short, Hobart was as careful as possible and doesn't deserve any blame.

8

On this morning, Prudence didn't stop. She walked right into the shop.

Her father and her brother Josiah and Gideon the apprentice didn't notice, so busy were they at their planing and awling.

"Good morning!" said Prudence.

"Prudence!" said Father. "What brings you to us this morning? Has Mother sent you with blackberry currants for our midday meal?"

"No," said Prudence. "I've come because I'd like to learn to be a cooper."

"WHAT?!" cried Gideon. "Why, a girl cooper?"

"Surely you're joking, Prudence!" declared Josiah. "Why, I could sooner imagine our American colonies separating from Mother England!"

The two boys laughed, quite meanly.

Father put his hard hand on Prudence's shoulder.

"Prudence," he said, "such foolishness doesn't become you. You know as well as I that young girls are made for milking, mending clothes, and baking pies. Let's be home with you, and hear no more nonsense."

But Prudence was very brave. She didn't move a foot.

"Father," she said, "I would like to be a cooper. And if you teach me, why, I'll make a barrel as well as might a boy!"

The cruel boys laughed again.

"Look, Gideon," cried Josiah, "at the barrel made by Prudence!" He was holding up a broken stave.

A tear welled in Prudence's eye.
"I *will* be a cooper!" she cried. "You'll see!"
She turned from the shop, and off she ran.

—excerpt from the unpublished manuscript
Prudence Whiddiecomb: The Girl Cooper
by Evelyn Ewart and Margaret Wrenshall

The next day I threw my laptop and a handful of underwear into my Camry and drove north, up 93 to Vermont.

An easy way to get credibility as an author is to live someplace rugged. Publishers live in Manhattan, so they consider southern Connecticut to be a hinterland. They're easily impressed, and it seemed foolish not to exploit that weakness.

Preston Brooks has West Virginia. Upstate New York is a popular choice. That's cordwood-chopping, run-down mill-town country. West Texas is fertile—cf. Cormac McCarthy, Larry McMurtry. Wyoming and Montana give a writer a lot of seriousness points. Nobody's gonna call you out when you start throwing around place-names like Bitterroot and Teton and Laramie. The point is to prove that your prose is as natural as a bushel of organic tomatoes or a cut of steak from a free-range longhorn.

Territories are going fast. Before long novelists will have to set up camp in Burkina Faso or Sakhalin Island if they want any credit for being genuine voices.

With a bottle of Reutical in my pocket, it wouldn't be long until I was putting *The Tornado Ashes Club* on the market. I'd need the publishing assistants to say to their bosses "you've got to sign this guy—he's a completely pure voice, he holed up in a cabin in like *New Hampshire* or someplace and wrote this fucking amazing book that's so lyrical you're gonna shit."

Plus I knew Hobart would almost immediately regret his decision, and I didn't want to be around to deal with it.

So I'd called up my Aunt Evelyn.

THE STORY OF AUNT EVELYN

Once Evelyn was a famously fierce lawyer. She wore pant-suits. She was in the papers and on TV a few years back when her firm had defended the city of Boston against some kids who claimed they'd been injured riding the subway. She was the one who tricked the main guy into admitting in court that their injuries were actually from filming a homemade break-dancing video. That was the same year she announced she was a lesbian. This didn't bother anyone in our family, a fact which I think disappointed her because she was fired up to smoke any opposition. After that she mellowed out. She got a girlfriend, Margaret, who was only a few years older than me. Margaret had captained the Smith College rugby team to the national championship. She's great. I did a bunch of shots with her at the commitment ceremony. A year or two later, Evelyn announced that she was quitting the law. She and Margaret were going to move up to Vermont to open a maple sugar distillery. That was the kind of thing you could do if you didn't have kids, my mom had commented ruefully.

At about six I turned down the gravel road in Tracton toward their house, a solid rectangle of local stone set back among de-sapped trees.

Margaret came out, the Joan of Arc dome of her hair bouncing as she ran up to me for the first round of hugs. Then into the kitchen for round two with Aunt Evelyn, who was ferociously eviscerating a cantaloupe.

I was treated to a magnificent welcome dinner: organic spinach salad, mixed fruit puree, locally raised Connecticut River salmon with apple-maple chutney, homemade seven-grain bread, followed by traditional Native American corn pudding. This wasn't what I'd expected. I'd imagined my stay in Vermont would be a hard literary asceticism, like a boxer in training camp. But I'd now been unemployed for almost two months so I ate like a grateful urchin.

"Try the wine," Aunt Evelyn said, "our friends Crispin and Lawrence sent it to us from Sorrento. It's made by Trappist monks."

"Those monks know how to stomp a grape," Margaret said.

"So Pete, I think it's wonderful that you're working on a book. We're so honored to have a young novelist for a guest. What inspired you to turn to matters literary?"

"Mostly to humiliate Polly, and impress people at her wedding."

Margaret laughed. "Right on." Margaret totally gets it.

"Plus I wanted to get enough money so I don't have to work anymore."

"Well, that doesn't sound especially noble," my aunt said, though she appeared at least slightly amused. "I'm considering embarking on a writing project of my own. A children's book. I really think it's a story that could be empowering to young girls. It's about a girl who isn't content to just become a wife and a mother. She wants to learn the trade of coopering. Barrel making."

"Huh."

"The best part is that it's a true story. Her name was Prudence Whiddiecomb, and she lived over in Spayboro in the late eighteenth century. And while her father was off fighting in the Revolution, she took over his business. She became quite a successful cooper and also did some light smithing." Evelyn told me about her explorations in the historical societies of local towns, in speech peppered with phrases like "the interesting thing about staves is . . ." and "now, in those days, Spayboro wasn't the county seat, which complicates things."

After the corn pudding, Margaret showed me an illustration she'd done for the proposed book. Her ideas of what makes a good illustration for a children's book are different from those of children. Her main influence seemed to be Eastern European movie posters and Victorian crime sketches. The etching was in charcoal, a terrifying, ghoulish close-up of Prudence holding a tool, with a quarter of her teeth exposed, about to stab a barrel.

"That's an awl," Margaret said, in answer to an unasked but reasonable question.

Aunt Evelyn never really figured out maple syruping. She told me about how there'd been an explosion in their neighbor's sugar shack, caused by poor ventilation. A basset hound had been maimed but was getting by now on three legs, an example of perseverance for us all. That was the kind of rural detail from which I could benefit. I made a note to add a part in *Tornado Ashes Club* where Grandmother draws inspiration from such a dog.

The next morning Aunt Evelyn and Margaret went into Spayboro to buy tapenades and such. Under a pot of Mountaineer Organic Slow-Roast Dark Blend coffee, Evelyn left me a note encouraging me to "make the sugar shack your writer's studio!"

So there I sat, among the empty vats. Evelyn had set up a metal desk and a wooden chair for me. On my laptop were my most recent pages. Luke was traveling from Tunisia to Peru in the belly of a steamer, his clothes soaked with bilgewater as he dreamed of home. It was great, messy stuff that had occurred to me while I was scouring my bathtub. Meanwhile, Silas, Genevieve, and Grandma were camped out in the Black Hills, and Genevieve was telling a Lakota legend (I'd made it up) about the stars representing the hearts of lost lovers.

All the inspiration and energy I needed to finish was, I hoped, contained in the little gray pill I dumped out of the Reutical bottle. I washed it down with a swig of coffee and waited.

EFFECTS OF REUTICAL, AS NOTED BY THE AUTHOR, MARCH 11

BEGIN 11:34 A.M.

0–8 minutes after ingestion: No effect. Boredom.

8–11 minutes: Slight anger at Hobart. Have I been hoaxed? Itchiness of scalp (probably unrelated).

11 minutes: Self-administration of second Reutical.

12.5 minutes: Need to urinate.

13 minutes: Even-paced walking into house, followed by normal urination.

14 minutes: Self-administration of small glass of MacAllister whiskey, to accelerate process.

21–34 minutes: Fascination with the hairs on my right hand. Sudden need to count them above the wrist.

Concern over where to demarcate as "above the wrist." Drawing of impressively straight line across wrist. Counting of hairs, followed by two recounts to ensure accuracy (78, 77½, 77⅓, avg. 77.61111)

34 minutes: Feelings of confidence and affection toward Hobart. Removal of stray .611111 hand-hair by means of salad tongs.

38 minutes: Return to sugar shack.

38.5 minutes: Discovery of a small spider on sugar shack floor. Observation that he, too, is covered by tiny hairs. Consideration of all the things in the sugar shack (vats, spiders, desk, electrons, etc.). Listing of things that are covered by hairs (children, monkeys, flies, etc.). Sudden fear of sugar shack explosion, maiming. Running out of sugar shack.

39 minutes: Feeling of safety. Unusually high interest in the patterns of stray leaves.

43 minutes: Sudden need to document effects of Reutical on subject. Beginning of documentation.

46 minutes: Feeling of energy. Anxiousness that I am squandering Reutical's power. Self-administration of additional ½ Reutical tablet. Compulsion to write.

46–318 minutes: Writing.

318 minutes: Dry mouth. Heavy sweating.

At minute 318 I noticed that my shirt was sticking to me like a coat of damp plaster and my tongue felt cracked like the dirt in a desert streambed. I stopped typing and noticed, too, that my wrists ached and it took me a painful minute to unbend my fingers.

During that bout of writing I hadn't checked my page count. But I now saw that I'd written forty-nine pages.

"Well young Hawthorne!" said Evelyn as I walked into the house.

"Wassup Faulkner," said Margaret, less earnestly.

That night, after a dinner of leftover salmon, I reviewed the work I'd done. A lot was garbage. There were strange repetitions. The word *taciturn* was used four times in one sentence. Genevieve was thrice described as *robin-throated*. The Black Hills were said to "rise from the land like the calluses and corns and warts from God's own foot." In the scene where Luke arrives on the dock in Callao, he passes some barrels. For some reason, in my frenzy I'd felt it necessary to list the contents of thirty-four of these barrels. But that was all for the editors to sort out. I'd covered ground. And there was some artful prose, too, like where I described Genevieve as singing "with the humble desperation of a grizzly wailing from a leg trap in the Alaska night."

Hobart and the folks at Lascar Pharmaceuticals were doing some fine work with that Reutical. Once it hit the market, America's boys would go from playing Halo 3 and quoting *Aqua Teen Hunger Force* to spending their days filling in multiplication tables and declining French verbs.

On the bedside table Aunt Evelyn had left a hardcover volume called *Hearts of Ice and Blubber*. "One of my *FAVOR-ITES*! For inspiration.—Aunt E." read a Post-it note attached to the cover, obscuring a watercolor rendering of a woman in a dress outside of an igloo. On the back were emblazoned the words THE BOOK THAT SCANDALIZED CANADA!

Under the quilt I read for a few hours, as my brain was in too high a gear for sleeping. The novel tells the story of Cassie

St. Hilaire, the widow of a Toronto lawyer who dies in a ghastly fishing accident. Cassie takes a job as a teacher at a school for Eskimo women on Baffin Island.

I found a legal pad in the desk and stayed awake for a few hours just copying out sentences from this book until the Reutical wore off.

And this was how I spent my week in Vermont. I'd wake up, tear off a piece of seven-grain bread, wash down two Reuticals with coffee, supplement with whiskey if necessary, and write. By four or five I'd be sopped like a racehorse, but I'd have moved my novel forward: Silas and Genevieve and Grandma down into the tornado belt, Luke to the Peruvian vineyard as Nazi agents slowly closed in on him. At night I'd cool off with Cassie, who as I might have predicted started lesboing it up with an Inuit girl named Talinquak.

By Sunday, I was out of Reutical, Cassie and Talinquak had met their unfortunate ends, and Aunt Evelyn had started giving me sample pages of *Prudence Whiddiecomb: The Girl Cooper,* so it seemed time to make my escape. I'd made stunning progress on *The Tornado Ashes Club.* Luke finally died of spine cancer while listening to his nurse call her son in Iraq from the phone down the hall. We jump forward, to Grandmother, Silas, and Genevieve, on the plains of Kansas, as a tornado comes across: *"a tremendous smudge against the sky, woolly and ferocious. Moving, as all things are moved, by unseen forces, greater still, that willed it across the grasslands in low uncertain bends."*

With a long round of hugs I thanked Aunt Evelyn and Margaret for their hospitality, presented them with a case of Upstream Ale in gratitude, and headed off.

*   *   *

"Jesus Christ Pete where the . . . crap were you?" Hobart threw an open-handed slap that flapped into my shoulder like an errant duck. "I friggin' . . . almost puked wondering where you were!"

The poor guy thought I'd gone on a Reutical binge. He was afraid I'd met some awful superfocused disaster, like I'd decided to study the workings of a garbage compactor from the inside and ended up a puddle of red muck. Or I'd started ranking cleaning products on the basis of taste and ended up dead in the aisle of Walgreens with a bottle of Clorox in one hand and a notebook in the other, leaving the coroner to unravel a maze of toxicology that led back to Lascar. I felt so bad about the whole thing that I took Hobart out for waffles. He got strawberries on his and seemed cheered up.

On March 19, in my spiritual home as an author, the downtown Barnes & Noble's, I finished *The Tornado Ashes Club*.

It's Christmas morning, on a Kansas plain. Silas and Genevieve hold each other, on the roof of the Ford Maverick. They watch as Grandma stands near the path of an onrushing tornado. She opens the coffee can that holds Luke's ashes, the ashes of Silas's grandfather. Grandma whispers, her voice caught and pulled away by the wind.

And she said the truest words she'd ever said, in a lifetime of pained and sacred honesty.

Good-bye, my love.

Sure it was crap. 331 pages of magnificent greeting-card-level crap.

But as I walked out through the shelves, I looked at the works of my colleagues. There was Hemingway—*A Farewell to Arms, For Whom the Bell Tolls*—all those pseudoepic titles with women dying in the rain, and bullfights, and Italian vistas. He knew the deal. He knew doomed Mediterranean romances would pay for a Key West beach view and a new fishing boat. And Fitzgerald, who'd tricked the eye with an Ivy League pedigree and convinced the world that a rich guy who threw parties was some kind of metaphor. There was Faulkner, a southern huckster in the Bill Clinton mold, who suckered you in with his honey voice and tales of landscapes soaked in tragedy.

It went on back to Homer, who'd written stories so ridiculous, so full of special effects and monsters and busty, half-divine sluts that Hollywood would be ashamed to make them. And he'd pulled it off! He'd punched it up with *rosy-fingered dawn* and the sickeningly cloying scene of Priam begging for his son's body. That blind old trickster probably got more chicks (or dudes?) than Pericles.

On through Dickens, with his pleading orphans and sweetheart aunts; Mark Twain, with his little cherub-faced rascals and mock-rural slang; James Joyce with his whiskey-soaked stage-Irish blarney—they were all con artists. They weren't any better than the guys who write beer commercials or sell car insurance over the phone. They just had a different angle.

And there, at the front of the store, on the BEST-SELLING AUTHORS table, was *Kindness to Birds* by Preston Brooks, still selling strong. I flipped open the back cover to the author's picture: Preston, his beard as sharp as a razor. He was sitting on a hay bale, whittling with a pocketknife, the West Virginia mountains rising behind him.

9

FICTION

Protracted by Jean Fung. A novel about hooking up and engineering at a prestigious university, written by the former sex columnist for *The California Tech*.

The Tornado Ashes Club by Pete Tarslaw. Love, loss, and the soul of truth are explored when a wrongly accused man goes on a road trip with his grandmother and a Mexican folksinger.

Blow by Derek Peter Nelson. On a deep-sea exploration vessel, an oceanographer falls in love with a trained dolphin.

Eva Gets Thin, Gets Rich, and Gets Over HIM by Lindsay Phebbs. An assistant at a Manhattan advertising agency loses weight, gets promoted, and learns to forget her no-good boyfriend over a Memorial Day weekend in the Hamptons.

NONFICTION

Back to Babylon by Jeff Claite. A comic travelogue of a trip through Iraq, in the Bill Bryson tradition.

Tax the Jihadis! by Donnie Vebber. The controversial radio host shares his opinions about tax policy, corporate scandals, the War on Terror, and why Hillary Clinton is worse than Hitler.

Dreaming of Buck Owens by N'Gome Tula. A memoir by the Nigerian human rights activist about his time as a diamond miner and his love of American culture.

How to Stop Being a Ho ... and Why by Tysha Coleran. A tough-talking former schoolteacher takes on Paris Hilton wannabes and shows them how to clean up their minds, bodies, and mouths.

Chili on Spaghetti: A Cincinnati Love Story by Myra and John Ritchey. A "generously proportioned" husband and wife describe their unusual love affair with each other and with food.

—excerpts from a press release announcing titles acquired by Ortolan Press in the month of April 2007

People who know about publishing will not find this part of my story strange at all—I predict they'll nod with glum recognition—but those readers unfamiliar with how publishing works may find the story of how I sold my novel to be crazy and implausible. But, trust me, this is how it happened.

Maybe it'll assure you that the world works in crazy and implausible ways if you consider how I even got to New York. In the earliest days of the Dragon Eight bus line, which runs from Chinatown in Boston to Chinatown in New York, it was not uncommon for a few of the passengers to be carrying livestock. I myself never saw pigs, so I can't confirm that personally although others swear to it and claim that the pigs were "tusked." Poultry was frequent. Once, in the row in front of me, a woman held a rooster in a bamboo cage.

But then word got out about the $10 bus ride to Manhattan. Chinese livestock transporters found some less visible service. Soon every ride included an unwashed hipster lugging a guitar and reading a biography of Woody Guthrie. The buses are still seldom-serviced incubators for typhoid and bird flu that have been known to burst into flames on I-84. And the drivers spend most of the trip squawking into walkie-talkies in Cantonese. But the price can't be beat. So I bought two pork buns, found a seat, and headed south.

Before leaving I'd given *The Tornado Ashes Club* a final pass, to make sure it was ready for the marketplace. I'd made a list of commercial elements to add: more dogs, booze, and coffee, all of which are popular among readers. Thick descriptions of passionate kisses. I'd tucked in hints at my Big Themes: love, death, tornadoes, crimes, the human heart, hints so obvious that even dumber readers would catch on. Then I e-mailed a copy off to Lucy, my confederate in the publishing business, along with a request to crash at her place for a few days.

By the time I got on the bus I was bored sick of my novel. I carried along a printed-out copy, because the weight of it in my backpack was satisfying. I even took it out a few times, to feel its mass in my hands with the kind of simplistic pride a toddler feels over his poops. But I certainly didn't want to read it. I ate my pork buns and flipped through an article about Monte Carlo in the seventies in *Vanity Fair,* then dozed off with my head against the filthy window. Next to me a Chinese woman crunched a bag of dried cuttlefish. When I woke up it was dark and we were stuck in traffic near Co-Op City. Deposited at last on a Chinatown street corner, I made my way through the pee-stained, box-strewn sidewalks of southern Manhattan.

The central events of my trip to New York took place in two bars.

THE FIRST BAR

Fitzgerald's, somewhere on Seventh Avenue, near the place that sells corned-beef tacos.

I jockeyed through the postwork crowd and found Lucy in the back, sitting at a table in the crook of the restroom line.

And by the redness of her cheeks and the jolliness of her voice, it appeared she'd started drinking without me.

LUCY

> She won't be offended if I describe her as pie-faced. In college she was a cheerful adorable presence down the hall, the kind of girl who would bring you back some eggs from the dining hall if you were hungover. On rare occasions she transformed into a hilarious drunken clown, but mostly she was a diligent student; senior year she won a prize for her paper on Charlotte Brontë. She went off to work at Ortolan with romantic dreams, but they assigned her to some desperate editor with a stitched-together list of authors—Lucy seemed to work mostly on gruesome horror paperbacks about vampirous detectives and werewolves on oil rigs.

Lucy bashed her knees against the table as she rose to give me her trademark stumpy-armed hug. "Books!" she said, and she waved at the walls of Fitzgerald's. And sure enough! The walls were covered with black-and-white portraits of intense, cigarette-wielding men from the era of capital-letter Writers. There were dust jackets from decades-old novels, the kind of assertive four-color designs that these days you only see on packs of cigarettes. Over the bar hung the namesake, F. Scott himself, looking forlornly at me as I ordered a raspberry cider.

"So how are things going?" I asked. It was important for my plan that Lucy remember we were good friends and not think I was just using her to get published.

"Oh, they're okay. I got new sheets that are supersoft!" she replied over the din. She mentioned Polly's wedding, and since she seemed genuinely happy for that traitorous hussy I kept quiet until she changed the subject.

"Do you like this bar?" she asked.

"Yeah, it's great. Is it weird to name a bar after a guy who drank himself to death?"

Lucy looked around confused. "That didn't occur to me." She took an impressive swallow of bourbon. "I think writers used to come here. James Jones and Norman Mailer and stuff. But these guys look like mostly consultants."

Then she grabbed my wrist with both hands and her eyes burst out as though suddenly remembering something. "Your book!"

I worked my face into writerly indifference. "Oh that. Did you read it?"

"It's going to get me promoted."

This statement so stunned me that I jerked my neck in a way that hurt for weeks.

"You thought it was good?!"

"Oh not *good* good," she said. "I mean . . . I was impressed, you know, that you *wrote* the whole thing, but . . . I mean, *tornadoes?*"

Now I pantomimed "hurt."

"So you didn't think it was good."

"Look, Pete." She leaned in close, and whispered. "I can't tell anymore."

"What?"

"I can't tell. I don't know if they're good or bad or what."

"Aren't you supposed to be an assistant editor?"

"Editorial assistant, but—I don't think anybody knows."
By now we were leaning in like two spies. "They can't tell, my
boss *definitely* can't tell, his boss *certainly* definitely can't tell.
Nobody knows. And we're in a lot of trouble."

"Wait—"

"Look, do you realize how many manuscripts we get? Thousands! Tens of thousands! Just stacks and stacks! Some people
don't have desks, they just have stacks. And there are people
whose whole job it is to throw them in the garbage. Huge bins!
They use shovels! But the manuscripts never stop coming in."

"But most of those have got to be terrible."

"You have no idea! Crazy terrible! Sometimes pages have
bloodstains on them. We have a group, an e-mail thing, me and
these other assistants, we e-mail around the worst sentences—
you can't believe them! You get just numb to it. But once you
sort those out, then there are the ones you actually deal with.

"Pete, listen, I'm smart, right?" She said this so pleadingly
that I nodded as fast as I could.

"I can't tell. I thought I could. I thought I knew good from
bad. I'd find these incredible, touching books, and I'd say how
great they were, and the editors would toss them. Or they'd
publish them, and they'd sell like fifty-four copies. Literally.
Fifty-four copies."

She finished her bourbon. "*Peking*. I sent you *Peking*? It
sold thirty-four hundred copies. That's it. Total. And that was
'above expectations'!

"And this, this is even worse. The bad ones! These bad ones—
terrible ones, ones that don't even make *sense* and have *adverbs*
everywhere and made-up words—they sell ten million copies and
they make movies out of them. I used to cry, every night, literally,

I would get a milkshake and put vodka in it and cry because I thought I must be stupid. I had these dreams, every night, where everybody speaks some foreign language and I don't know it."

"What kind of milkshakes?"

"And I thought I was gonna quit. But then I sort of got it. *Nobody* knows. None of them. Editors, writers, agents, nobody. You know like when a kid is just screaming and screaming, and the mom just keeps throwing toys at it, but the kid keeps screaming, and it looks like the mom's about to cry, too?"

"I think so—"

Lucy slapped the table. "That's what it's like! The editors are the mom! Readers are the kid. And the editors just keep throwing stuff at them, but they don't know what to do!"

Lucy made it sound like the ruins of a postwar city. A nightmare where a crafty fellow could make a fortune.

"My boss, he's crazy. He's literally crazy. Do you know what he made me do? Monday, he told me to go on MySpace. Just spend the whole week on MySpace. And find something —a sentence, anything—something kids want. Just anybody he can sign."

"Did you find anything?"

"And blogs! Jesus! Blogs! If I hear the word *blog* one more time I'm gonna put my neck on the subway tracks."

"So how's business?"

"Oh it's terrible. They're going to fire people. They said so. These guys from England, these guys who own a liquor company? They bought the whole place and announced they're going to fire people. That was the first thing they did! 'Cheers, 'ello, we're going to make redundancies!' And everyone who'd seen the British *Office* knew that meant fired."

Then her eyes burst out at me again. "But *you*! You're going to get me off the desk! Because you meet the Checklist!"

"What's the Checklist?"

"It's this thing, this form you fill out now. The corporate guys made it up. Look!"

She produced a document from her messenger bag.

ORTOLAN PRESS NEW TITLE ASSESSMENT

Title: The Tornado Ashes Club
Author: Pete Tarslaw
Reader: Lucy Etten
Genre: Literary / Crime

(3.5) Readability

(2) Potential for sequels

(5) Potential for movie sales (visuals, action, casting, filmable locations)

(5) Potential for spinoff cookbook

(4) Potential for branding

(2) Potential for merchandising

(1) Potential for video game

(4) Potential for ancillary material (reader's guides, etc.)

(3.5) Author appearance

(5) Author interview

(5) Author blog / web presence

(4) Awards potential

(5) International marketability

( ) SR (if applicable)

RECOMMENDATION (5)

"Look at these scores! We'll have to make you a blog at some point."

"How come I got a three-point-five in appearance?"

"Believe me, compared to most of these guys you're at *least* a three-point-five. But look at this!"

"I'm a four in awards?"

"We're gonna make Genevieve Mexican. She'll sing ranchera music. Trust me."

"What's SR?"

"That's your sales record. Believe me, you don't want to have that. Unless you're Pamela McLaughlin or Tim Drew, it won't help." Lucy slapped the checklist against the table in joy. "You see?! Now we just convince Dave. But he'll buy it. 'Young talent, young talent!' He's always screaming that at me. He sounds like a porn producer."

I went back to the bar trembling.

Lucy and I kept drinking and talking, although not necessarily to each other. She, I remember, went on a rant about why people bother to write at all. She pointed vaguely at dust jackets. "Look at these people! Vance Bourjally. Charles R. Robinson. Forgotten! Dead! Nothing! All that work! All those cigarettes! Their books are *pulp* now. Their books are these *napkins*! They *literally* turned their books into toilet paper. Literally. You wipe your ass on their books. And those are the good ones! But it's the bad ones! The bad ones muck up the whole field. No offense."

None was taken. I for my part recall holding forth with invective against Polly peppered with embarrassing revelations. I remember leaving, and propping up Lucy for half the stumble back to her place. She suggested getting corned-beef tacos at this place that was right nearby.

"If it's so bad," I asked her, as we looked for the tacos, "why do you want to keep doing this anyway?"

It took her a long time to answer. "Sometimes, you find something that's so *good*," she said. "I don't mean good like yours is 'good.' I mean good good. 'You can tell' good. Like *Peking*. But, mostly—"

Then she vomited on her shoes.

THE SECOND BAR

The Cafeteria, in Brooklyn somewhere.
That morning I had woken up on a purple futon in Lucy's apartment at about noon. I washed my mouth out with some grapefruit juice I found in the fridge, and I knew I was in a girl's apartment because the shower was free of pubes.

I have no idea how anyone gets any writing done in New York—I found just getting a slice of pizza to be emotionally exhausting. But when I got back, there was a message on my phone from Lucy, whose misfortune it was to be at work in a rough state of mind, body, and liver. But she sounded excited—she told me to meet her and her editor at a bar called The Cafeteria at seven that night. "I told him you insisted on meeting in Brooklyn," Lucy said, which I didn't understand but at this point she was quarterbacking.

The Cafeteria, which I found next to a Polish bakery, was done up like a school lunchroom: the bar had a glass sneeze guard, the floors were gray linoleum, the chairs were plastic, and the bartender wore a hairnet. People carried Pabst on colored trays.

Lucy's boss, David Borer, an editor at Ortolan, was sitting next to her. Yards away in the semidarkness, you could still see the fear in his face. He was zipping his eyes around the room, as though somebody were about to reveal the secret of publishing and he was terrified of missing it. He was older than we were, fey and beaten. He looked like an elf who's gone through a bad divorce.

"Guess this is the popular kids' table!" he said, and then he laughed the kind of laugh a guy laughs when he knows he's made an awful joke.

"So, Pete, I loved your draft. Read it at lunch, loved it."

"You read it at lunch?"

"When you're in my business, you gotta read fast. Sometimes I read two, three drafts during lunch. And Lucy told me you just nailed this voice, this voice of your generation, that's really moving back toward what's real."

"Yes," I said, in what I imagined were Abe Lincoln tones.

"Really *owning* earnestness."

"Yes, yeah."

"So you just holed up in a cabin in Vermont and banged that sucker out, huh?"

"Yeah. I mean, I've been musing on it for years. A lot of it is very much my own family history. Stories I've heard from shut-ins I visit."

"It's real. You can feel that."

"Very, very real. Definitely."

"So, I'm always interested—what's your process, how do you work?"

What followed next was a game of Bullshit Poker. David asked me questions that I assumed were traps. I gave the writerest answers I could think of on the fly. Lucy, for her part, was somber, nursing her beer, from time to time staring hard at me in horror.

Luckily, on the subway, I'd written down a list of writery statements.

WRITERY STATEMENTS

- I've always felt that writing a novel is like doing surgery on yourself.
- I try and stake out territory where the real and the transcendent meet.
- *Tornado Ashes Club* is really a story of an American pilgrimage.
- Grandma is a spirit guide; she is to Silas as Virgil is to Dante.
- Every morning, before I wrote, I'd read a page from *Leaves of Grass*. Whitman speaks in such an American cadence.
- Before I started writing, I spent a year just trying to picture Luke's face. Then one day, as I was taking a walk by the river, he walked past me. And I sat down on the grass and started writing.
- I aspire to be as prolific as Dickens, as subtle as Henry James, and as lyrical as Toni Morrison.
- Writing, to me, isn't a hobby. It isn't a job. It's as necessary to who I am as breathing.

Some of these were hard to say out loud. I saw Lucy's forehead start to shine with sweat. But David kept nodding. And he kept drinking, more than you'd think a little guy should drink. He almost tripped once as he got up to go to the bathroom.

"Hey, Faulkner, don't blow this," Lucy scratched at me when he was gone.

"You're the one who told him I'm the voice of a generation."

"He's buying it, he's buying it."

We saw David walking back. He looked wobbly on his feet and he sat down hard.

"God," he said. "Writing. You know, probably shouldn't tell you this. But you know, Lucy knows this, everybody knows this. We're in trouble."

"I . . . uh. . . ."

"We're in trouble." He looked at Lucy. "Worse than you know." He chugged what must have been half a beer and slammed it against the table. "Fuck!" He looked at Lucy. "They're thinking of having a pledge drive, like PBS. Like, 'If you like this book, send us a check and get an Ortolan tote bag.' It's that bad."

He burped a couple times, then looked at me. "Why don't you write screenplays?"

"What?"

"I mean, you know, Lucy says you got the chops, why not screenplays?"

"Well, the novel, as a form, for me as a writer, is just so much more—um, suited to exploration of—"

"I've been working on a screenplay. I've been working on a short, too. Maybe get some actors, put it on YouTube, see who bites."

A long pause.

"Fuck!"

Then, "Look, I'm gonna take your book to my bosses. I want to buy it. You know why?"

"Um, because you responded to—"

"Because that country stuff, all that stuff, and the religion —I think we can place it with Wal-Mart. I think they'll sell it. That's what you gotta do these days. Make the math work, sell it big. I'm hoping."

"Uh, thank you."

"But what do I know? I'm a Jewish kid from Scarsdale."

Just then a Sasquatch tapped David on the shoulder. That may sound like an exaggeration—it is not. This guy's face was hidden with matted, untended hair and the air around him seemed to quiver from his body stink, like heat rising from a desert highway. He smelled like the most poorly tended organic farm in the world.

David said "hey!" and they shook hands.

"How's it all going, with the thing?"

"Oh, it's pretty good. Getting pretty sick of chicken!"

"I bet."

"And my dentist, he's not too happy."

"Oh yeah."

"But all in all."

"Cool, man," said David. "Shoot me an e-mail sometime, bring me up to speed."

"Can't, man, remember? No computers."

"Oh right, right."

The Sasquatch left.

"That guy," said David, "has some nuts on him. He kept pitching me these books—he'd go for a year only eating fried chicken. A year of only drinking soda. A year of never showering, no computers, all these ideas. I could never sell them individually. But then finally he came up with the idea of doing them all at once. Sold it, he's off and running."

David took a big sip of beer. "Dude's having a rough year. Anyway—your book! Lucy, she's good. I'm gonna get her to clean a lot of it up."

I could see objections forming behind Lucy's eyes, but she stayed quiet.

"She's gonna cut a lot of the crap out. But—it's good. People will buy it. I think."

Another pause. David looked up at the bar, then stood up.

"All right." He shook my hand.

We walked outside, the three of us. As we neared the subway, David told us to follow him, and he started off down a side street. Lucy and I looked at each other and followed, and he led us down a slope to a small square of park. On one side was a row of three-story brownstones.

"You see that place?" David pointed at the one on the corner, which stretched back for nearly a block. "That's Josh Holt Cready's place. Three point five million dollars. *Manassas* paid for that place." Then he turned, and locked me with his eyes. "I passed on that book! Fuck!" We gazed at the place for a minute.

Then David yelled "You suck, Cready!" We all ducked behind a bush. We waited for maybe ten seconds, then peeked our heads over the top. No reaction from Cready's house.

Then a light came on upstairs. We all freaked out and booked down the street.

"Shattered my confidence," David said, as we scurried away. "Confidence! That's the one thing you need to be an editor! Never again, I swore to myself."

We got to the subway. David shook my hand. "All right. Good stuff. I'm gonna see if I can make this happen. Don't fuck me on this."

And he walked off. Lucy was holding her head in her hands.

"Um, is he okay?"

"Oh no." She took her hands away. "But I think you just sold your book."

10

The Roman Empire. For two millennia, it's stood as the symbol of value. Of virtue. Of integrity. Of lasting strength.

Our very word—investment—is derived from Latin. It means the same things today that it did two thousand years ago. Security. Stability. Your financial future.

At Via Appia Funds, we combine the values of ancient Rome with a forward-looking 21st-century approach to investment. Our goal is simple: to build an epic empire of wealth for all our clients.

When you invest with us, you'll feel the strength, the confidence that comes from turning your future over to dedicated, devoted professionals who can respond to your needs. Professionals who can adapt to an ever-changing marketplace, while always staying true to the core principles that last beyond years.

Choose Via Appia Funds. Choose integrity. Choose strength. And choose a financial future that will stand, proud and sturdy as the Coliseum.

—excerpt from an introductory letter for
Via Appia Funds by Pete Tarslaw

What I assumed would happen after I sold my novel

Some editors would take me to someplace that made cocktails with elderberries. I'd get drunk and hold forth. As I left I'd see a model on the street waiting for a cab.

"Can you only write, Pete Tarslaw, or can you flag a cab as well?"

"I can flag a cab."

"Then let's go."

Back in her apartment, in Gramercy or somewhere, wherever models live, she would press her lips against my ear.

"I know you can write love beautifully, Pete Tarslaw. Can you make love beautifully as well?"

"Why don't I show you?" I would do so.

Two months later, at a dinner in London (I'd be in London for the UK launch of *T. A. C.*, and the restaurant would be called something like the Fatted Calf), Zadie Smith would lean across the table to me.

"You know, I'm on to you, you bastard." Then she'd smile. "Takes one to know one. I won't tell on you if you don't tell on me." Later the two of us would do coke off a manuscript.

Also I would be on Charlie Rose.

What Actually Happened After I Sold My Novel

When I saw my contract I learned why writers dwell on hard-luck characters who fix busted boilers and squabble over grocery bills. It's because writers don't get paid very much. Ortolan offered me $15,000 for *The Tornado Ashes Club*. Most of that I wouldn't see until the book came out. Lucy drew a graphic that explained the finances of the publishing game:

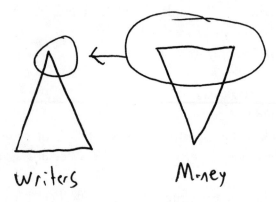

The few writers at the top, the Tim Drews and Pamela McLaughlins, take all the money. There's not much left for the lots of writers at the bottom.

My book was set to come out in early November. David Borer told me that the British owners of Ortolan believed that Americans did a lot of reading over Thanksgiving, "They buy books to take with them on the train to Cleveland and so on" was their logic. With layoffs looming no one was brave enough to tell them otherwise.

* * *

Once, in ninth grade, I made a model of the Eiffel Tower out of toothpicks for a big project at school. When I finished the whole thing was lopsided and warped, but it was so fragile that I dared not tamper with it, I just hoped it would stay together long enough for me to get a grade.

That's how I felt about *The Tornado Ashes Club*. Lucy spent the summer editing my manuscript, while I watched Red Sox games in my underwear, indifferent to the outcome. She'd e-mail me a question almost every day. "How did Luke learn Spanish?" "Why doesn't Silas just explain to the police that he didn't kill his boss?" "Does a dying deer really smell *faintly of cinnamon*?" "You use the word *sallow* four times, and I'm not sure you ever use it right." She seemed to be catching on to the slapdash nature of my work: "On page 41 you say that Albuquerque is 'a hot, blast furnace of a city,' but then eight pages later you say that 'mountain breezes kept it cool as a treehouse in October.'"

Finally I had to tell her she should just do whatever was necessary and stop bothering me with it.

I had nightmares where I saw copies of *The Tornado Ashes Club* staring up at me from the remainders table, crowded next to other rejects, their covers pathetically desperate, like the faces of misshapen girls at a middle school dance. The image haunted my afternoon naps. It was amazing how quickly my swagger had turned to cowardice.

Then, in June, I got a call from Jon Sturges. When he called I was taking a bath, which is an inexpensive way of eating up time. He started telling a story about how high-born Roman women paid extravagant sums to sleep with famous gladiators, which was interesting but not relevant to anything.

"So, I'm expanding on a new frontier. Really pushing aggressively."

"Right on."

In fairness to what would eventually transpire, I'll note that in his description of his new business plan, Sturges used lots of terms like "malleable" and "freely structured." So I should've realized he hadn't done the legal legwork. But what he described sounded to me like the kind of low-level, you-don't-get-caught sort of illegal.

The job he offered me was writing out some sales materials for a mutual fund he had founded. He claimed he had a long list of "serious investors" who were already involved.

"See, I'm great at picking companies, you know? I just have a talent for it. But I can't always—you know—articulate their strengths in written form. That's your talent, bro."

"Right."

"So, I'll send you some—you know—basics, and you write it up. Rome—that's the theme. The strength of—you know—Rome."

"I think I can do that."

"We're really dynamically shifting the way capital is gonna flow, Pete. It's a fully integrated system. But we need somebody with your kind of focused clarity."

"How much will you pay me?"

"A thousand dollars."

"Okay."

I should stress here that I didn't know what happened to my writing when I was done with it. I assumed it ended up in some kind of newsletter I never saw.

The truth is, I just didn't worry about it. On the Web site there were stock pictures of Roman ruins and a place to type in your credit card info. I'd work for one hour every day during the 11 A.M. airing of *The Price Is Right*. Most of that summer I spent on the couch.

In August, Lucy sent me a mock-up cover design: a tornado that looked like it'd been done in fingerpaint against a green field. The font was simple and all-American, like on an IHOP menu.

11

It's long been my contention that the most influential man in the history of American fiction was Henry Ford. Ever since the first Model T rolled off the production line, narratives of road trips have been a mainstay of popular literature. One imagines all the drivers of American fiction of the past fifty years on the same freeway. They'd form a traffic jam as congested as downtown Los Angeles at 5:45 P.M., with Sal Paradise leaning on the horn.

Unfortunately, not all authors who take to the road are Homers and Kerouacs, nor is every meandering journey an odyssey. Consider *The Tornado Ashes Club*, the debut novel of one Pete Tarslaw. Beginning with a gunshot in Las Vegas, Tarslaw launches his characters on a dizzying zigzag trip across time and space that leaves one reaching for the car-sick bag. The convoluted plot is rife with all manner of roadside oddities: French peasants, high school football, blossoming love. But it's much like a Las Vegas buffet: everything's there, but none of it's very good. Tarslaw's prose seems to never catch its breath. He squanders the reader's patience by rendering every loose hubcap and half-eaten cheeseburger into a listless rhetorical faux-exuberance, all of it weakly undergirded with a primer of vague Christian metaphor. With a slurry of mixed images and tiresome characters, in language as worn out and withered as the sixty-some-odd bar slattern nursing a cigarette and a whiskey sour at a cheap casino, his is a road trip that makes you wish you'd taken the plane.

—excerpt from Charles Meredith's "Of Books" column in the
San Francisco Chronicle, December 1, 2007

There's a neat book called *Panned!: Bad Reviews of Great Works*. It's made up of excerpts from contemporary reviews that completely missed the point. Slams of books, music, art, and movies we now recognize as genius. Like *Huckleberry Finn*: "Mr. Samuel Clemens, who styles himself 'Mark Twain,' has penned a riparian folly which, in its vulgarity and crude language, does discredit to himself as well as to the Negro race, the intended beneficiary of these strained efforts." And *The Great Gatsby*: "One hopes Fitzgerald, whose lamplight burned so brightly in *This Side of Paradise,* can recover from this misstep. For beneath the jaundiced view of American enterprise and the juvenile obsession with the cocktail-and-party set, we sense the hand of a competent writer of romantic fiction."

Maybe the best one is of *Moby-Dick*: "It is best read as a lesson in the inevitable failure of a writer of no Ambition. Mr. Melville wastes his labours. He chooses no grand theme, nor bothers much with the human condition, save a few comic sketches of the mad captain. Instead he bores the Public with a chronicle of whale-fishing, accounts of which are already numerous. Those wishing for an education in cetology will prefer Mayhew's *Whales of the Atlantic and Pacific Oceans.*"

There's a final chapter, too, made up of wildly positive reviews of now-forgotten works: "*Odeon Unbound* is that rarest of things, a novel in which greatness can be perceived in every sentence. It is our firm prediction that alongside Shake-speare and Dr. Johnson, our children will study the works of Gilbert Pentweed, and his name will be etched in the ranks of literary immortals."

Aunt Evelyn sent me a copy of *Panned!* along with a batch of maple cookies. Her accompanying note was full of "buck up" platitudes. She was of course too polite to mention Charles Meredith's review.

I try not to hate anybody. "Hate is a four-letter word," like the bumper sticker says. But I hate book reviewers.

Book reviewers are the most despicable, loathsome order of swine that ever rooted about the earth. They are sniveling, revolting creatures who feed their own appetites for bile by gnawing apart other people's work. They are human garbage. They all deserve to be struck down by awful diseases described in the most obscure dermatology journals.

Book reviewers live in tiny studios that stink of mothballs and rotting paper. Their breath reeks of stale coffee. From time to time they put on too-tight shirts and pants with buckles and shuffle out of their lairs to shove heaping mayonnaise-laden sand-wiches into their faces, which are worn in to permanent snarls. Then they go back to their computers and with fat stubby fingers they hammer out "reviews." Periodically they are halted as they burst into porcine squeals, gleefully rejoicing in their cruelty.

Even when being "kindly," book reviewers reveal their true nature as condescending jerks. "We look forward to hearing more from the author," a book reviewer might say. The prissy tones sound like a second-grade piano teacher, offering you a piece of years-old strawberry hard candy and telling you to prac-tice more.

But a *bad* book review is just disgusting.

Ask yourself: of all the jobs available to literate people, what monster chooses the job of "telling people how bad different books are"? What twisted fetishist chooses such a life?

This isn't Don Rickles at a celebrity roast, where everyone's having a laugh over shrimp cocktail and a Tom Collins. People still quote Dorothy Parker, because she was the last book reviewer who was funny. That was eighty years ago.

Nor do I cut book reviewers any slack for "advancing the arts" or "calling good work to our attention" or "keeping the culture of letters alive." If a guy drove around your neighborhood with a bullhorn, pointing out which people were too fat, he would be advancing wellness, and calling fitness to our attention, and keeping public health alive. But you would hate him. You would throw rocks at him, as well you should.

Which brings me to Charles Meredith.

Charles Meredith is something of an institution at the *San Francisco Chronicle*. He writes a weekly column called, with appropriate pretension, "Of Books." In that space, for seventeen years, he has issued jackass pronouncements in an obnoxious high-English patois of his own invention.

I'd never heard of Charles Meredith before he wrote a review of my book. But since he picked on me, unprovoked, it's fair for me to pick on him.

It's not hard. Go ahead and do a Google image search for him. Gaze on the picture of his folds of fat forming oceanic heaves and swells through his turtleneck. Look at the way his neck is sheathed in a foreskin of flesh like an uncircumcised penis. It will be easy for you to envision him as I do: sitting at

a restaurant alone, banging his breadbasket against the table
to demand more rolls.

Why should Charles Meredith care if I wrote a bad book?
Why go out of his way to point it out to people? Maybe he has
some psychological problem. Maybe when he was a kid, the cool
kids used to call him "fattyfattyboomballatty." Maybe I should
feel bad for Charles Meredith.

But I don't.

How *The Tornado Ashes Club* swam into his ken I'll never
know. David sent me an e-mail, with the link and the message
"any press is good press."

It's not "good press" to have your book described as "a slurry
of mixed images and tiresome characters, in language as worn
out and withered as the sixty-some-odd bar slattern nursing a
cigarette and a whiskey sour at a cheap casino."

The review appeared about three weeks after my book
came out. The morning *The Tornado Ashes Club* had first appeared on Amazon, it started out at #253,477 in the sales rankings, between *The Calendar Stones of North Wales* and *The
Horseman of Alsace: A Novel of the Franco-Prussian War.* By
the time I got out of the shower, it had jumped to #128,980,
I think because Aunt Evelyn and my mom bought copies. A
pace of 124,000 spots every twenty minutes was solid, but it
tapered off after the first leap. For comparison I checked on
Peking, which Lucy was always raving about. We were in a
close duel, so I ordered a copy of mine, bumping myself 2,156
slots.

At the downtown Barnes & Noble there was a "Staff Rec-
ommends" shelf. Under a copy of Toni Morrison's *Beloved,*
"Edward" had written, "A sweeping, powerful love story from

one of the all-time best. Full of passionate, evocative prose that veers toward poetry, it touches on all of our most crucial national themes." When nobody was looking, I swapped in my book—everything still applied.

I never reread my book—huge chunks of it made me cringe —but back home I set it on my coffee table next to a copy of William Faulkner's *The Sound and the Fury*. They were both about the same size and shape. I think, asked to choose, an illiterate person would've picked mine.

And then Charles Meredith had to prowl in and fling his feces. Doubtless Polly saw that, and she and James cut it out, and put it on their fridge, and laughed and laughed and laughed.

So that night I got rocked at The Colonial Boy, and woke up in an apartment in Southie with the sinewy arm of Liz the bartendress across my chest. I'd started hitting on her, I remembered, because I'd asked her if she liked reading books and she said no.

I squirreled out of her bed, afraid that if I turned on the light to find my sweatshirt I'd wake her up, so I went home freezing and minus a well-loved sweatshirt.

The T across the river was full of hollow-eyed commuters who stared at the ground or read. Some of them read Tim Drew and Pamela McLaughlin and one guy had Nick Boyle's thick latest. But nobody was reading my book.

The train stalled at Charles/MGH with a mumbled announcement over the speaker. I was cold, and my brain scrunched itself into a painful knot, and my stomach felt foul as if filled with fetid pond water.

My moniker was slapped on a book, but none of my problems had changed. Ghosts of literary suicides danced in my head—Hemingway and some French guy with a mustache whom I didn't recognize.

Soon every copy of *The Tornado Ashes Club* would do the slow death march to the remainders table and the bargain bin, and then to Buck-A-Book, and then to the pulpery, to be shredded and boiled down and turned into egg crates. There'd be nothing for me but to keep drinking, and grow fat, and keep working for Jon Sturges until I died.

The train doors snapped open, and some sort of blonde aristocrat woman in a stylish purple trenchcoat dashed on. She sat down across from me, opened her heaving leather handbag, and took out a copy of *Kindness to Birds* by Preston Brooks.

12

Your boss getting shot might sound like a comic dream—for instance, if you work for Donald Trump. But for the hapless Silas Quilter, it's a nightmare, especially when the cops finger him as the triggerman. The murder is just the starting point in Pete Tarslaw's debut novel, *The Tornado Ashes Club*. It sends Silas to the arms—and Ford Maverick—of his storyteller grandmother, who leads him on an escape across twenty states as she tells a tale of her own lost lover. The story can get cloying, and Tarslaw's awfully ambitious—Mexican ranchera music, World War II, and Peruvian vineyards are all crammed in. But he's done his research (want to know what Tunisian fishermen eat? pages 213–217). And some of the dreamlike descriptions—an Iowa night is described as "a graceful ballet of grass entwined with starlight"— leave you asking for more. **B.**

—review of *The Tornado Ashes Club,* published in the December 8, 2007 issue of *Entertainment Weekly* magazine

Anyone who's paying attention in America can tell you it's strange which things become famous and popular and why. I like to imagine that, around 800 B.C., somewhere in ancient Greece, a guy, let's call him Linus, wrote an epic poem. It was pretty good, full of adventures and strange animals and sexy goddesses and five-armed monsters and all the stuff epic audiences go for. Linus started orating it, or whatever they used to do. But somehow, people just liked *The Odyssey* better. No one could explain why. Maybe a particular king or something insisted on the Homer version, and everybody went along. Maybe Homer got there first, or had a better orating voice, or ran a better marketing campaign. But 2800 years later, we've all heard of Homer and nobody's heard of Linus.

You could argue that *The Odyssey* was the better work. More intelligent or poetic, or addressing universal themes—and that's why it lasted. But I don't think so. There's not much evidence that fame and popularity follow any kind of logical pattern. And who can tell these days anyway? The whole thing's more or less a crap shoot. For every Charles Dickens who catches a break, there's probably some guy named Bartles Osbrook who was just as good but less lucky. In some alternate universe they gather and read Osbrook's classic *A Christmas Fable* around the holidays.

There are probably twenty books better than *The Great Gatsby* that we've never heard of. The only remaining copies are rotting on the shelves of those crammed used bookstores off country roads where everything smells like sawdust. Nobody's bothering to read those books. Just because eighty years ago, F. Scott Fitzgerald gave a better interview or had cooler friends, or because he's made for better biographies in the years after.

If you think I'm wrong, I'd invite you to take a good hard look at what becomes popular. See if it makes any damn sense.

Or consider the example of my own book. *The Tornado Ashes Club* is a case study in the pinball route to fame.

I've mostly cobbled this together from gossip and hearsay, but as I understand it, there were four distinct stages.

First Stage:

One of the marketing people at Ortolan Press was an insomniac. He lived out in New Jersey someplace, and when he couldn't sleep he'd go out to the garage and walk a few miles on a treadmill while clicking around on an old TV. One night he got to watching one of these Christian talk shows, paid programming at 3:30 A.M. Around the office they'd been getting memos about appealing to the evangelical demographic, so he figured he'd see what the deal was. It was the Reverend Gary Claine, one of these tanned guys with the perma-grin. Gary Claine's whole deal is that he used to play tight end for the University of Oklahoma. He still has an athletic energy—from the pulpit he waves his hands all over the place like he's bidding at an auction. Anyway, the marketing guy watches Gary Claine tell smiley stories about the Good News. And he hears him advertise his magazine, called *The Way*.

The marketing guy thinks that maybe an ad in *The Way* would be a good angle for selling Christian books. Those seem like the kind of cranks Ortolan's trying to get at. Maybe they could even send a review copy to the Reverend Gary Claine himself. He jots down a note to himself.

About a month after *The Tornado Ashes Club* comes out, after it's been panned by Charles Meredith and reviewed nowhere else, and it's tanking on Amazon, the British bosses at Ortolan call a big meeting. They start chewing everybody out for not doing a better job of reaching "alternative markets." They open the room up for ideas.

And the marketing guy stands up. Lucy was there, and she heard him tell about his insomnia, and the treadmill, and the Reverend Gary Claine, and *The Way*. Why waste our money on expensive ads in the *Times,* says the marketing guy. These are the customers we're trying to reach, and we can reach them at cut-rate prices. One of the British bosses nods and says to the marketing guy, "Congratulations, you've just saved your job."

So they take out a full-page ad in *The Way*. Most of the readers of the magazine are lonesome old women, the kind of ladies with nightstands covered with pill bottles. They can't tell the difference between a full-page ad in *The Way* and the explicit blessing of the Reverend Gary Claine himself. So they send their sons-in-law off to buy them copies.

Meanwhile, the Reverend Gary Claine receives a copy, with the compliments of Ortolan. Now, this part is just speculation, but I think it checks out: the Reverend Gary Claine is one of those ex-football players who resents that people have always treated him like an idiot. He frequently references the days when he was "lost in sin" back in college. Maybe he even regretted not hitting the books a little harder. So when a Manhattan publishing company sends him a review copy, he's flattered. He takes it seriously. He's a salt-of-the-earth Christian, so he doesn't want to insult the sender. He reads the book, and starts making bland positive remarks about it on his show—"What a loving story of faith—you know, it got me thinking of First Thessalonians 5:8"—that kind of thing.

And slowly my sales numbers start to rise. On Amazon, I drifted into the low thousands.

Second Stage:

Georgina Maddox was a small-town librarian who loved books. "I consider Scout and Jane Eyre and David Copperfield as some of my dearest friends," she wrote. Georgina herself had never published anything before her essay in *The Atlantic* magazine. Entitled "A Reader's Request," it was written in clear schoolmarmy English. You could picture Georgina in a puffy dress, writing it longhand at her kitchen table.

What set Georgina to writing was the state of book reviewing in America. There was too much savagery and bile. Book reviewers, she wrote, "are becoming nothing more than bullies. Like malicious boys pulling the wings off butterflies for cruel laughs, reviewers seem intent on destroying the most fragile and beautiful of all creatures: books."

She really took aim at Charles Meredith. And she cited his review of me as an example.

You can practically smell the vinegar on Mr. Meredith's breath as he calls one novel (*The Tornado Ashes Club* by

Pete Tarslaw) "a slurry of mixed images and tiresome characters, in language as worn out and withered as the sixty-some-odd bar slattern nursing a cigarette and a whiskey sour at a cheap casino." A clever phrase, perhaps, but why attack so viciously a promising young author?

In this age when literate culture is threatened, where young men and women would rather shoot each other in video games or watch the fake drama of "reality" television than read, we don't need more bile. We need careful, loving readers who are prepared to grab at small miracles in prose, wherever such treasures can be found.

"A Reader's Request" prompted the most letters *The Atlantic* had ever received. There were counterattacks, and counter-counterattacks. Book blogs got especially fired up about the whole business. Georgina Maddox even went on the *Today* show to stick up for earnest writing.

Suddenly, buying my book was equated in readers' minds with protecting a butterfly from a bully. Ortolan printed a whole second run of *The Tornado Ashes Club,* with a quote on the back cover:

"A promising young author."
—*Georgina Maddox,* author of
A Reader's Request

On Amazon I hit #843.

Third Stage:

In the late 1980s Cheerios Cheer Patrol commercials, Hazel Hollis is the blonde one in pigtails, with the belt of freckles

like the Crab Nebula smeared across her nose. VH1 sometimes shows these commercials in "Before They Were Famous" specials. They acquired a camp value after Hazel's
single "Clean Me Up" broke out in 2000 and was closely followed by the even more suggestive "Down There." But it was
playing Sister Bertrille in a sexed-up 2003 movie remake of
The Flying Nun that put her on that global, Super Bowl–
Coke-commercial level of fame.

And then of course came the inevitable cocaine-fueled tail-
spin. She was videotaped calling a nightclub bouncer a "chink
dago." Then she backed her Hummer out of the parking lot at
Tick-Tocks in Malibu and landed in the Pacific. She had to be
fished out by the fire department.

That's where *The Tornado Ashes Club* enters in. Her agents
and managers decided that what she needed was a classy movie
project. Somebody at some studio must've pitched them my
book: it's got the whole Christian thing, it's a book so it's Oscar
bait, a perfect reputation-rehab role. She could play Genevieve,
put some singles on the sound track.

Somehow, a copy got into Hazel's hands. And she had it
with her when she was leaving a hair salon and got into a screaming match with a paparazzo. She went at him, wielding my book
like a hatchet.

On the cover of *US Weekly* three days later, the title was
too blurry to read. But it's there, in Hazel's hand, next to
her face contorted in Gorgonic fury. And celebrity journalists, always with their eye to detail, made sure to mention it.
The Tornado Ashes Club was even mentioned in the court
documents.

When the week was out I was #212 on Amazon.

Fourth Stage:

The alleged child molester was played by a guy I recognized. Only days later did I remember from where—he used to play the jolly gay guy on this short-lived sitcom about a convenience store called *Inconvenienced*.

But in this particular episode of *Law and Order: Criminal Intent,* he was playing a Christian youth group leader accused of killing an eight-year-old he'd molested. He played it really creepy—I think he'd been miscast on the convenience store show. In the scenes where the cops were scowling at him through the two-way glass in the interrogation room, he's sitting in the metal chair, waiting for them to come back—and reading *The Tornado Ashes Club.*

I didn't see the show when it aired. But Lucy called me immediately afterward, as I was flipping through some old X-Men comics and preparing for bed.

"Did you see that?"

"What?"

"*Criminal Intent*! We'll send you a tape. This is gonna be huge."

The key moment in the episode comes when Vincent D'Onofrio comes into the room. The alleged child molester puts down my book.

"Good book?" says D'Onofrio.

"Not bad," says the molester.

D'Onofrio flings the book across the room in a rage.

"Certainly not *that* bad," says the molester, icy calm.

"Maybe you can start a book club on Rikers Island," says D'Onofrio.

It's a great scene. Later it turns out the guy's guilty.

I'm not sure if the recommendation of a fictional child molester on a TV detective show counts as "word of mouth." You'd think it might hurt book sales. But once again David Borer claimed, "Any press is good press." Maybe it was just a matter of getting people to recognize my book at the store. Or maybe there's a lot of Christian child molesters out there looking for a good read.

Whatever it was, copies kept moving. Tell that to anybody who thinks Homer got there on merit alone.

As research for my novel, I'd read almost all of the Wikipedia page about tornadoes. As a tornado develops, something called a rear-flank downdraft gets going. That's when the trouble starts. The tornado gets stronger and stronger, feeding on itself until it hits the ground and things really get crazy.

That's what it felt like. Like a tornado, it's hard to reconstruct in your memory; you just remember flashes. When I got the twenty-third spot on the *New York Times* best-seller list, Jon Sturges took me out to the 99 Restaurant for lunchtime steaks and we pounded fists. Derek and Hobart started asking me to sign copies for their coworkers. David Borer would call me twice a day to talk about movie offers. I started a correspondence with the Reverend Gary Claine, and he promised to keep praying for me. I would go down to Barnes & Noble every day, just for the thrill of seeing my book on the BEST-SELLING AUTHORS table. Ortolan sent me on a twelve-city book tour. Somebody else was picking up my minibar tabs so I was blitzed for a lot of it.

What I remember clearly is Philadelphia.

I stood at the podium of BookStew or whatever the place was called. I stared out at eighteen people who listened as I read.

"Sometimes it's the simplest of things—a faint melody heard and remembered, the feel of your grandmother's soft hand, smelling of baking, touching your cheek; a return to a place you dreamed of as a child; a bend in a tree worn from climbing. Memories that open up the chambers of your heart. Suddenly your soul fills up, like warm cow's milk filling a pail on a chill November morning."

I paused reverently before closing my book.

After the applause had died down, and I signed copies, and people started to filter away, I saw the girl with the scarf.

"Hi, I'm sorry," she said. "I just—I really loved your book, and I just wanted to, I dunno, say thank you."

I put on my best writer face, the face I'd been practicing in the mirror for months: reflective, concerned by the world's sorrows, amused by the world's folly. And I invited her back for a drink at the Ramada.

It all would've been creepily perfect, exactly true to my predictions, except this was like the worst Ramada in the entire world. We were making out in my room, and I pulled back the comforter, and there was this sort of octagonal stain on the sheets, a kind of electric yellow color, nothing natural, as though a highlighter had exploded. So I had to get that sorted out, which put the brakes on things. And then later, at around 2:30 A.M., there was a fire alarm. So we had to go out into the parking lot.

The girl with the scarf, of course, treated this like a great adventure. She held my arm and leaned her head on me.

"Write a poem," she said.

"What?"

"Write a poem about this. You're such a great writer. I bet you could totally write a poem about this."

Christ, I thought. *What have I done?*

A Brief Note

I want to insert something here, because obviously, I'm describing some pretty bad things that I did, and it's going to get much worse. I have a lot to answer for, I know that. But let me just tell you, Reader, three things:

1. Ever since I'd broken up with Polly, I couldn't listen to the song "I'll Never Find Another You" by the Seekers without bursting into tears.
2. Sometimes, on lonely nights, I'd brush my teeth with one of Polly's old toothbrushes, which I'd saved since college.
3. At my lowest point, when I was writing *The Tornado Ashes Club* and not getting anywhere, I was 49/51 on whether or not to kill myself. I went so far as to go online and find out how many aspirin you need to take to finish the job.

Just remember all that.

PART II

DECLINE AND FALL

13

Admiral Jameson watched the flicking counters move across the CentInt Action Station. Tonight there was more movement than he'd ever hoped to see.

He reached into his pocket and took out a Marlboro cigarette. He was a four-star admiral, Commander in Chief, Atlantic Fleet, with thirty-five years in peace and war. He'd seen combat in Vietnam and nuclear standoffs from the White House. And he still had to hide his cigarettes in the sock drawer so his wife didn't find them.

But tonight, he'd known he'd need one.

A Belgian officer leaned over. "Sir, it eez not permitted to smoke, according to regulations."

Jameson looked him over. He saw the stripes that indicated a staff captain. He'd seen that face a thousand times before. The brash face of a man who never left the office.

"Son, tonight you're going to see a lot of things that go against regulations."

AH-1 Cobra Helicopter, over the Tyrrhenian Sea

Lieutenant David Brandshot turned around in his chair. He jerked off one earpiece of his headset.

"We just got word—can't take you in any closer. Too much air traffic."

Flynn strained to hear over the whir of the propeller.

"How the hell am I supposed to get into Venice?" he yelled back.

Brandshot pointed straight down. Flynn looked out the bay door to the sea below him. A Zodiac CZ7 boat was bobbing below. Fifty, maybe forty feet.

"You're gonna have to jump!" Brandshot was struggling to yell back while still keeping his ship level.

Flynn hesitated. He hadn't taken a real swim since lifeguarding on Cape Cod, twenty years before.

"Dammit, am I gonna have to come back there and push you?" Brandshot shouted. Holding the stick with one hand, he swiveled his head. Flynn was gone.

—excerpt from *Teeth of the Winged Lion* by Nick Boyle
(Copyright © 1984 Anchorage Maritime Books and
Nick Boyle, reprinted with permission of the author)

"Yuhp! Yuhp! Yuhp!"

She let out yelps both wild and regular, like a jackrabbit being electrocuted in time with a metronome. Astride me she was bouncing at a lively clip for a woman of her age. My role in the whole business was more or less passive.

"YUHP!"

Then she slapped me hard on the chest. She pressed down with both palms, as though squeezing me out like the drained rind of an orange.

"Yuhp."

The matter thus concluded, she hopped off, padded to the bathroom and slammed the door. A moment later she came back wearing a robe and carrying a glass of water.

"So which one are you again?"

"*The Tornado Ashes Club.*"

She took a sip. "Which one is that?

"It's about a guy and his grandmother, and there's a country singer, and then there are parts in World War II—"

"Right, right. Christian stuff." She took another sip. "Not *that* Christian, I guess."

"Um, I guess medium. The editors changed it a lot."

She pulled her jeans on, but she still wasn't wearing a shirt. This look I've never found flattering on a woman.

"Editors are accountants with red pens," she said, as she pounded over to the hotel-room desk and picked up the phone.

"Dana. Yah, Pammy McLaughlin here. Listen, do me a favor hon. Have the kitchen send up a fuckload of roast duck."

Then Pamela pointed at me. "You want something?"

"Uh, I think I'm good."

"You stickin' around?"

"Uh, no."

"Yeah just the roast duck, maybe some mashed yams or sweet potatoes or something. Some kind of legume." She hung up the phone, informed me she was going to take a shower, and wished me luck.

I put my clothes on and left.

When I got into the elevator to go back down to San Diego BooXpo, I realized my junk was bumping directly into my jeans, so I must've left my underwear in Pamela McLaughlin's room.

Here's how that happened:

I spent Christmas with Mom and Aunt Evelyn and Margaret. Everybody made a big fuss over the young author. Mom had asked me to write a poem for the occasion. I humored her and scratched out a few lines about "honored turkey, noble bird." It was a big hit. I was nervous that I'd be called upon to say witty things, but instead everybody assumed the regular things I said were witty. I would ask for the corn, or whatever, and my mom would be, like, "Well! We've got to feed the young author's brain!" and she'd pass the corn. I made up a story that Faulkner always ate the dark meat, because he considered it to be more truly suffused with blood and history.

Then things really started cooking, and next thing I knew I was invited to the San Diego BooXpo.

I was surprised to learn people in San Diego cared enough about books to have an Xpo. I only knew the place from *Simon & Simon* and Sea World.

But the marketing people at Ortolan told me that not only did they have such an Xpo but I was an invited guest. I was supposed to be on a panel called "Of Blogs and Books: Young Authors on Technology and Literature." Lucy and I had never gotten around to starting a blog for me—luckily nobody had checked—but just being under thirty, I qualified.

This was to be the first stop of a three-stage West Coast promotional tour. I was all for it. Things with Hobart had gotten a bit chilly ever since I freaked him out about Reutical.

But at the last minute, I got bumped for Josh Holt Cready. He'd deigned to come back from Gstaad or wherever the fuck he was wintering.

Still, plane tickets had been bought, things were in motion, the BooXpo people were apologetic and let me keep my hotel room. So I'd have a whole weekend to myself, bought and paid for, in San Diego. Sitting on the plane, I remember thinking "everything's coming up Tarslaw!"

WHAT I SAW AT THE SAN DIEGO BOOXPO

- Downstairs in the Convention Center, people carting tote bags strolled through alleys formed by booths of publishers, an Arab bazaar for the mild-mannered and middle-aged. The place was dense with banners and cardboard cut-outs of authors and gleaming editions to flip through. It was a bonanza for free pens and key chains.

- There was a display about Tim Drew's latest, *Ararat*. It was about biologists who discovered Noah's Ark was real, and how that might unlock the cure for various diseases.

- There was a whole Nick Boyle section. Huge cardboard stand-ups advertised Nick Boyle's new nonfiction work, *Nick Boyle's Psych-Ops*. People were deep in line waiting to meet a real psych-ops guy, standing there in fatigues.

- Along one wall were booths for hardware companies, where you could try out little hand-held iPod-style devices for reading. I picked up the Toshiba Dante and the girl showed me how to scroll through. I started reading one of the Harry Potter books on the light-up screen, but I found myself missing the feeling of dominance that comes from cracking the spine in two. I suggested she add a perfume dispenser that emitted the stink of dye and cut paper. She didn't seem interested.

- Tucked discreetly in a corner was a stand for Reizvoll Press, producers of intense erotica. One cover showed a man who had crab claws instead of arms, clutching a chesty woman in some kind of stone dungeon. I would've liked to have learned more, but the lady working the booth was a monstrous titan with dyed black hair, about ten rings on each hand, and a mouth like the Joker (Jack Nicholson version), and she spooked me.

- I had the most fun looking at the displays from Ramrod Publishing, a company I'd never heard of. They specialized in alternative history thrillers. Their big one was *Blood for Quetzalcoatl,* which imagines the Aztecs invading Europe in 1491. It's full of human sacrifices and big battles between knights and warriors, and the hero is an unknown merchant sailor named Christopher Columbus. But they had dozens. Their covers were the best: a steam train driving past a medieval castle, Abraham Lincoln in an astronaut suit, biplanes flying around the Pyramids, cave men fighting aliens, samurais fighting Eskimos, Adolf Hitler kissing Marilyn Monroe. Those guys seemed like the real geniuses. But the only other person who paid them any attention was a twelve-year-old Asian kid almost crushed beneath his giant backpack. He was arguing with the bearded fatty behind the desk about whether an AK-47 would really stop one of Hannibal's elephants. It sounded like they'd both done a lot of research. The Asian kid kept saying, "I'd just shoot at the knees! I'd shoot at the knees!" And the bearded guy would say, "Kid, do you know *anything* about how strong the skin and skeletal structures of elephants are?"

Preston Brooks was not there in person, unfortunately. As I walked through the aisles, I fantasized about crossing paths with him—the two of us looking each other in the eye and squaring off. Maybe there'd be a final showdown.

When I saw his new book, I held myself back. I played a game of trying to imagine what new heights of sentimentality and emotional prostitution he'd reached: little children going to look for long-lost brothers with hobo satchels over their shoulders. Two orphans falling in love and trying to raise a child the way they'd wished they'd been raised. A veterinarian who travels the country healing the hearts of old worn-out dogs.

But my wildest flights of shamelessness could not outdo the Master.

Preston Brooks's new book was called *The Widows' Breakfast*. Amazing, right there. He'd beaten me with the title alone. But the subject was five widows—yes, one of them was black. They meet in 1942, when their husbands are all training to be pilots in World War II. And starting in that year, they have a tradition of getting together for breakfast on the morning after the funeral, anytime one of their husbands dies.

The widows' breakfasts go through the years, and changes and grandchildren and that sort of thing, the kind of stuff that sells Kleenex by the cartload to aging women who can barely keep it together at the mere mention of the passage of time.

What a tremendous genius he was. He made it look so easy. If I'd met him in the aisles that afternoon, it wouldn't have been a showdown at all. I'd have shaken his hand.

That set the tone for the rest of my afternoon.

Up the escalator on the second floor, I stood at the back of a big auditorium and heard the panel I was originally on.

There was Josh Holt Cready, in the flesh. He was a tiny squirt of a thing, and his wire-rim glasses made him look like some kind of termite or poisonous beetle.

He spoke in a low, reedy whisper, so the packed-in crowd had to crane forward to hear him issue pronouncements: "Sooner or later, everybody in my generation will grow up. They'll get tired of Shakira. They'll turn to Saul Bellow. They'll weary of *South Park* and they'll remember *Mansfield Park*."

Kudos to him for that. Great material and well delivered. A few eager school-principal types stood up to try and spark a standing ovation.

I leaned back against the far wall of the auditorium and pretended the applause was for me.

Having spent the day so far in cultural betterment and self-congratulation, I decided it was more than okay to start drinking.

TWO TERRIFIC THINGS THAT HAPPENED, AND THEN THE NEXT MORNING:

The First Terrific Thing

Down one of the touristy streets, across the train tracks and around the corner from the Convention Center, I saw one of those prefabricated Irish pubs with the Guinness signs and the etched lettering, this one called Bobby Sands'.

I walked in, and from the San Diego sunlight it took a minute for my eyes to adjust to the dull darkness favored by daytime drinkers. My attention was drawn to a loud monologue being delivered around the corner of the L-shaped bar.

"If we're gonna be an empire, then fuck it. Let's be an empire."

This was being delivered by a jowly man in sunglasses. His audience was the bartender. Not one of those glass-shining bartenders you see in old movies and New Yorker cartoons—this was a young guy with a pile of curly hair, grinning at all this as though it were a comedy show specifically for his amusement.

"But an empire needs to get its hands dirty. Decimate. You know where the word decimate comes from? Ancient Rome.

When they'd conquer a city, they'd go like this: one two three four five six"—the jowly man counted off among the three of us—"seven eight nine ten *thwack.*" He stared at me and mimed chopping. "Chop off his arm. Do that in Iraq, no more insurgents. That's power. Imperium. Something they can understand. 'Course you can't do it there because the goddamn TV cameras are in your face."

The bartender slid down to me and asked me what I'd have.

But I was staring at the jowly man. He looked familiar. His flesh hung off his neck and bunched together like the curtains at my aunt's. The skin around his eyes was cracked like poorly kept pavement. He was drunk or crazy or some epic combination.

"Here, wait, we'll ask him," said the jowly man, "see if he knows." He fired a firm point at my face. "Which way is east?"

Just as he asked this, I realized who the jowly man was. I remembered him from his picture, driving the amphibious landing craft. It was Nick Boyle, author of *Talon of the Warshrike.*

"Which way is east?"

The bar was running perpendicular to the street—I was facing the bottles—I'd come from down the street—behind me was the ocean—so—

"That way!"

"All right, you pass," said Nick Boyle. "*That* way's the Chinese, and *that* way's the Iranians. And *that* way, God help us, is the fucking Mexicans."

"I hate to tell you, but there's plenty of them that way too," said the bartender, pointing north.

"Every fucking way, the Mexicans."

I ordered a hard lemonade. This was a panic decision.

"Hard lemonade, Jesus Christ," said Nick Boyle. "Give him a fucking vodka or something. Stolichnaya. Put some hair on his balls."

"I guess I'll put some hair on my balls," I said.

"Don't underestimate the Iranians," said Nick Boyle. "They've got some very good submarines."

"Excuse me," I said, "I'm sorry—you're Nick Boyle, right?"

"Depends who's asking. If you're the IRS, no. If you're my ex-wife, no."

"I think your ex-wife would probably recognize you," I said. I accompanied this with the nervous laugh of male submission.

"After a bottle of red wine and a couple Xanax she wouldn't recognize fucking Santa if he punched her in the tits."

This sentence stunned me such that I spit up a little.

"So that's pretty much anytime after eleven in the morning." Nick Boyle looked me over. "You don't look much like my ex-wife though." Long sip from his glass of vodka. "You're about thirty pounds thinner."

Nick Boyle! Stumbled upon in a San Diego bar! Surely this was it. This was what literary life was meant to be like!

"I don't mean to be a gushy fan," I said, "or, you know, sure you hear this but I loved—love—your books. I remember one summer just sitting on this horrible scratchy couch we had, you know, ninety degrees out, rattly air conditioner going, and just plowing through them. And I didn't want to get up, even though my legs were just horribly itchy."

Didn't need all that detail. But the sense memory of it was strong—I couldn't think about *Talon of the Warshrike* without feeling the spiky burrs of that couch, upholstered with sixties rug sample seconds.

"*Arma virumque cano,*" Nick Boyle said, with a tired cadence, as though this were a cliché as worn as *That's the way it
goes* or *Can't win 'em all.*

"What?"

"*Arma virumque cano.* I sing of arms and the man."

"Right."

"It's what's worth writing about. Half these fucking critics don't get that. But tree houses and sewing clubs aren't worth
writing about. *Arma virumque cano.* I sing of arms and the man.
You know where that's from?"

Nick Boyle pointed at me but didn't give me enough time
to answer wrong.

"That's the first line of the *Aeneid.* That's what it's about
and there's no apology. Oldest story in the world."

So now the ice was broken, and I was treated to

THE THOUGHTS AND OPINIONS OF NICK BOYLE

- ON GOVERNMENT REGULATION: "This bar
  should have peanuts. Every bar in America ought to
  have peanuts. Why can't the government regulate that?
  In the shell, too."

- ON HOW HE CAME UP WITH HIS IDEA FOR
  TALON OF THE WARSHRIKE: "I went to Venice
  with my ex-wife. We were taking a night cruise, and
  looking back at the city I thought, What if somebody
  blew this place up?"

- ADVICE FOR A YOUNG WRITER: "Thing of it is,
  I'm not a good writer. Prose, sentences, that stuff, I
  don't know about it. I had a lawyer's training, a business training. So I wrote clear and direct. But let me

tell you something. Prose, frills—people don't care about that stuff. They want stories. This is why Hollywood's kicking their ass. It's why I can make the switch over to movies, video games—all I do is sketch out the story."

- ON VIETNAM: "The Viet Cong were desperate! The Tet Offensive wiped them out! And then we pull back. What kind of nation pulls back on the verge of victory? Any boxing coach could have told you it was a shit way to win a fight."
- ON HIS CAREER AS A BUSINESSMAN: "Writers love to knock capitalism. They'll write five hundred pages about some hard-working farmer, but a guy working in a corporation to give his family a good life is a worse criminal to them than Stalin."
- ON THE CURRENT STATE OF AMERICAN LETTERS: "Half the books these days are about smoking dope, masturbating, and crying about your girlfriend."
- ON HIS OWN WRITING: "Here's the thing—I didn't know this when I was writing. But it came through anyway—everybody, *everybody,* wonders if they have it in them. What's a hero? What's a story ever been? It's a hero proving himself. Delve into the psychology shit all you want. That's been the backbone of stories since cavemen around a fire."
- ON WHAT IS THE BEST "KILLING PISTOL": Smith & Wesson 640.
- ON PRESTON BROOKS: "A sentimental faggot."

He said it, not me.

If the reader is having trouble picturing any of this, he or she should note that we kept drinking through it all and the statements were delivered with greater vigor and reduced precision of pronunciation.

Toward round three or four, he described to me the amphibious landing craft he owned, the one I'd seen in his picture in the *New York Times Magazine*.

"That's a Higgins boat. Ike said those boats won the war. Two-inch draft! Goes right over coral, obstacles, anything!"

"A two-inch draft!" I exclaimed, with the thinnest understanding of what that meant. He told me how he'd bought his from a crusty Coast Guard coxswain who'd lost an arm ramming one into Tinian.

"At Omaha Beach, one of those boats, the whole damn thing, men, metal—vaporized! Completely gone. Ran over a mine or something. Goddamn if that isn't courage!

"I tell you," he said, now leaning in on me, his breath leathery and thick, "that's all I'm doing with my books. Moving around men and machinery.

"All right," said Nick Boyle finally, looking at his watch, "I gotta go give a talk at some high school. Tim was it?"

"Pete."

"Stay the course."

He waddled out, and I sat there beaming. I'd done it. From the scratchy couch to bending elbows alongside him, Nick Boyle himself. The bartender presented me with a lengthy bill for both of us, which I paid without complaint.

The Second Terrific Thing

I'll understand if the reader finds it a little coincidental that I met two famous authors on the same day. But remember that this was, after all, the BooXpo, and famous authors were swarming around all over the place. I'm pretty sure I saw Alexander Solzhenitsyn, too, although it may have just been a homeless person. I saw Tom Wolfe, or at least a Tom Wolfe impersonator. Stephen King was walking around, and I would've tried to talk Red Sox with him except he was eating a pretzel.

By midafternoon, something about the air of the place was getting noxious—all those packing crates of unread pages, and the smell of coffee encrusted in the mouths of manic readers, cycled through their breath. I walked outside to catch a Pacific breeze, turned to do a walking loop of the Convention Center, and saw Pamela McLaughlin.

She wearing a thick leather jacket the color of an old record, with her mussed-up half-blonde hair flopping around on her shoulders. At the second I saw her she was simultaneously lighting a cigarette and blowing her nose. My first thought was *That's very efficient!* and then I thought, *It's also very dangerous,* and then I realized, *Hey! That's famous paperback mystery writer Pamela McLaughlin!* and then I thought, *Pamela McLaughlin lights her cigarettes and blows her nose at the same time? That's very odd,* and by then I was almost on her and I had to say something.

"I'm a real fan!" is what I ended up saying.

"Huh?"

"Of your books." This wasn't true. As of yet I hadn't done more than flipped through them derisively in the grocery store. "You're Pamela McLaughlin, right?"

She issued a dismissive, let's-hurry-things-along nod.

"Yeah, yeah."

It was going very badly, this, and I needed to say something coolly casual to recover.

"You just in town to see the pandas?" I said this with a smile twisting into place, because I was proud of how clever it was, but then the smile untwisted as I was finishing, becoming almost a frown as I remembered I was stealing that line from an old *Simon & Simon*.

But I guess she hadn't seen that episode, and the twisting of my face maybe just came off as lascivious, because she shot a line of smoke above my left ear and said:

"I've been meaning to go to Sea World. Feed the penguins," and it was clear then that she was game to play along.

"I'm Pete Tarslaw. I wrote *The Tornado Ashes Club*."

"Pammy McLaughlin. I didn't read it."

Awesome. Kudos for her for saying it; that was my attitude. I pointed at her cigarettes and said—because this is what a cool guy would say, right?—"Those things'll kill ya."

"They're not the only ones trying."

Up close it was clear how much airbrushing had been done by the *New York Times Magazine*. Her face looked like a baseball mitt. A new baseball mitt, mind you, not some old worn-in glove on display at Cooperstown in an exhibit about "Hope and Sorrow: Baseball in the Depression." Her cheeks looked like the palm of a new Wilson before you've had a chance to break it in. There was a dense thicket of wrinkles, some of them so deep I'd wager you could stick a penny at least a third of the way in. Her hair was blonde, but not Viking-wife blonde, more the color of a pale wood cutting board. She was muscular, too. Shoulderwise she could pass for a field hockey coach.

But she also possessed a brazen adult confidence I wasn't used to, and it made me kind of giddy and afraid, like a high school sophomore getting hit on by one of those creepy divorced teachers you hear about in Florida.

Pamela had said in interviews that she always carried a gun, and I wondered where it was right now.

In retrospect this moment was also the height of my own confidence. I mean lifetime—that exact minute, too. So maybe I was projecting some alpha-male pheromones, and she was projecting queen-bee chemicals, or whatever, and they were mingling in the air. That would explain the next thing that happened, which is she stubbed out her cigarette with the bottom of her black boot and looked me square in the eye.

I realize, by the way, that this is all beginning to sound a bit campy. But that was the exact appeal. It was that thing of *How long can this possibly be sustained?*

"I'm going to Mr. Fung's," she said. "Bar near my hotel. Are you coming?"

Yes, of course I'm coming, you fantastic nose-blowing smoking boot-wearing mitt-faced vixen! is what I thought.

"I'm always in for a dumpling," is what I said. I'm not sure that's any better of a thing to say.

A STORY PAMELA MCLAUGHLIN TOLD ME AT MR. FUNG'S

"All this was brain splatter." She indicated a section of cocktail napkin meant to stand for a murder scene she'd been to, near the Liberty Bridge on the south side of Pittsburgh.

"By the time I got there, a rookie had picked up most of the skull chunks. Probably thought he'd impress the bosses by doing the dirty work. So when I rolled up, the detective was screaming at him. 'Cause all that's crucial; you want to map the blast backward, locate the shooter.

"Not that it really mattered. Shooter was in a car, fired out his window. The real question is how they got the victim, Evan, how they got him out of *his* car.

"In a murder case, you always start with the husband or the wife. This guy's wife was a wispy toothpick. Very mannered—she'd been born in France. Right there everybody's suspicious. Her family had a wine importing business. So that didn't play well either, in a city of beer drinkers. But she had tiny little spider arms—no way she could have fired a shotgun. And why would she do it out here? So then you start looking for affairs—his or hers. When you shake that tree, you always get some apples."

Pamela really said that.

"Every murder, every one, is a soap opera. You're just watching it backward.

"That's where the toxicology matters. They ran this Evan's blood work downtown. Turns out he'd taken some amyl nitrates. They relax the anus. He was down here for sex." She laughed. "When that report came back, the detective had to pay me twenty bucks. He couldn't believe he was gay.

"The wife, she had a close friend, Kent. Very handsome guy. Gym muscle. One of these upscale gay hustlers you hear about. Anyway, they got the computer whizzes on it. In a few hours they figured out this guy Kent roped in Evan on the Internet. Two hours more and they found the receipt for the shotgun. Here's the best part: this guy Kent, he bought the shotgun over the counter at Bear Mountain Hunting Supply! If I put that in a book, readers wouldn't believe anybody could be so stupid. I mean, if you'd seen this guy—he probably walked in wearing a Charvet shirt or something. Whoever sold it to him must have known he wasn't going duck shooting.

"Anyway, just seeing the cops he was a blubbery mess, gave the whole thing up in about a minute and half, said the wife paid him. She's got a smart lawyer, still awaiting trial. But when they showed her the shotgun receipt, she muttered under her breath about 'that stupid little shit.' Like I said: you start with the wife."

Then Pamela finished her drink.

"So, are we doing this?" she said.

That's how I ended up fornicating in the W Hotel and then feeling my wang bump against my jeans in the elevator.

On the W elevator I did wonder if maybe, if I'd played it right, Pamela would've invited me to Bellissima Haven. But other than that I was pretty pleased with myself.

The Next Morning

On Sunday the Convention Center had a picked-over look. Copies of the *New York Times Book Review,* fliers about new titles, and catalogs were scattered around on the floor, like popcorn boxes and peanut shells on the ground at a closing carnival.

Outside I found a cart selling coffee and breakfast burritos, and I headed up the escalator to find a place to sit and eat. In the smaller conference rooms, they were still holding panels. Through an open door I saw one that was nearly deserted, so I settled down to breakfast in the back.

Onstage a man who looked like seventy-year-old retired Charlie Brown was softly answering the questions of a few gathered readers.

"Literature is important. It matters. It sounds a bit corny, perhaps, but I *believe* that."

Jesus, this guy sounds like a Nick Boyle character, I thought, as I unwrapped damp tinfoil.

"You have to get it right, or you shouldn't do it at all. When I was younger, of course, I wanted to be a novelist, you know, Hemingway, all that. So I decided: I'll write one million words. That seemed like the number I should write before I tried publishing any. It took me thirty years."

A jet of grease shot me on the thigh as I took a bite of my burrito. These were my only nice pants for the whole trip, so I left the burrito on my seat, slunk out, got some paper towels from the bathroom, and did a quick mop-up.

When I slid back in again Old Man Charlie Brown was still talking.

". . . so I was in China, in the Foreign Service—this was 1980 or so—and I think I started making my notes then," he was saying.

"And I started thinking, and working them through, more as a hobby than anything else. It's slow. You have to be very careful, and very slow. I find, anyway. But slowly, it started to take a bit of shape. Then I retired, and my wife, God bless her, she said 'you waited thirty years to be a writer. Give it a good try.' She made me sit down and write every morning."

I'd sort of gotten a sense of the burrito's landscape now, so I could eat while watching Old Man Charlie Brown talk.

"It's funny," he continued. "I was writing, here, about paleontology, excavations, digs. And that's what writing a novel is. People think of it as slapping words down on paper, the stack of sheets and a pile of cigarettes and so forth. Or conjuring things up, closing your eyes and seeing it in a flash, or something."

There was too much egg in this burrito.

". . . but, *excavating*. That's a much better metaphor, I think. You peel back layers, slowly, and brush off the dirt, and gradually, very gradually, it becomes clear to you. You see more and more of it."

Abandoning half the burrito I sipped my coffee as he kept going.

"And it is careful work. Tedious work. And, just like with a dig, if you try and go too fast you'll ruin the thing. You can't rush it. You might dig for a day, and just find a tiny piece of pottery, or what have you. Just learn one small thing about one of your characters. But that's the only way to do it, slowly. So it's slow work, down in the dirt there, but if you do it well, then hopefully you'll uncover something—that's really the word, you *uncover* a novel I suppose—you'll uncover something that's worthwhile."

Yikes, I thought, *this guy is working too hard.*

"So, I suppose I'll go at it again, get in the dirt again, because I do enjoy it. That gradual—gradual discovery. And if you do it well, I think, then you almost don't feel you have any part in it. Any more part in making it than a paleontologist has in making a fossil."

I could see why they saved this guy for Sunday. Old Man Charlie Brown shuffled offstage as the audience clapped politely.

As we were leaving I asked a besweatered spectator who that had been, talking.

"Bill Lattimore," he said.

"Bill Lattimore . . . what did he write?"

"He wrote a novel called *Peking.*"

"Oh right, right. Thanks." *Peking,* Lucy's favorite book, which at that moment was doubtless being used as a trivet for Hobart's lunchtime mashed potatoes.

I made a note to tell Lucy to tell Bill Lattimore to stop knocking himself out "excavating" and just crank out a book with a murder and some Christmas stuff.

With a few hours to kill before my flight, I wandered around downstairs. A few booths were still up, and a few stragglers poked about. At the Ortolan table, I picked up a copy of *The Tornado Ashes Club* and flipped through it. I read sentences at random. *The gold light seeped between the cracks in the peaks, pouring through in heavy streams, the heat of it popping and melting the snow along the rims of rock.* Or, *Silas, the taste of old beer still plastering his mouth, looked down into the white checkermallow and the greasewood, and saw how the earth rebuilds itself.*

I could still hear Nick Boyle thundering about "men and arms," and Pamela pointing out on a cocktail napkin where the Pittsburgh cops had found brain splatter. At the very least, those two seemed like they meant what they wrote. I was having trouble finding a single sentence in my book that I'd truly believed. But hey—I'd pulled it off, right?

There was a woman near me, thirty-five maybe, looking at another copy of my book.

"That's a pretty good book," I said.

"Yeah," she said. "I had to read it in my book club. I didn't finish it. Couldn't really get into it, you know?"

"Oh. Well I thought it was pretty good."

"Yeah, it just seemed like one of those books that's trying to pack too much in. I got about halfway and decided, meh."

"What about the language?" I asked. "Didn't you think the language was lyrical?"

"I guess, but, you know, at a certain point, it's just—you know—words."

"Huh. I'm sure people said that to Faulkner." This came out pissier than I'd intended.

"I love Faulkner, actually. I wrote my master's thesis on the theme of race in *The Sound and the Fury*."

She continued looking at my book as though it were a catalog for clothes she didn't like.

"You know, I wrote that book."

She looked up at me, and then down at the cover, maybe checking to see if the name matched the face.

"Hey, when the police think Silas killed his boss, why doesn't he just wait and explain what happened?"

"Well . . . Silas is confused, and he's a timid soul, of course—"

"I mean, I'm sure if he explained himself they'd figure it out. Wouldn't that make more sense than running all over the country? Because then he really seems guilty."

Angry blood rushed about my body. But I kept my cool, turned on my writer voice: patient, pedantic.

"These characters take shape on the page. All I do is observe, and record. I wait for the story to tell itself to me."

"Mmm," she said.

"I excavate," I said. "I'm like a paleontologist. I get in the dirt, and I dig. This book, really, is just a dinosaur bone I uncovered."

She put my book back on the stack. "Maybe it just, you know, wasn't for me." She gave me a schoolteachery smile. *Super* condescending.

"Do you know Pamela McLaughlin?"

"Pamela McLaughlin—she writes those mystery books? Yeah I've heard of her."

"Well I had sex with her last night."

"Um, that's great." She backed away, looking for exits.

"And I talked about boats with Nick Boyle. Higgins boats. Ike said those boats won the war."

"That's great. Congratulations."

"So I think I know a thing or two about writing."

I'd won the exchange. That dumb-ass woman with her master's thesis. "Race in *The Sound and the Fury*"? Real original theme. I would've pointed that out if I didn't have to catch a flight.

She wouldn't have been so cocky if she'd known I was flying to Los Angeles to talk about *The Tornado Ashes Club* movie.

14

INT. POE'S APARTMENT - THAT NIGHT

The place looks like Ted Kaczynski's cabin, transplanted to the basement of a Brooklyn brownstone. Strewn sweatshirts, old towels, Chinese food boxes that have been there since the Clinton Administration. Rush *Chronicles* plays on a beat-up stereo. Dead center, on fruit crates, is the chessboard.

CLOSE ON POE, crouched over the board—black side, pieces unmoved.

> POE
> How'd you do it, you bastard?

A POUND comes on the door. Poe doesn't move.

ANGLE ON the door. Another POUND, and the door bursts open. SERGEI enters. He's followed by YEGOR—built like a brick shithouse, two-fifty, easy, and with arms that could crush a skull like a Fuji apple.

> SERGEI
> You shouldn't leave door unlocked. Not
> such a safe neighborhood.

He smiles. A smile you don't want to see. Only then does Poe look up.

> POE
> I don't have it.

> SERGEI
> You don't have what?

POE

The money.

SERGEI

Money, money, Americans always
rushing to the money. "Show me the
money," ah? Maybe we just come by to
see you practice.

POE

It's gone.

SERGEI

Maybe we come by, I show my friend
how you play your game.

Yegor crosses, and looms over Poe from the opposite side of the
board.

SERGEI (CONT'D)

Maybe we play social call.

POE

Well then, I'm sorry I don't have any
chardonnay and brie.

Suddenly Sergei reaches out and smacks Poe across the face.
Poe reels, then jerks back, nose bloodied. Sergei takes a gun out
of his pocket. He puts it in the middle of the chessboard.

SERGEI

Or maybe we play this game.

Sergei crouches in front of Poe.

SERGEI (CONT'D)

You are not so smart.

Sergei picks up a pawn from the board, and stands up.

SERGEI (CONT'D)
This one is called in English, pawn, yes?
Pawn is very easy to give up. To give up a
pawn is nothing.

POE
(Nursing his nose) You know a lot about chess.

SERGEI
I played chess, when I was boy.

POE
Ever hear of Garry Kasparov?

Sergei stands.

POE (CONT'D)
Once Kasparov played Bela Nadosy, the
Hungarian champion. Nadosy was
white, Kasparov was black. The first
three moves went like this.

Rapid-fire, Poe makes six moves—pawns, knights, rooks. None
of the moves touch the gun. One of the pawns lands in the
trigger hole.

POE (CONT'D)
Three moves. That's it. And Nadosy said,
"You've beaten me." These aren't very
dramatic moves—nothing a good amateur
would've thought of. But Nadosy knew
he was beaten. Do you know why?

SERGEI
Tell me why.

POE
Because he could feel Kasparov's
confidence. He could see it

in the way he played. And he knew he
could never beat a man that confident.

> SERGEI
> And Kasparov became world champion.
> Wonderful story.

> POE
> And Nadosy—

Poe reaches across the board—right under Yegor's chin—and
tips over the white king.

> POE (CONT'D)
> Nadosy drowned himself in the Black Sea.

Poe stands up.

> POE (CONT'D)
> You're white. You just made your first
> move.

Suddenly Poe pulls a Tec-9 out from under the chessboard.
Before the Russians can react, he has it on Sergei's forehead.

> POE (CONT'D)
> Do I seem confident to you?

—excerpt from the unproduced screenplay
"Black/White" by Miller Westly

"I'll tell you *the* Marlon Brando story. Actually, more of an Elia Kazan story. They're filming *On the Waterfront,* the scene in the hold of the ship, where the squealer's just had a crate dropped on him, and Karl Malden shows up, and all the longshoremen are looking at him. So Kazan sets up the shot, gets everybody in place. And then he goes around, starting with the extras first, and gives them backstory: motivation, fleshing out every man there into a full character. 'You're a Czech. You don't speak English that well. You know these guys resent you, but you're lucky to be on this crew, and you're saving money to bring your wife over.' 'You were a smart kid, teachers told you to apply to college. Your dad encouraged you, said he'd figure out a way to pay for it. But then he busted his leg. Nobody helped him, and you had to start working.' Stuff like that. Kazan goes through every actor, fifty, sixty guys, and gives them each something. Starting with guys who don't have lines, extras. He finally gets through all of them, and the minor characters. Then he talks to Karl Malden for twenty minutes, walking him through everything: how he should be thinking, how he's never seen a body this bad before, what he *ate* that day, everything.

"Then, when he's finally done with Karl Malden, Kazan says, 'Okay, we're ready, shoot it.'

"And Brando, who's been standing there watching this for three hours, says, 'Hey, Elia, you never said anything to me.'

"And Kazan wheels on him. Points at him. In front of everybody.

"And says, 'You just stand there and say your fucking lines.'"

Miller Westly has only one level of intensity. The whole time he was telling me this, he chopped his hands through the air as though he were smashing a series of invisible boxes that flew at his face.

"That's how you make a movie!"

The Standard Hotel in Hollywood seems like a joke. The upside-down sign seems like a joke, the shag carpeting seems like a joke, the 2001-style pod chairs that hang from the ceiling seem like a joke, and the constant thumping Euro-infused trip-house seems like a joke. The pool looks like a retro-cool '70s über-designer's joke of a pool. But everybody acts like it's totally serious: the Swedish-haircut guy behind the desk acts like it's serious, and so does the model dressed as a mermaid posing in a giant fluorescent fish tank.

Miller Westly certainly seemed to take it seriously. At 3:13 P.M. he swooped in, and from a black ceramic bowl on the lobby table, he scooped up some wasabi peas. Without apology he told me he might smell a little bad because he'd been with his trainer that morning, "An Israeli guy who will kick your ass and make you like it."

We sat down poolside, and he told me he'd been drinking a lot of mojitos lately with Appleton rum, asked a waitress if she had Appleton rum, made her promise that the mint was fresh, and ordered two mojitos and a Negro Modelo. As the waitress walked away, he made a study of her ass, the way a botanist might look at a rare orchid.

"That is exquisite. It is primal. Primal reaction. One of the core principles I'm always keeping in mind in my writing is that men are primal, visceral animals. Wrap it up in all the bows and fifteen-hundred dollar Savile Row suits with silk pocket squares from Milan, but there is a *primal* animal at the core. Given the chance he will act and behave like an animal. If you keep coming back to that basic fact you will never run out of stories."

This was all said with incredible velocity. Miller talked as though he were reading off ideas that were racing past his brain on an electric ticker. Only hours later, replaying the tape in my head at half speed, could I reconstruct it.

"Look at Brando," he said. "For my money, the best actor, period. Just on a pure, raw, visceral level. No one touches him. I would give both my nuts and three inches of cock length to have him for one scene. I've written entire screenplays just as an exercise, just so I could think about how Brando would say it. And I've spent months working out problems in screenplays that Brando could solve just by standing there. He *seizes* the screen. Eats it. *Fucks* it. The screen *begs* Brando to fuck it. And here's why. He's always playing that tension, the exact line between a man in society and just a raw animal. You can feel it. You can feel him restraining himself. You've seen *Streetcar*?"

"Yeah."

"The first time Brando met Tennessee Williams, he took off his fucking *shirt* and fixed Tennessee's *toilet*. And Williams called Kazan, who was directing, and said, 'This is the guy. This is Stanley Kowalski. The guy's got grease on his hands and he's fixing my toilet.' Primal."

Then the mojitos came and Miller told me *the* Brando story.

I'd been sent to Los Angeles to meet Miller Westly because he was interested in writing and directing the movie version of *The Tornado Ashes Club*. I'd read up on him to prepare and concluded he was a great man for the job. In the men's bathroom at the 2000 Oscars, Miller Westly allegedly tried to stab Russell Crowe. Westly had just lost the Best Adapted Screenplay award; he wrote that biopic of Ethel Merman that Renee Zellwegger won the Oscar for.

Then he and Russell Crowe got into an argument— apparently, if the Internet is to be trusted—about Crowe backing out of Westly's next project. It was an updated version of *The Merchant of Venice* set over a Super Bowl weekend in Las Vegas. Crowe allegedly called the screenplay "a hundred pages of coke-addled bullshit," and Westly took a swing at him with a Bowie knife he had in his cumberbund. Westly was wrestled to the ground by Harvey Weinstein, Ian McKellen, or Kathy Bates, depending on which story you believe. After that, Westly disappeared for two years and went to live in Japan.

But the way I figured, you have to be a certain level of famous to get into an argument in the bathroom with Russell Crowe. And coke-addled or not, you must take your scripts seriously if you're willing to stab for them.

The Ethel Merman movie was good. Or at least, what was wrong with it wasn't Miller Westly's fault. I'd seen it in college with Polly. For many weeks afterward, when we were bored in my room, I would demand that she do the scene where Renee

Zellweger tells the producers that she won't change how she sings, *"Not for nobody!"* Polly would frump out her chin the way Renee did.

I tried to watch the movie again before flying west, but I got to the scene where Ethel finally tells Ernest Borgnine (Val Kilmer) she loves him, and I knew it would be just too sad.

According to IMDb, Miller Westly had recovered from his sabbatical. He'd sold a screenplay about Alaskan crab fishermen for $2 million. He adapted *Sister Carrie* for Martin Scorsese. As a sample, his agent had sent me his next script: "Black/White," about Russian mobsters who extort a chess prodigy in Brooklyn. Russell Crowe was attached to direct.

It hadn't been easy to set this meeting up. I'd had twenty-seven phone conversations with his agent's assistant, Aaron. He took to calling me "baller" and told me that when I got to LA we'd have to "Scotch it up." I think that meant drink Scotch somewhere, but, unsure, I didn't commit.

Poolside at the Standard, Miller clinked my glass and sucked down his mojito. He started mashing up the mint with his finger.

"Not sure this was fresh."

Then his Treo started rumbling through his pocket, and he ejected up to answer it.

This was exactly how it was supposed to be. Here I was, drinking a mojito, with a guy who wanted to make my book into a movie. I had some definite ideas for the film. I also wanted to hear about the Russell Crowe stabbing. But surely the best strategy for a novelist was to act aloof, slightly repulsed with the whole place and the whole process of turning my work, Art, into a movie, Commerce. The mojito should be treated as unsatisfactory.

That would be my presentation, anyway. Internally I was focusing on *Which movie stars will I get to meet?* and *How much will I be paid?*

Even deeper—I barely dared think it—*What if I win an Oscar?*

Miller hung up or pushed the End Call button or whatever and strode back.

"Listen, bro, I gotta bounce. I gotta e-mail a draft of the chess thing to one of the EPs before he gets on a plane to London, and my assistant's up in Santa Barbara picking up a Modigliani. You got enough, right?"

"Enough? Enough for what?"

"Enough for your article."

"What?"

"Aren't you the kid from *Entertainment Weekly*?"

"No—I . . . I talked to your agent? To Aaron? I wrote *The Tornado Ashes Club*."

"Oh, fuck!" he said, and he sat down. "The book! Shit!" He punched me on the shoulder. "*Tornado Ashes.* Hazel Hollis loves this shit, right? Crazy fucking bitch."

He popped an ice cube in his mouth.

"Also a crazy-*fucking* bitch, from what I hear. Ha!" He slapped me on the shoulder. "Seriously. Charlie Sheen told me that. Anyway, your thing—thing was fucking balls-out genius."

He took a copy of my book, with colored Post-it notes sprouting from the sides, out of his bag.

"I want to fuck your book. Literally. I want to cut a hole in it, smear it with lube, and fuck it. Is that intense? I'm a pretty intense dude. I have notes."

MILLER WESTLY'S NOTES

- "Look, I've got a lot of gay friends—this is Hollywood, we all messed around in college, gay producers, gay dentist—but Silas needs to be butched up. If only to lure better actors.

- "The Vegas stuff, opening scene: Silas walks past a drunk, degenerate gambler. We establish that this guy is outside the hotel every day. He asks Silas for a couple bucks—and Silas gives it to him. *Knowing* he's just going to gamble it away. That establishes the whole thing: inevitability, kindness, love, the whole deal.

- "Silas's grandfather, the guy Grandma marries after Luke dies? He needs to have been a real bastard. Psychological abuse, slapped Grandma around, drank. We'll have a scene in the car, where Grandma tells Silas about it. 'Your grandfather was a son of a bitch.' Cut to flashback, him slapping her, hard. You see what I mean?

- "Grandma—see, this is a great role for your Ellen Barkin, whoever, one of these actresses who's always complaining that there aren't any parts for 'mature' women. Academy will *love* that. But viewers, they need to know Grandma was *hot* when she was younger. Maybe Renee. Maybe some new girl. Foxy, but *elegant* foxy.

- "Esmeralda—folksinger, great character, we'll sell four hundred thousand copies of the sound track the first week. But she should be an addict. Recovering. She doesn't tell Silas. Then on the road, when things get tough, she has a relapse. *Great* third-act complication. Silas nurses her back to health, beats the *shit* out of the guy who gave her the stuff.

- "The bounty hunter. He has to be sympathetic as hell. One of these Christian reforming guys, you know? He's got a little girl at home. We see that in his bag of guns and grenades and shit, he's got one of those drawings out of macaroni she made him at school. When he catches up to Silas, he gives him this great speech about redemption.

- "The stuff in World War II, Luke in the Resistance, all that—great. But get this: one day he's on a mission with the Resistance guys, and they take him through the woods and show him this place—barbed wire, Nazis all around. What is it? It's a concentration camp. You see that? 'Here's what we're fighting for,' that sort of thing.

- "Luke in Peru, when he's dying—they bring in this old Catholic priest. Old guy. Gives him the last rites. And the priest tells him, 'I had a long life, you had a short life, but soon we'll be together in Heaven.' Can you picture *that*? Awesome scene. Tension.

- "The ending, Grandma's letting go of the ashes—great scene. Here's the thing: she should be holding Silas's hand, and she lets go and just walks right into the tornado. That's the end. That's your last shot. This woman walking into a fucking tornado. Huge impact."

It's difficult to convey the speed with which Miller Westly gave me all these ideas. In between he was taking sips of his Negro Modelo, and when he was done with the beer he was done talking. He took a dark glass bottle out of his pocket, and from it he administered three drops to each of his eyes.

"What do you think?"

What I thought was, *This man is a genius.* Maybe greater even than Preston Brooks.

He was so brazen! So unabashed! He didn't try to pack his frauds into lyrical language. The literary con game was to write some bullshit and convince readers it's good. But the Hollywood game seemed to be to tell its customers, "Here's some bullshit. You'll pay for it, and you'll like it."

I was humbled. I realized he was much better than me at this.

Miller looked up at me with a swaggery hint of a smile.

"You're realizing I'm much better than you at this, right?"

"Yeah," I said, quite stunned. From across the table he punched me in the shoulder.

"I have to be. Your book sold—what—thirty thousand copies? Something like that?"

It was significantly less than that, but I gave a modest shrug to suggest he was in the ballpark.

"And that's a success for a book," he continued. "But I deal in movies. I need to get four, five *million* people watching, minimum, or I'm on my *ass* in this town. I can't afford to fuck around like you can."

Miller picked up his Treo, looked at it, then slammed it back against the table.

"Shit. I gotta get to the Palisades, get the draft, and send this thing out in the next seventeen minutes. You wanna take a ride? We'll talk in the car."

*   *   *

Curbside, Miller tossed the Mexican valet a twenty, told him *"rapidamente,"* and the valet shot off like an Olympic sprinter.

As we waited Miller took out his eyedropper again and reapplied. He offered it to me.

"You want some?"

"What is it?

"Distilled condensed liquid THC. Put it on your eyes. Full-body high without having to smoke weed. That shit's terrible on your lungs."

I declined, now terrified of getting into the car. But I didn't say anything because I didn't want to seem uncool.

The valet brought the car around—a BMW 6 Series—we got in, and Miller floored it down Sunset.

Outside a row of boxy offices, we got stuck behind a slow-moving van and were blocked on the left by a Prius. Miller's solution was to shift into reverse, cut into the right lane before an Escalade caught up to him, and then floor it. As he did this he reached across me and pointed at a road that bent up into the hills.

"I was at a party up there once—no idea how I got home, but I woke up and found ten eggshells on my bathroom floor. I'd eaten ten raw eggs. Shit."

That "shit" was directed at a traffic light.

"Here's the fucked-up thing—the party was on Saturday. When I woke up, it was fucking *Wednesday*."

I suspected Miller might be the kind of guy who's a better driver if he's maintaining a steady rant. So I tried to keep him going.

"Did you always want to write for movies?" I asked.

"When I was a kid my dad took me to see *Dr. Strangelove*.
Fucked-up movie to take a kid to. But my dad was a fucked-up
guy. I was twelve when I saw that movie, and it just clicked:
Yes! I gotta be a part of this! I wanted to be a screenwriter ever
since I learned Arthur Miller was fucking Marilyn Monroe. She
wasn't fucking John Updike, was she?"

I conceded the point.

"Look, I'm a competitive Type-A intense guy. You get one
spin on this planet. Nobody knows that better than me. I wasted
a lot of time. I blew most of the midnineties up my nose. But
think about this: no society, ever, has been better at anything
than America is at making movies. The Ming Chinese made
vases. The Renaissance Italians made frescoes. We are the best
at making movies. We're fucking geniuses at it. In Iran they
stomp on American flags and then they go see *Shrek* 3 and
X-Men. In a market in Mongolia you can buy a DVD of *Pirates of
the Caribbean*. It is our cultural fucking genius, dude, and we
are spreading like seed across the entirety of the fucking globe."

We were zipping now through vegetated curves.

"You're a smart kid, wrote a good book. Let me tell you something. In a generation, novels are finished. 'Film is twentieth-
century theater. It will become twenty-first-century writing.'
Ridley Scott said that. He ought to know—you ever read a book
that shook you up more than *Alien*? I mean, primal shake-you-
to-your-core. That movie shook flecks of poop out of my in-
testines, I mean specks of steaks that had been up there for
decades.

And we're still figuring out this form. We're getting so
much better. Eighty years ago, movies were piano chords over

title cards, and fainting women, and villains with mustaches. Eighty years from that to *Alien*. You think the novel's had a pace like that? You think the novel can keep up? Let me tell you something. Novelists are gonna figure this out. There is no greater thrill for a writer than hearing your words boomed out in THX. You're a writer. Think about what that's like. Your scenes, sixty feet across. Fucking *Shakespeare* never felt *anything* like that. . . . Shit."

That last "shit" was directed at the clock in the BMW, not at Shakespeare.

Miller put in a focused three minutes of driving before breaking to say, "Half of them already were screenwriters! Dickens, Tolstoy, Twain, Dreiser—these guys were writing cuttos and cold opens and pan shots and battle scenes. They just didn't have the technology. When F. Scott Fitzgerald died he was under contract at MGM. Imagine what Shakespeare could've done if he'd known Brando. Or Dickens with Julianne Moore. Fuck, give Dickens Rob Schneider and Jennifer Tilly and it'll be a fifty-million opening weekend. If those bastards were alive I'd be living in fucking Downey and working at Blockbuster."

Miller left me to figure out how that follows as he dialed his phone.

"How we doing? . . . I'm passing Will Rogers . . . It's gonna be close, maybe I should call you in a bomb threat . . . she's in Santa Barbara picking up a Modigliani . . . dude, I'm maybe seven minutes out . . . nice."

As he was talking, I wondered if I would die in a fiery car crash. On the plus side, if that happened, sales for *The Tornado Ashes Club* would skyrocket. I'd be back on the best-seller list for sure. And an air of mourning would ruin Polly's wedding.

On the downside, *I* wouldn't get the money.

I joke, but I was nearly wetting myself from fear.

"But the key is this." Miller hung up his phone, and this was to me. "It's not about talent and sound and special effects and camera work and lighting. It's about economy. I don't mean movie writers getting paid more than novelists, because that's so fucking obvious I don't need to point it out. It's about story-telling *discipline*. Which sounds crazy, because *discipline*? Everybody out here's getting blow jobs from Estonian models during a five-hundred-dollar deep-tissue massage and eating sushi flown in from the Aleutians, right?"

Here Miller took a hard right at a stoplight, onto a narrow snake of a street. He accelerated as though trying to find a flaw in his German suspension.

"But you know why screenplays are tighter? They have to be. Because when the director's shooting, he's burning money every second. You cannot have waste. Imagine if every sentence in a book cost two grand. Are you sure you're gonna leave it in? You *sure* you need those adverbs? Best writing school in the country is watching daylight burn on a shoot and just *hearing* the expenses tick up."

We pulled up in front of Miller's house. From the drive-way I could see only two rectangles of white wall split by a glass door. But I followed him inside, and the back of his cavernous living room was a pane of glass, and over dots of roofs I could see the Pacific. On the right the floor opened up to a black-tiled pool, with a waterfall that dropped into another pool.

"Fix a drink. I gotta send this shit."

There was a tidy bar under a giant framed poster for *Nosferatu*. Original, it looked like. A German Expressionist vampire loomed over me as I tried to decide what kind of vodka to have.

I realized the back of my shirt was soaked with terror sweat from the drive with a THC-fueled mad genius. Worried I might stain the white couch, I just stood there and looked at the pools. Miller was on the phone in the other room.

"Boom! I just sent you gold. Go in the Elite Class Lounge or whatever and print that . . . Have the pretty stewardess get you a nice Johnnie Walker, double, rocks, read that, and by the time you're over Newfoundland you're gonna be wondering what picture you want them to use on the cover of *Variety* . . . nice safe flight."

Miller came back into the room, stared me in the eye, and pointed behind me.

"Thomas Mann used to live right down there." Then he turned and said, "How many novelists you know have two fucking pools?"

Liquefied THC must have a sedative stage, which kicked in by the time we drove back to the Standard. There was less swearing at traffic lights, and I had to exert less energy exerting the muscles in my sphincter to keep from soiling myself.

"I'll tell you a story about novels," he says. "I went to lunch at Campanile with Sam Mendes. And we got to talking, and he says [here Miller did a very good British accent] 'Miller, there's something I've been just *itching* to take on, and I want you to adapt it.' It's *Madame Bovary*. So he makes me an offer, I take it, I go up to Vancouver for a couple weeks and take a look at it. Mark up the thing, pull out scenes, sketch out dialogue, he doesn't say anything but I know he wants to put Kate in it—Winslet. So I think I've got a take. There's affairs, there's botched surgery, Paris, death, stuff to work with. I start writing.

"Here's the thing. I get through 'Interior—Rouault's farmhouse, north of France, 1850s, et cetera, he's working on the broken leg, Emma enters. But then I realize I've got nothing. Because here's the problem: it has to be internal. You can't dramatize it all. And there's no actress, not even Kate Winslet, who's that good. There never will be. There's always going to be that distance. You can watch a movie. But you can't live it. And *Madame Bovary,* you need to live it.

"So I call up Sam, tell him I took a swing and couldn't connect, he says we'll find something else, et cetera.

"Just to clear my head I wrote a movie about a biracial car thief who gets caught up in a gang war in prison. It's in turn-around at Paramount."

We drive on through the green that hides the houses in Bel-Air.

"You know, I probably could've done it, *Madame Bovary.* Could've pulled something off, Sam and Kate would've made it look good. But you know what? It wouldn't have been *true.* I couldn't have made it *true.*

"And let me tell you—I'll lie about just about anything. But I couldn't make myself turn *Madame Bovary* into a lie.

"Flaubert," Miller said. "That guy deserved two pools."

After I left LA I never heard from Miller Westly again. I traded a few calls with Aaron, who acted mock resentful that we had failed to Scotch it up, and through odd evasions over several months I eventually understood that Miller had lost interest or gotten too busy or somehow given up on *TAC*.

Which was too bad. Some of the things that happened to me later I would've liked to discuss with him.

15

The hot-tub jets still whirred, blowing indifferent fountains of water against the slumped face, bobbing it about like some awful buoy, or a horrible children's pool toy. The face of Heavenli D'Jones, who'd danced on her last bachelor's lap—in this life anyway. A single gunshot, like a red wax seal on an antique document, was centered in her forehead.

Officer Ted Kobler was watching the scene, while a few higher-ups conferred on the patio. Kobler had never been in a house this nice, not in eight years of traffic stops and beat walking, not in his entire life. It had never occurred to him someone might have a Jacuzzi right in their backyard—not in Pittsburgh anyway. Beyond it, the grass, trimmed as tightly as a marine's haircut, sloped down before revealing an incredible view, a Christmas tree of city lights, dots spaced out to the horizon, broken only by the dark waters of the Allegheny.

But with all that to look at, Kobler couldn't take his eyes off that gunshot.

Then he felt someone slide past him. It took him a second to notice. A hell of a lot longer than it should take a cop.

A woman—straight black hair, tight khakis, leather jacket—bent over on the Spanish tile by the Jacuzzi and took out a notebook.

"Hey! Hey! You can't be here! Lady!"

Then he felt a firm hand on his shoulder.

"Relax, Kobler."

Detective Mitch Frilock stepped up next to him, drinking coffee out of a Styrofoam cup.

"Hey, Trang," Frilock said. "You think those tits are real?"

Trang Martinez looked up from her notebook.

"I dunno Mitch. Maybe you should come over here and feel 'em. Probably be the first action you've had in a while."

—excerpt from *Strip Tease* (a Trang Martinez Mystery)
by Pamela McLaughlin copyright © 1997 Pocket Books,
reprinted with permission)

The next stop on this Western junket was Montana.

I picked up *Strip Tease,* one of Pamela McLaughlin's books, at the LA airport and read it on the flight to Billings. By the time we were over Denver I'd finished.

The basic plot: Trang unravels these murders that are designed to disgrace various city councilmen. She realizes they're being committed by this eccentric old guy who wants to keep his rotting rodent-infested house from being condemned. Once she's cracked it, everybody thinks the matter's settled. But Trang discovers the real reason the old guy doesn't want his house condemned is that if they tear it down they'll find the body of his wife, whom he murdered in a case that's long since gone cold. So Trang solves that one, too. Also Trang is sleeping with a veterinarian who works with tigers at the zoo. That part's just filler.

But the point, for me, wasn't reading the book. It was that I, Pete Tarslaw, Famous Novelist, had slept with Pamela McLaughlin. That was how things went in the world of letters. Now I would do what Famous Novelists do: read with derision the works of former lovers.

This was all prep work for my appearance at the Great Plains Writing Program at the University of Billings.

I'd found the time in LA to Google myself and seen some new reviews. The *Brooklyn Eagle* said I had "a rare ear for the rural voice." If there's anybody who knows the rural voice, it's a book reviewer in Brooklyn. The *Miami Herald* said my book was "flawed in conception and overwrought in execution." The same thing is true of the city of Miami, but people seem to like *that*.

There was some intellectual backlash, too. Some blogger who called himself "The Pathetic Fallacy" wrote this long essay pointing out that my book was "everything that was wrong with contemporary fiction." Which, given my method, was kind of a compliment. I mean, I'd hit all the bases.

But I was hoping to go over huge at the Great Plains Writing Program. This was one of the nation's premiere graduate schools in writing, apparently. I'd never heard of it, but I gather it's a big deal among your tea-drinking academic literati. Tom Buckley, who runs it, is a legend. He'd written a book of well-received short stories called *Bird King,* then settled down to teach the craft for fifteen years. He taught other people who wrote other well-received short stories.

The point being that winning him over could be the first step toward landing a sweet teaching job and beginning a long career of pipe smoking and sexual hijinks.

Along with his invitation to be a Guest Writer, Tom Buckley had sent some copies of the literary journal, *Prairiegrass Review*. After I finished with *Strip Tease,* I flipped through a few of those.

The contrast could not have been sharper. Consider this simple chart:

	Strip Tease by Pamela McLaughlin	Typical story in *Prairiegrass Review*
Begins with	Trang Martinez examining the boobs of a murdered stripper.	A guy eating grits in a hospital.

Characters	Corrupt city councilmen, one-eyed prostitutes, imprisoned serial arsonist, Trang's former lover (Dutch soccer star).	Suicidal girl. Retired plumber. Old man who watches a crow out his back window.
Sample sentence	"The medical examiner sawed through the victim's rib cage, and Trang listened to the sound like a thousand crunching potato chips."	"They sat and faced each other for a while with restful, blank smiles."
Ending	Trang helps a state trooper zip up a body bag, and says "Too bad scumbags aren't recyclable."	The old man eats a bag of almonds. Some kind of muted epiphany is hinted at.

They each have their flaws, I guess is my point. But you can't get *Prairiegrass Review* at the airport.

Those folks in Billings were trying to write earnest honest fiction about crows and almonds. If they were willing to try, I was willing to cash their modest honorarium.

The University of Billings had promised to send a student to pick me up. At the airport I had some exciting moments following the vectors of passing young women until they veered off toward baggage claim or to hug some mulleted slackjaw.

My student ride finally found me and introduced herself as Marianne. They'd at least had the common courtesy to send a girl, but she was hardly the specimen of coed loveliness I'd hoped for. Thankfully she didn't want to talk about writing. In fact, as she led me to her pickup truck, she mentioned she hadn't read my book. Not pointed or anything, she just put it out there. I respected her for it.

I'd written about Billings in *The Tornado Ashes Club,* despite never having been there. I'd had Silas, Grandma, and Esmeralda (née Genevieve) drive through, and I'd written that *in Billings he could hear rattling metal and the rumble of truck engines, the chords of unashamed American work.* True enough, although I'd made the place sound a lot more romantic than it actually was. Billings appeared in fact to be pristinely worthless, nothing but Pizza Huts and oil refineries. The passenger-side window of Marianne's truck was made of cardboard and packing tape, and the March wind seeped in around the edges. Not in any kind of interesting way, just enough to make my ride unpleasant.

THE READING

We were late getting to the lecture hall. About forty people were shifting around in their seats, above average attendance for one of my readings. A third of the people were seniors who probably come to every event they see a flier for, just to keep their juices going.

Tom Buckley shook my hand. He was handsome in a pared-down way, as though years of prairie winds had blown off any excess from his face.

"Pete, welcome. Thanks for coming to Billings."

"Thanks. Good to be here."

"We're so glad to have you as one of our guest writers. We're all eager to hear you share some work with us. I've got some beginning writers here who I think could really benefit from engaging with it. We'll open up some discussion."

Part of me wanted to lean in and say, C'mon, guest writer? You're a smart guy, you've obviously got a sweet gig for yourself here. But we both know I'm just a punk kid who cranked out a cheesy book instead of getting a job. *Share? Engage?* I'm gonna read a couple paragraphs, and your students are gonna sit glass-eyed and think they're getting their tuition's worth. Then we're gonna get some beers."

Tom Buckley jogged to the podium and introduced me. This was always an uncomfortable minute. Nobody ever had much to say about me, except that I was young. But Tom Buckley's presence alone enlivened the crowd; I could see them shift forward as he delivered some impromptu remarks about how I'd come all the way from Boston to give a reading. Tom said that he always liked to use the word *give,* because that's what writers do. The students and the old women nodded at this beautiful notion as I gulped some water.

My set piece for readings was a flashback scene in France during World War II. Luke and some Resistance types are going through a forest, and they come across a pregnant woman, a collaborator who's been kicked out of her town and is about to give birth. Some of the Resistance guys want to shoot her, but Luke decides to stay behind and help her.

This bit works well for readings. There are some funny parts where the woman swears in French as Luke ineptly tries to help and gets freaked out by all the mess. I do the French voice in an accent—an impression of my high school French teacher, Madame Bouchand. This always gets laughs. But the scene wraps up with emotional punch, as Luke holds the baby in his hands. Everyone loves babies. Sometimes mothers in the audience are almost crying at the end.

Except at U. Billings, I was distracted. Tom Buckley was sitting right in the front row, halfway out of his chair, smiling a smile a kindly priest might give to an atheist.

I kept losing my place. For a patch I forgot the French accent, and started doing something like Scrooge McDuck.

Finally I stumbled through to the end. Luke wipes the baby's forehead with a rag still stained by gun oil. The audience applauded for the exact amount of time basic etiquette required.

Tom Buckley pounced up and grabbed me on the shoulder.

"Any questions for the author?"

There was a pause, four coughs long. Then an old woman stood up.

"Do you ever write mysteries?"

"Uh . . . no, I never have."

As she sat down she shook her head *no* at her sister, who I guess didn't hear. Two more coughs. A kid in the back who was maybe seventeen stood up.

"My name is Edward. Luke's rifle, would that be a standard M1 Garand or an M1A1 carbine?"

"Uh . . . the latter."

No one else had any questions.

Tom Buckley thanked me. There was tempered applause. Under it he leaned in to me and clasped me on the shoulder.

"It's tough to really craft a scene, really breathe air into the lungs of it, isn't it?" He said this as though no one had ever meant anything more. "This writing's a tough craft! Tough set of tools. You gotta get 'em and keep 'em sharpened, all the time."

THE CLASS

As it happened, it was Marianne's day to read her latest story in class that afternoon. She intoned it as though it were the Apostles' Creed.

"She felt the chocolate against her teeth as she heard him splash water from his hands against the cracked tile of the bathroom sink. She knew he would dry them as he always did, against the back corner of the towel, the patch of fabric still firm."

As Marianne droned on I was really wishing I could've skipped this part of the afternoon. If this was what teaching writing was like, I was going to have a very hard time. When she was done, what was I supposed to say? The whole thing was kind of a mess. She was clearly worried about getting every detail right. That's a stupid and time-consuming way to write.

After our silent ride I'd come to like Marianne. I wanted to tell her, "dude, it's called fiction—just make something up!" I wanted to wave Pamela McLaughlin's book at her, and say "people are perfectly happy with this crap! Why are you knocking yourself out getting some detail right about towels?!"

Her story was called "Caramel," and it was about struggling parents on Hallowe'en who've just taken their autistic kid trick-or-treating. They've finally gotten him into bed, and they sit at the kitchen table, smoke a joint, and decide to eat his candy. All of it, Milky Ways and M&Ms and Skittles.

Which is not a terrible premise. You could make somebody cry with that premise, easy. But Marianne was insisting on making it a slow evocation of ambiguity or something. Keyword slow.

"Jesus, we get it!" I wanted to tell her. "Is eating the candy some kind of cruel revenge? Is it childish? Is it a tender act of love between the parents? Whatever."

One guy who was not having my problem was Tom Buckley, at the head of the table. His whole body was spread open, filling his chair. He was listening to her with such focus that he practically sucked words out of her.

"He put the back of his hand against the cold linoleum of the tabletop. She dropped two Milk Duds into his hand. They stared at each other, and then away. Their jaws pulled hard at the caramel."

Marianne put her story down. Tom Buckley held his pose for a silent minute, just in case there was more listening to do.

"Okay! Thank you, Marianne, for giving us that story. Let's all take a breath! Then let's see if we can't dig out the *meat* of this story. Who's ready to dig? Pete, how about you?"

The last thing I wanted to do was dig the meat out of anything.

"Well, there's a real texture here, isn't there?" I said. "It's almost . . . tactile."

I saw a few of the students write *tactile* in their notebooks.

"'Tactile,'" nodded Tom Buckley. "Let's hear more about that."

"Well," I said, "there's a quality to the language. You can almost . . . feel this story. You can almost—put it on, like an old sweater."

Would that stave off these weirdos?

"There's a comfort to it," Tom Buckley said. "A familiarity."

What? I thought.

"Exactly," I said.

Different students started to chime in. Easily, at first, but then it ratcheted up. People were damned hard on her. Her prose was called *wooden* and *somnolent* and *irritable*. Someone accused her of being "derivative to the point of plagiarism." People kept saying they were going to make "prescriptive comments," and then they'd tell her how she needed to fix everything.

This southern kid named Ethan, who had a chin that curved out far enough from his face to resemble a winking crescent moon, attacked Marianne's use of the word *vaporous*.

What the hell are you guys talking about? was what I was thinking.

Not on the story level—the story was crap and they were right to tear it up.

But what was the point of any of this? Let's say, after a year of polishing and rewrites and edits, this story gets published in *Prairiegrass Review*. Then what, Marianne gets like five hundred bucks? That's how much America values a great short story. It's worth less than a PS3.

An hour passed. Still more criticism and comments.

Jesus H., you guys! RELAX!

Finally Tom Buckley ended it all.

"Pete, thank you for joining us and for giving us your comments," said Tom Buckley. "Anyone who'd like—and Pete, I hope you'll join us—why don't we keep the discussion going over an adult beverage or two, down at Cullock's?"

"Oh I'd love to," I said. I still wanted to get a job. Maybe not here but in, say, Florida or someplace.

THE DISCUSSION CONTINUES
OVER ADULT BEVERAGES

I rode—silently—with Marianne in her pickup truck to Cullock's.

At one unusually long stoplight I felt I had to say something. "You really—I think you really hit on something with your story."

"Thanks," said Marianne, with an air of not-at-all believing me.

At the bar the writers of the Great Plains Program were sequestered in a back room, a square brick polyp attached to the corner of Cullock's. They huddled over a table already forested with pitchers of Bud. Tom Buckley was pressing his back against the wall and grinning a suspicious grin of wisdom.

Marianne squeezed in, lit a cigarette with one hand and with the other took delivery of a shot of whiskey. She danced it down her throat with shakes of her head, the careless performance of someone who intends to get super drunk. I could hardly blame her.

Ethan had bought her the whiskey—it was his job to do so because his criticisms were voted to be the most devastating of all. That was the tradition, to keep everybody from getting too pissy.

Discussion of Marianne's story was safely capped, but every conversational line and thread seemed to weave back to writing and authors. These people apparently couldn't think or talk about anything else. Supertramp would come in from the main bar on the jukebox, and somebody would mention they'd had this tape in junior high, and I'd liven up a little, thinking maybe we could hang out and talk about Supertramp. But within two redirections everyone would be talking about Alice Munro.

Somebody tossed off Nick Boyle's name as a derisive adjective.

"Nick Boyle is awesome," I said into the din. But this seemed only to confuse everyone. Ethan laughed, and another guy looked at me much too long, as though trying to figure out if my statement was some kind of Zen puzzle. So I shifted policy, deciding to drink steadily and hope my silence would be mistaken for wisdom.

Josh Holt Cready came up. Marianne made a scoff and a derisive flutter with her cigarette hand. But then she shot her eyes at Tom Buckley, afraid he might have heard.

Tom Buckley, for his part, said nothing bad about anyone. When he spoke you could feel the table sag as everyone leaned in. He mentioned "Rick Yates" and "Ray Carver" as though reciting the lineup of a championship team from his boyhood.

After a few hours the place thinned out. This was a mystery to me, because where could writing graduate students possibly have to go?

There were only five of us left around the table when Tom Buckley said, "Talking about stories"—we'd been talking about stories—"what's the *lonesomest* story you ever heard?"

I considered getting up and putting Supertramp back on.

Tom Buckley's question was to everybody, and he looked around at Ethan, Marianne, and me, defying anyone to try and bore him.

No one rose to the challenge.

"I'll tell a *lonesome* story. I used to have a friend out in Butte. 'Bout ten years or so ago I got to know him. Out in Butte, that whole area is studded with copper mines. This friend of mine was a miner, a real old-timer by the name of Bill Stubbs. Bill liked his bourbon, and sometimes I'd get a bottle of Early Times, knock on Bill's door, and say, 'Bill, why don't you get us some water and some glasses, and we'll sit on the porch, and we'll drink a glass of good bourbon.' He'd come on out, we'd sit and talk."

C'mon, dude, save it for Prairiegrass. It was hurting my face to look interested.

"One night Bill got to telling stories of the mining days. He said once an explosion went off—methane—just as he was coming up. Most of the fellas got out. But one guy—Jack, his name was—got trapped in the mine, caved in. They dug, and they brought cranes in, hoping Jack might have enough air to keep alive. His wife waited there, wringing her hands as they dug."

At this point I slipped my eyes around the table, not quite sure that this was really happening. *Is this guy for serious?* But they all kept staring at Tom.

"Three days later, they finally dug through. Jack was dead. But they found next to him a count pad and a broken-down pencil. Jack musta known he was finished, and while he was trapped, he wrote a note to his wife, now widow. Started out *Know that I love you.* And there was a message to the kids, too, and some of that. But then the writing trailed off, it grew all scratchy, hard to make out. What Jack had written about was the smell of washed linen. Paragraphs and paragraphs about it.

"The miners, they figured old Jack had kept it together to say a word to his wife and kids but then the gas got to him.

Driven crazy down there, writing in the dark, his mind had just caught hold of something at the end. But Bill told me that the widow couldn't believe that. She read that note over and over, trying to find something in it, thinking it must be a message, a cry out from just at heaven's door, I guess. The widow, she started to wash her linens, twice, three times a week. And every time she did, she'd grab neighbors, and tell 'em, 'I think I'm getting at it. I think I know what Jack was trying to tell me.' One week she'd say, 'He was trying to tell me life's like clean linen.' Next week she'd say, 'I finally understand it now, he was asking me to forgive him, it was a message about how we all need to be washed clean before God.' And the neighbors, they'd just smile and nod and agree. 'Cause what else can you do?"

Tom Buckley finished his story, and took a big sip of beer.

"That was old Bill's story anyway. Here's to him."

What? What the hell was that? I expected everybody to frantically make excuses and leave. 'Cause, seriously, what a fucking downer! We're all just trying to drink some beers!

Tom Buckley turned to me, and said, "How about you, Pete? You know any *lonesome* stories?"

Now, if I'd taken a minute to think about it, I could have come up with something terrific, with earthy blue-collar touches.

But Tom Buckley's eyes made me jumpy. Stupidly, I started with the first thing I thought of. And once I was launched I was committed.

"This one time my mom took me shopping at the mall, I was maybe five or so. I was completely bored, of course. I'd just seen *Empire,* so I was pretending I was Luke Skywalker, and I'd crawl around under the racks of dresses and pretend I was with Yoda in the swamps of Dagobah. Which was awesome. It was dark and crazy under there. But then suddenly it seemed like a lot of time had passed, and I didn't know where my mom was, and I looked out, and I couldn't see her, and I freaked out."

I drank more beer, which everyone interpreted as a dramatic pause rather than a conclusion.

"Then what happened?"

"Oh, she was just over arguing with the returns lady. She heard me crying and came over."

Awkward shuffling could be felt around the table. Tom Buckley gracefully ended it by slapping me on the back and announcing, "Being a kid can be lonesome!"

But I knew what I'd done wrong. I'd profaned the evening. These people treated stories like sacraments. They looked sorry for me that I didn't.

Marianne spoke up. "I had a boyfriend who used to work for the Forest Service. We broke up—long story, different story. Anyway, one time he told me this. The Forest Service used to hire college kids in the summer, to hike out to towers way far out in the woods to watch for forest fires, one guy to a tower. They'd pack up three weeks of food, supplies, and stuff and hike out there. And they'd just sit, with a radio, and call in to the station if they saw anything—lightning strikes, brush fires starting up, whatever. Three weeks later, replacements would hike out to start the new shift, and they'd hike back. Anyways, obviously this job attracted sort of weird guys, loners, philosophers, poets, guys getting over women.

"So, Mike—my boyfriend—told me guys would bring out just libraries of books, chessboards, crossword puzzles, whatever, because they were gonna be sitting, alone, for three weeks. Guys would bring just stacks of paperbacks, like ten Nick Boyle books. But one summer this guy came in, weighed about a hundred and ten pounds, little pale guy from the East Coast somewhere. And Mike was helping him set up and he asked him what he was bringing with him. And all he was bringing was a copy of *Leaves of Grass* by Walt Whitman. And Mike looked at it, saw how thick it was, and said dude, this book isn't gonna last you more than two days. You're gonna go nuts out there. And the guy looked back at him, dead serious, and said, 'This book could last forever.' So anyway, Mike figures it's not his problem to keep this guy entertained, wishes him luck, sends him off.

"But that was the summer they had those freak snowstorms up in the mountains, 'cause of that volcano in Indonesia or whatever. Most of these watchtower guys, they hear about what's coming over the radio, and they get out of there when the snow first starts falling. And by the second day, the Forest Service is radioing everybody in the towers and telling them you better get back here stat. But this kid, the pale kid, his radio's out. And he doesn't get the message. On the third day, it's just a *blizzard,* and they decide they better go out and get him, but they make it about four miles before the snow is just too bad. They turn back, and they figure he's just gonna have to wait it out.

"So it snows for a week, and this is in *June,* so nobody was ready for it. Then the snows melt, and there's floods, and that washes everything out, and it's July before they can even get a rescue party together to go out and relieve this poor kid that's been stuck in a watchtower in a blizzard.

"Mike was one of the guys that went out there. He's worried sick about him, and they hike as fast as they can, but it still takes a day and a half to get to the tower. The whole way they're wondering how this kid made it. So they get to the tower, they climb up the ladder, and they find the kid. He froze to death. Mike used to have nightmares about it, because by then the flies had got to the body. And the weird thing was, they had a little hut in the tower, so that would have been some shelter at least. But the kid was outside. He was outside, on the deck. And Mike told me the kid died just sitting Indian style, outside. And he was slumped over his copy of *Leaves of Grass.*"

For a while nobody said anything. I certainly didn't, because, fuck. That was a story, all right.

Then Tom Buckley said, "The disdain and calm of martyrs." Ethan nodded.

I skipped *Leaves of Grass* in high school but I'll make a confident guess that's what he was quoting.

After that the drinking continued. Even a few jokes. Tom Buckley told a story about helping John Cheever find an alley to pee in in Iowa City. But I certainly didn't say anything. I was feeling a vague but palpable kind of pretty bad. We closed out the place.

In the stories in *Prairiegrass Review,* the characters' epiphanies are muted and subtle. I don't know if that's an official rule for publication or just an informal agreement, but that's how it is. You don't spell it out. The *Prairiegrass Review* version of my trip to Montana would end with me lying on my bed at the Super 8, watching a rebroadcast of an especially uneventful Colorado Avalanche game, eating Funions because I'd resolved to give Funions another try.

But Pamela McLaughlin spells everything out: why people do stuff, what they're thinking about, and so on. It may be worse, artistically, but it's what people prefer, so that's what I'll go with here:

As I lay on my bed at the Super 8 watching a rebroadcast of an especially uneventful Colorado Avalanche game, reconfirming that Funions are terrible, I thought about Marianne's story. Ethan, Marianne, Tom Buckley, all of them—they were living up here in this shit hole, damn near pulling their hair out, driving around in trucks with duct tape on the windows, telling each other these awful stories they'd accumulated, because of one idea. Because they believed that getting a story right, telling it right, holding it, was a holy duty. They seemed to believe that getting a story right could save the world somehow. Or at least make you a better person. And to fail to tell a story honestly was sacrilege.

The story I'd put down, whatever it was, wasn't honest. It was a fraud. For the first time, I wondered if that was a kind of crime.

I'd spent a decent chunk of my advance on it. *The Tor-nado Ashes Club* hadn't afforded me a house, but a 54-inch flat-screen was a fine substitute.

I went to one of the HD channels, showing aerial footage of British Columbia, and flipped through the mail that had accumulated.

There was a note from Polly. "Pete," it said, and I could hear it delivered in the newly nasal tones she'd acquired since leaving me. "I saw your book at our [*our! That bitch*] local book-store the other day. I was so proud! Always knew you had it in you. I haven't had a chance to read it yet—this wedding stuff is nuts—but I'm looking forward to it. And I'm so glad you're coming to the wedding. It'll be so nice to see you again. Best, [!] Polly."

What a despicable she-monster she was. It was all the worse because I admired the craftiness of it—the mock-kind note, the gentle tone, the reminder of the wedding. It was a counterintuitive strike worthy of Sun Tzu. It was an attempt to reverse my victory, to pretend to be proud (PROUD!) of me so that at her wedding my precocious success as a famous novel-ist would seem to bolster her grandeur rather than outshine it.

It shook me, in any case, and I'm embarrassed to admit here that I took my vengeance out on the pizza guy, tipping him less than a dollar, although I tried to make it up a few weeks later when not only did I overtip but I ordered some breadsticks I didn't even want.

All of my problems could've been solved, or at least tem-porarily removed, by a round of daytime drinking with Derek. But he'd gotten back together with his Mount Holyoke girl, the

16

Dad didn't know much about Vietnamese food. Brats, sauer-kraut, and Chicago dogs, heavy on the chili, were more his style. If you couldn't order it at Bo Merrick's Sports Bar and Grill on West Addison, it wasn't worth eating. We were the only family I knew that glazed their Thanksgiving turkey with Miller Genuine Draft.

But as I grew older, Dad decided that maybe I ought to know something about the culture that I came from. He took out the Yellow Pages and found a restaurant called Pho 54 up in Evanston. "Authentic Vietnamese Cuisine." So one Sunday, the three of us set off for what would prove to be a very memorable brunch.

The waiter sat us down in friendly but garbled English, no doubt wondering what this awkward little black-haired girl was doing with the big guy in the Bears jacket and the lady with the permed blonde hair. Some kind of kid exchange program maybe.

Opening the menu, Dad immediately looked daunted. I hadn't seen him so confused since our doctor gave him a pamphlet on menstruation.

"Spring rolls, those sound good, as an appetizer," Mom suggested, as usual trying to be helpful. Dad ordered those confidently—at least they had an English name.

The waiter dutifully brought over four little logs wrapped in rice paper, set them down, and wandered off. He trusted us to know what to do. Big mistake.

Mom figured the best course was to plow ahead smiling. So she cut the roll into slices, like a butcher carving up a salami, and ar-ranged them neatly about her plate.

"Look Dennis, cucumber!" she said, offering some much-needed encouragement.

Dad, however, didn't want to be fooled. He knew perfectly well that, Vietnamese or not, nobody eats paper.

So his picked up a spring roll and unwrapped it, like peeling a banana. He dumped out the contents on his plate. A messy pile of shrimp, cucumber, and lemongrass sat in front of him.

"Boy they sure don't give you much, do they?" he said, obviously disappointed.

Mom practically gasped in horror, and looked around to make sure no one had heard.

"Dennis!" She leaned in close and whispered. "They do the best they can."

> —excerpt from *The Luckiest Polack in Chicago*
> by Ellen Krapowski (Copyright © 2006 Doubleday,
> reprinted with permission)

y emotional rope was already frayed on tl
sode of *Oprah* made me cry. Now, I know
ing about *Oprah* is like a sinner talking about C
with me here.

The flying schedule that took me from Bill
Boston was one of these awful stop-in-Phoenix cc
such that I landed at Logan in purple predawn, bel
Donuts had even opened. When I turned my phor
had a message from Jon Sturges.

"Pete, Jonny Sturg here. Listen. You might get
the US Attorney's Office. They got these bureaucrat:
who are hounding us, completely trumped up; this
thinking of moving the whole thing to one of tho:
Anyway, just play it cool. I'm sure it'll blow over. But–
took a look at some of the computers and they do
name, so—whatevs, I'm sure it'll blow over."

So I had to file that away in the "Things That N
come a Huge Nuisance Later" section of my brain.

Back at the apartment, Hobart wasn't in his roor
kitchen I found a pot of untended instant mashed pot
appeared they'd been left for several days, because h
above them were several unidentifiable exotic varieties
crawled into bed in my pants.

When I woke up, around two-thirty in the afteri
found solace in my Panasonic 54-inch flat-screen TV.

16

Dad didn't know much about Vietnamese food. Brats, sauerkraut, and Chicago dogs, heavy on the chili, were more his style. If you couldn't order it at Bo Merrick's Sports Bar and Grill on West Addison, it wasn't worth eating. We were the only family I knew that glazed their Thanksgiving turkey with Miller Genuine Draft.

But as I grew older, Dad decided that maybe I ought to know something about the culture that I came from. He took out the Yellow Pages and found a restaurant called Pho 54 up in Evanston. "Authentic Vietnamese Cuisine." So one Sunday, the three of us set off for what would prove to be a very memorable brunch.

The waiter sat us down in friendly but garbled English, no doubt wondering what this awkward little black-haired girl was doing with the big guy in the Bears jacket and the lady with the permed blonde hair. Some kind of kid exchange program maybe.

Opening the menu, Dad immediately looked daunted. I hadn't seen him so confused since our doctor gave him a pamphlet on menstruation.

"Spring rolls, those sound good, as an appetizer," Mom suggested, as usual trying to be helpful. Dad ordered those confidently—at least they had an English name.

The waiter dutifully brought over four little logs wrapped in rice paper, set them down, and wandered off. He trusted us to know what to do. Big mistake.

Mom figured the best course was to plow ahead smiling. So she cut the roll into slices, like a butcher carving up a salami, and arranged them neatly about her plate.

"Look Dennis, cucumber!" she said, offering some much-needed encouragement.

Dad, however, didn't want to be fooled. He knew perfectly well that, Vietnamese or not, nobody eats paper.

So his picked up a spring roll and unwrapped it, like peeling a banana. He dumped out the contents on his plate. A messy pile of shrimp, cucumber, and lemongrass sat in front of him.

"Boy they sure don't give you much, do they?" he said, obviously disappointed.

Mom practically gasped in horror, and looked around to make sure no one had heard.

"Dennis!" She leaned in close and whispered. "They do the best they can."

—excerpt from *The Luckiest Polack in Chicago*
by Ellen Krapowski (Copyright © 2006 Doubleday,
reprinted with permission)

My emotional rope was already frayed on the day an episode of *Oprah* made me cry. Now, I know a writer talking about *Oprah* is like a sinner talking about God, but bear with me here.

The flying schedule that took me from Billings back to Boston was one of these awful stop-in-Phoenix combinations, such that I landed at Logan in purple predawn, before Dunkin' Donuts had even opened. When I turned my phone back on I had a message from Jon Sturges.

"Pete, Jonny Sturg here. Listen. You might get a call from the US Attorney's Office. They got these bureaucrats over there who are hounding us, completely trumped up; this is why I'm thinking of moving the whole thing to one of those islands. Anyway, just play it cool. I'm sure it'll blow over. But—um, they took a look at some of the computers and they do have your name, so—whatevs, I'm sure it'll blow over."

So I had to file that away in the "Things That Might Become a Huge Nuisance Later" section of my brain.

Back at the apartment, Hobart wasn't in his room. In the kitchen I found a pot of untended instant mashed potatoes. It appeared they'd been left for several days, because hovering above them were several unidentifiable exotic varieties of fly. I crawled into bed in my pants.

When I woke up, around two-thirty in the afternoon, I found solace in my Panasonic 54-inch flat-screen TV.

I'd spent a decent chunk of my advance on it. *The Tornado Ashes Club* hadn't afforded me a house, but a 54-inch flat-screen was a fine substitute.

I went to one of the HD channels, showing aerial footage of British Columbia, and flipped through the mail that had accumulated.

There was a note from Polly. "Pete," it said, and I could hear it delivered in the newly nasal tones she'd acquired since leaving me. "I saw your book at our [*our! That bitch*] local bookstore the other day. I was so proud! Always knew you had it in you. I haven't had a chance to read it yet—this wedding stuff is nuts—but I'm looking forward to it. And I'm so glad you're coming to the wedding. It'll be so nice to see you again. Best, [*!*] Polly."

What a despicable she-monster she was. It was all the worse because I admired the craftiness of it—the mock-kind note, the gentle tone, the reminder of the wedding. It was a counterintuitive strike worthy of Sun Tzu. It was an attempt to reverse my victory, to pretend to be proud (PROUD!) of me so that at her wedding my precocious success as a famous novelist would seem to bolster her grandeur rather than outshine it.

It shook me, in any case, and I'm embarrassed to admit here that I took my vengeance out on the pizza guy, tipping him less than a dollar, although I tried to make it up a few weeks later when not only did I overtip but I ordered some breadsticks I didn't even want.

All of my problems could've been solved, or at least temporarily removed, by a round of daytime drinking with Derek. But he'd gotten back together with his Mount Holyoke girl, the one who'd taken pity on him when he came down from his tree those years ago. So he couldn't be rallied.

So alone I ate, and clicked around on the HD TV.

On a TV like that, almost everything is engrossing. On MSNBC, Olbermann looms Godlike, leaning forward into your living room with a definitive pose. On the Spanish-language talk shows you can see the details of the flimsy sets, the lines where they stopped painting or bent back the boards. On *Hotrageous Celebrity Couples* on E!, Angelina's image covers the screen and dominates the room like an Easter Island head. I'd gotten good speakers, too, so on the bass-fishing show you could hear the echoing thwack of desperate fins against the steel deck of the boat.

I stopped clicking to make a study of the face of an Asian woman, midthirties maybe, whose makeup artists had counted on a blurrier resolution than my Panasonic provided. As a result there were pockets of her forehead much shinier than others. Stopping to analyze, I realized I was watching *Oprah*.

Turning the sound down, I made a game of trying to decide why this Asian woman was there. She wasn't quite thin enough to be an expert on dieting. She was too young and unharried to give marriage advice. She appeared too cheery to be offering warnings about child molesters or why boys are lagging behind in school. But Oprah—on whom a much more balanced makeup effort had been exerted—listened with one of her serious faces. A psychologist of friendship maybe? I surrendered and turned the sound back up.

". . . how about at school, did the kids treat you any differently?" Oprah was asking.

"Well, when I was really young, kids were just curious. Because my eyes were different, they'd ask me if I could see everything, or if it was like I was always squinting. 'Can you see up here?' Yup. I can," said the Asian woman.

The audience laughed at this. I laughed, too, because I remembered John Whitbeck giving a similar eye exam to Chris Pai in second grade, the results of which were considered to be a baffling but decisive scientific rejection of our understanding of how eyes worked.

"But most kids just treated me like everyone else. And I *was* just like everyone else—birthday parties, school, I was a huge Cubs fan, I had a crush on Kirk Cameron . . ."

The audience laughed again.

"Now just like everyone else, you had a bully, all kids have bullies," Oprah said. She looked to the audience. "Raise your hand anybody here that didn't have a bully." The camera didn't catch this, but Oprah said "You few were probably the ones doing the bullying!" Everyone laughed again, and Oprah turned to her guest. "You tell a great story about a bully in the book."

"That's right, Mitchell was his name."

"Mitchell, that can be a bully name," Oprah said. Very astutely observed! I agreed with laughter as did the audience. There *were* certain bully names, and Mitchell was definitely one. Why did people condemn their child like that?

"Mitchell used to call me names and chase me home from school, and I complained about it to my dad. Now, my dad, of course, classic Chicagoan, he tells the story to his buddies at the bar. Big guys, factory workers. And they form a plan. So one day after school, Mitchell follows me home, calling me names and throwing twigs at me. Just as I'm running up to the door, my dad comes out. And I'm crying, and Mitchell's standing there trying to look innocent." The Asian woman did a funny impression of Mitchell trying to look innocent.

"My dad says, 'So, you like to bother girls, huh?' And Mitchell shakes his head. Then my dad says, 'Well, my friends and I, we like to bother bullies. Why don't you meet my friends?' And out the door of our house come about a dozen of the biggest, toughest, meanest-looking Chicago guys you've ever seen. And Mitchell takes one look at them and *starts crying*."

The audience enjoyed this very much. They laughed loudly, and so did I. Some of the audience started applauding. I did not, because I was alone and it seemed inappropriate.

"That was the last day he ever bothered *me*!"

Oprah held on to the Asian woman's knee, by way of "let's-hold-it-right- there."

"When we get back, we're going to <u>meet</u> <u>Ellen's</u> <u>dad</u>!" Oprah said these last three words in a chant that got the audience riled up as the commercials came on.

I didn't even change the channel. Maybe if I had—if I'd just thought to check back on British Columbia—everything might've played out differently.

"We're back with Ellen Krapowski, a Hmong—am I pronouncing that right?"

Ellen nodded.

"A Hmong-American who at age three"—Oprah pronouncing all this in her solid from-the-lungs voice—"was adopted by Bill and Denise Krapowski right here in Illinois. She's written a memoir about that experience called *The Luckiest Polack in Chicago*. Now Ellen, you've written that your dad was your greatest inspiration growing up."

"He was, absolutely. He taught me moral values and the importance of doing something greater than yourself. He wasn't always *talkative*"—here the audience laughed on account of Ellen's funny delivery—"but he taught me, really, through his actions, and how he was always there for us, always keeping our family together, and letting us know we were safe and loved."

This was a high-impact statement. Even I needed a second. Oprah herself took a pause, a nodding pause, before continuing.

"Reading this book I thought, I for one have got to hear from this man, this father, who, in his own funny way—and it is a *very* funny book—but he, your dad, really teaches us what it means to be a father. So we've brought him here. Please welcome—Dennis Krapowski!"

A shot of the audience, with their eyes wide and suddenly expectant. You could see the wrinkles and the widening pupils.

Out came a sixty-something man with a broom-end mustache. He walked as though his hip was just a bit out of balance, with his eyes down as though following an invisible rehearsed line across the stage. But Oprah stood up and caught him and gave him a hug as he sat down, and so did Ellen. Inspired perhaps by the comfort of his plush chair—and they looked very comfortable indeed—he grinned up toward the back row of the audience.

"Thank you for being here—"

"Thank you, Oprah, me and all the guys—" The audience was already laughing because his Chicago accent was so thick.

"That is a Chicago accent!" said Oprah. "You heard it here, if you're coming to town, get ready." Everyone laughed.

"So Dennis, you and your wife knew that you could not have children of your own, and you decided to adopt."

"Yeah, that's right, and we went to the agencies, y'know, and there's paperwork and all that. And then through a friend of ours we heard about this program, to adopt kids from Vietnam over there that needed homes. And I'd had buddies go over there, guys I went to high school with, and we'd seen it on TV, y'know, the tragedies there." *Da tra-jiddies dere.* "And I mentioned it to my wife, and we thought it was something we could try."

Oprah tapped his leg just lightly.

"Tell me this, Dennis, how did you raise such an amazing daughter?"

Everyone clapped and Oprah looked at them, nodding as though the crowd itself were a chorus of her own emotions.

"Well now, she did most of it herself! But we just—my wife and I decided we ought to raise her just like everybody else, and we were here in Chicago, so I took her to the Bears games when she was little, and taught her to eat sausages and all that, and we just tried to show her that you know we never thought of her as different or anything like that. As far as we were concerned, she was a hundred percent Krapowski, and that's how we tried to raise her."

Now picture me, sitting alone, crusts now accumulated in an open pizza box, but I've stopped eating. And this man, probably thirty-eight or thirty-nine inches on my screen, saying that. And a pause, the hush picked up perfectly by my speakers.

My eyes felt all salty and heavy.

"Dennis, in the book Ellen talks about how much of a Cubs fan you are, and how you try to get to as many games as possible."

Dennis nodded. "Oh, yeah, I took her to a lot of games. I think she only came for the popcorn half the time!" Everyone except Oprah laughed.

"All of us here, after reading this book, thought, 'We have got to do something for this man, who put up with all the crying, all the late nights, took her shopping for her *prom* dress for heaven's sake, when your wife was in the hospital, this guy'— she pointed at him—"deserves something."

The audience clapped eagerly. And I felt my mouth muscles smiling, almost against my will. The whole thing, the whole choreography, was so impossibly lame. But, hell, this guy did deserve something. He was terrific.

"So we asked a friend of ours, Mary Blazek, she's the head of public relations for the Chicago Cubs, if she might not have something for you, too."

A big-shouldered blonde lady in a Cubs jacket came out. My speakers picked up each happy gasp of realization from the audience as Mary Blazek handed Dennis an envelope.

"We just wanted to thank you for your support," said Mary, "and for your daughter's support, and for raising another generation of Cubs fans. And from the Chicago Cubs family to the Krapowski family, two generations of fans, here's a little token of our appreciation."

Dennis opened the envelope, and at just the moment he was figuring it out, Oprah said, "Season tickets, first row, right behind the dugout. You're gonna be buying a lot of popcorn now Dennis!"

Dennis stood up and half hugged Mary Blazek, he was so happy. The crowd was losing it with righteous delight.

Here's the thing about all this: later, over beers with Derek, I would describe the whole thing, in thick ironic tones. I would do an exaggerated, Chris Farley version of Dennis's accent, and around the Colonial Boy I'd waddle as he had, like a dancing bear. I'd tell how the whole crowd of needy menopausal women had gone bonkers to see some schlub win a prize for being a good dad.

Derek and I would talk about how Ellen Krapowski must have seen what a marketable story she had, about her tragic Hmong past and her new life here in America, full of deep-dish pizza and baseball. She must've teamed up with some packager, who saw how her touching 190-page tribute would burn up the shelves on Father's Day AND Mother's Day. Some ghostwriter sanded down the edges and played up the prom dresses and popcorn.

But at that moment, as Dennis held those tickets—and he didn't know what to do so he tried to shake Oprah's hand, and she looked at the crowd with a "c'mon!" and then gave him a big hug, and then Dennis kissed Ellen on the forehead—my cheeks were wet. I was crying. I hadn't cried since the days after Polly left, when I rolled around on a mattress like a helpless seal pup. But these tears were helpless in a different way, helpless in the way we all are before the purest, best things in the world. I was crying, full-on *crying,* tears streaming down my face like a sinner at a revival.

This woman, this somewhat doughy Asian woman, had told a story, a story about mothers and fathers and daughters that drew out the incredible, ordinary miracle of raising a child. How hard it was, how goofy your dad seems, how the whole thing is so human and messy until, years later, you can see how magical it was, how saintly your parents were, even as they wore their pants up to their rib cage and farted sometimes and snored like camels down the hall.

Above all, we could see it in front of us and we could tell it was true. We could feel the near-religious power of a true story.

Afraid almost, I panicked, turned off the TV, and went out to buy some beer without even putting on a jacket.

It only took a minute to pull it back together. I scoffed at how Oprah had stage-managed the whole thing, choreographed it all with Busby Berkeley precision, even Dennis's clumsiness built in to the routine. I pictured the Cubs' bosses, getting a call—probably on a special red phone they saved just for Oprah. And calculating how it would all play out, they'd jumped on it, seeing a brilliant PR opportunity and sending out their flack, Mary Blazek, who probably took a class on "Community-Corporate Interaction," in business school and knows how to make her bosses look like good citizens and good neighbors.

The whole point of it after all, the timing, the staging, everything, was to sell—and this is a real list, I wrote down the commercials—Special K protein bars, Lumineers porcelain teeth veneers, Oscillococcinum flu medicine, Lunchables Extra Cheesy Pizza, Children's Musinex, Walden Farms Chocolate Syrup, Oil of Olay, and the local news, which was of course itself just a minor-league version of *Oprah*. This human connection was just a ploy, a shameless effort to lock in eyeballs, and the sole end was to turn our affections into revenue for food conglomerates and manufacturers of toothpaste.

But they'd told a story, and they'd made me cry. They'd shaken me up in some deep human throb center. Possibly this is the "soul" everyone's always talking about.

17

Listen, listen. Hey . . . everybody, listen, I'm gonna say some stuff. (*to a stranger in a front table*) You—no more chewing. Chew chew chew you're like a squirrel. Or a beaver. A chewing beaver. Yes—thank you, shut him up. Hi, so listen. I'm Pete. Peter Tarslaw. I know some of you. Others, you know, whatever, we're gonna become friends. I just, you know, the movingness of the occasion, and this is a wedding, and I thought what the hell I'll give a speech. Keep it short, that's the advice they give and I will. I'm a novelist, by the way.

Polly and I—Polly Pawson, you know her as "the bride" or "Polly"—we used to date. In college. And, you know what, it was the best. The best time for me. Honestly. Remember in college when you could still just make out? (*Here Derek stands up and does a 'cut it' motion*) No I won't. You know, Polly, you're beautiful. The black hair, and the skin—it works for you. And I'm happy you're happy. James, you're from Australia. But that's okay, so are a lot of people. (*Derek approaches, along a side wall*) I can see you. Just because you're not in my field of vision. I see *motion*. I'm like a dinosaur.

Hey, George. That's George. George and I had a throwing contest earlier. I won handily. But he's from a boomerang culture not a baseball culture, so. Also, obviously . . . you know.

And thank you to the Pawsons for footing the bill on all this.

Look, this wedding, it was honest. That's the thing. You can feel the honest. And you know maybe Lincoln, probably his ghost was here. You two love each other. And I'm totally, one hundred percent happy about that without grudges.

So, I'd like to say, a toast. To honest (*Derek now embracing me and whispering in my ear to stop*) no, this, let me do this. To honest, and love. And Polly. You're fucking the coolest. Seriously. Everybody knows it now.

—text of a speech I delivered at Polly Pawson's wedding reception, as reconstructed from the memories of witnesses

Dignity. That was to be the watchword. At Polly's wedding, I would ooze and secrete dignity out of my very pores.

Dignified behavior, what they used to call *class*, would be the most elegant revenge. Confidence and success would waft off me, the Australians would be shamed, the aunts would be admiring, the bridesmaids would be lustful. As her guests fluttered around the famous novelist who'd deigned to come, Polly would know I'd won.

A famous novelist such as myself couldn't travel to his ex-girlfriend's wedding on the Chinatown bus, stinking as it does of cured ethnic delicacies and Brooklynism.

I had to take the Acela, because you can't say just *Amtrak* with an air of cavalier detachment. I drank a Heineken—a dignified beer—from the café car.

I heard a man and a woman talking about a meeting they'd been to in Boston, presenting some marketing plans to a consulting company. I thought of how I'd weave that into an anecdote for deployment at the wedding, wrapping it in worldly irony like bacon around a date. *Here we were going through the country of the Puritans, of Jonathan Edwards and Nathaniel Hawthorne, and they were talking about marketing,* I'd say with a smile wise beyond my meager years.

God, I was going to *kill* at this wedding!

But the best thing of all was my genius wedding present. Every time I got bored acting like a famous novelist riding the

train, I thought about it. By now it had probably arrived: the
Oenophile Select Temperature-Controlled Dual-Zone 28-Bottle
Wine Refrigerator.

The Oenophile Select Temperature-Controlled Dual-Zone
28-Bottle Wine Refrigerator wasn't on Polly's registry, so right
there I was sending the message that the various tacky items
she'd chosen herself were something of an embarrassment, and
for their own good I'd had to use my own exquisite taste. It was
also expensive, but it was the kind of thing where most people
don't really know how much it costs. Polly would wonder, but
she'd think it beneath her dignity to go on the Internet and find
out. At least for a few months, and then she'd crack, and find
out. She'd learn the price, it would be less expensive than she
thought, but still expensive, but she'd know she'd lost just by
looking.

But the best part was she'd have this thing in her house,
and it would never be full! Why would newlyweds James and
Polly ever have twenty-eight bottles of wine? Gradually, Polly
would start to think about this. She'd look at James, and
wonder why he wasn't the kind of guy who needed space for
twenty-eight bottles of wine. And she'd think about me—her
ex-boyfriend, the Famous Novelist, who must assume everybody
needs space for twenty-eight bottles of wine. She'd realize she'd
missed out on the Oenophile Select Temperature-Controlled
Dual-Zone 28-Bottle Wine Refrigerator lifestyle that I would
have provided.

At Penn Station in New York, Lucy joined me for the ride on
to Washington. She looked weary from months of trying to save

her job at Ortolan as the British guys slashed away. With battle-hardened dispassion she reported that last-quarter numbers were in, and sales had tapered off for *The Tornado Ashes Club*. Preston Brooks, that avuncular bastard-genius, was back on top with *The Widow's Breakfast,* which apparently half the readers in the country had seen fit to stuff in a stocking.

But this fact did not in the least affect my efforts at dignity. In fact, by the time we were out of New York, I'd worked it into my whole Polly's-wedding persona. It made perfect sense. Preston Brooks was a strictly *commercial* writer. But I, Pete Tarslaw, the famous novelist, was something much more. If I could pull it off without seeming obvious, I planned to suggest to the aunts and the bridesmaids that *most* great novelists weren't fully appreciated in their own time.

While I was working all this out Lucy had fallen asleep on my shoulder, and drool was beginning to seep out.

As we were pulling into Baltimore, she jerked awake. Her cheek was all smooshed up from my jacket. The nap must've invigorated her, because now she was full of girl-going-to-a-wedding energy and she got chatty.

"Pete?"

"Mmm?" I said, practicing a sonorous Novelist's Tone.

"Can I ask you something, honestly?"

"Of course." The Famous Novelist is always honest.

"How do you feel about, you know, this? Polly getting married?"

Ordinarily I might've given Lucy a straight answer. But the wedding was less than fifteen hours away. So I turned to her, looked her in the eye, put on my Novelist face, and belted it out of the park.

I gave her an answer about how "people change," and there
are "always regrets, bittersweet regrets," but that any kind of
"real love matures" into a love that can be "happy in another's
happiness," even if it's not with you.

She so completely bought it that when I was done she
rubbed my arm.

"I'm so glad to hear you say that," she said, "because Polly
actually asked me if I thought it was a good idea, to invite you."
She rubbed my arm again. "I told her I thought it was."

If I'd been telling her the truth, of course, I would've told
her I thought Polly was a vicious harridan and that while she
may have thought she'd outwitted me by landing this James
fellow, I'd proved myself the better con artist by writing a best-
selling *book*, which was a hard scam to top, and that I was
waiting with delicious anticipation to see Polly cringe in defeat
on her own wedding day.

As Lucy and I went to sleep that night in the DC Radisson,
I was sure that was how it would play out.

But the next morning I saw the Buddhist monks.

Lucy and I were sitting, in our wedding finery, on the shuttle
bus Polly's dad had hired to take guests from the hotel to the
chapel. Then two Buddhist monks got on.

They both had shaved heads and glasses, and they wore
orange robes the color of traffic cones. Lucy of course started
talking to them, and it emerged that they were friends of James's
family from Australia and had come all this way to perform a
blessing at the ceremony.

"This is our first time out of the monastery in three years," one of them said to Lucy. "Tomorrow we are going to see the pandas at the National Zoo!"

It began to dawn on me that this was not going to be the wedding I had anticipated. Because not even I believed I could impress Buddhist monks.

There was a lilt, a genuine happiness, in the voices of people walking up to the chapel. Women were snuggling up and tucking their hands into the pockets of men's overcoats. Lucy tried to do this to me, but I shooed her away, as I didn't want any potential hook-ups to think we were a couple.

The wedding was held in a simple clapboard chapel from the 1840s, plank boards and white pews. According to the program, this was the very chapel where Abraham Lincoln had gone to services with several freed slaves on the morning after he signed the Emancipation Proclamation.

I began to feel very itchy inside my sportcoat.

For ushers I'd expected a flop-haired, meathead band of James's Australian Rules cronies. But, while Australian, they didn't look meatheady at all. They were all thin. And clean-shaven. They had soft, cottony cheeks. They didn't look like they'd been shooting dingoes. They looked like they might be in a glee club together. They weren't eyeball-molesting brides-maids. With gentle accents they were offering arms to old women.

Our usher was in fact a literally retarded kid—legitimate Down syndrome—who was taking his responsibilities very seriously.

"Bride or groom?" he asked Lucy.

"Bride," she told him. "Are you by any chance James's brother George?"

"Yeah, I'm George," he said.

"I'm Lucy! Are you excited about your new sister-in-law, George?"

"Yeah, she's a great sister-in-law," George said. The Buddhist monks, already seated, looked back at us and smiled. Lucy turned to me with a "how great is that?" expression, and I fake-smiled as best I could.

"There's James!" said George.

And there he was indeed, my first sight of him, up at the altar. He looked, in a word, innocent. Like Macaulay Culkin, but with perkier eyes. The manliest things about him were his shoulders, which jutted out wide under his tuxedo. I watched him wave to his kid brother as he took his place.

The wedding started to come into focus for me, like a Polaroid developing. My illusions slipped away. I saw Polly's dad, a lawyer with an unfortunate patchy baldness, smiling and shaking hands as he worked his way around the aisle. Polly's mom, dyed black bun of hair on top, a woman who'd told me in a private moment that I seemed like a "great guy," smiled behind him in a royal-blue dress. Once the two of them had taken Polly and me out to Legal Seafood, and Polly had told me afterward that they'd found me "disarming."

I saw Polly's kid brother, a twenty-two-year-old fuckup who lived in his parents' basement and smoked pot all day. But even he had scrubbed up, and he led in his grandmother, a woman who'd once pinched my cheeks and told me I looked like "a healthy young Irishman."

Derek whispered hello as he slid in next to me, and he brushed off the pew before letting his Mount Holyoke girl sit down.

Then the organ blasted everyone alert, and we turned our heads around as Polly came in.

I'll spare the reader a bullshit description of how beautiful she looked coming down the aisle. Beautiful wasn't the key aspect. She did look beautiful, so beautiful that seeing her it occurred to me in a flash that somewhere in my past I'd ruined my entire life.

But worse than that was that she looked really, purely, happy.

In our time together, I'd seen Polly fake a lot of things. After our friend Alaina had paced around on a poorly lit stage for two full hours in a stupendously disastrous one-woman show about Dolley Madison, I'd watched Polly deliver fulsome and false compliments about how "captivating" it had been. To a distinguished professor of American history I'd seen her brilliantly allude to a false pregnancy, just to get out of sitting through a screening of *Birth of a Nation*. To my own mother I'd seen her deliver lengthy and baseless testimony on my remarkable diligence as a student. No one could fake someone out like she could. She was amazing. I'd loved her for it.

But walking down that aisle, beaming, she was not faking. I could tell. And it broke my heart all over again.

The Reverend—a woman—read the ceremony. There were readings from *The Prophet* and First Corinthians. The Buddhist monks chanted out a blessing in Tibetan.

The Reverend invited James and Polly "to share their vows with their friends and loved ones and with each other."

They stared into each other's eyes.

"I, James," he said in an Australian accent, more rounded and genteel than I'd expected, "vow not to spend *every* Sunday morning watching rugger and cricket on SkyTV." Happy laughs from the assembled. "I vow to remember to drive on the right side of the road." Happy laughs. "I vow not to complain too much when you play Britney Spears."

Again laughter, and then it got serious.

"I vow to support you, Polly, in everything that you do. I vow to protect you, Polly, and everything that you cherish. I vow to listen to you, to look after you, to be with you, when you wake, when you sleep, as a comfort, and a strength. I vow to love you, Polly, in everything that you are, in sickness and in health, till death do us part. I vow to give my life over to you, Polly, so we can make a new life, together."

Lucy dabbed her eyes. They were as red as beets.

"I, Polly, vow to at least *try* to like Vegemite," she said. Cathartic, happy laughs from choked-up throats. "I vow to appreciate the cultural achievements of Australia, such as Kylie Minogue, Kath and Kim, and INXS." Relaxed laughs. "I vow not to always point out that Budweiser is *vastly* superior to Victoria Bitter." Laughs and scattered cheers and friendly boos, hovering just within a reasonable volume limit.

"I vow to support you, James, in your every endeavor. I vow to comfort you, James, in every care and worry. I vow to listen to you, to look after you, to be with you, when you wake, when you sleep, as a comfort—"

Here Polly's throat snagged and she wiped her eye. She took a breath, and let out a soft laugh. You could feel the crowd pulling for her. With a tremble she pushed on. "I vow to love you, James, in everything that you are, in sickness and in health, till death do us part." She took another breath, and then her voice was calm and strong. "I vow to give my life over to you, James, so we can make a new life, together."

Some Australian let out a genteel "Hurrah!" and joyous cheers erupted. Lucy badly defaced the sleeve of her dress mopping up tear-water and snot.

In months of working on *The Tornado Ashes Club*, I'd gotten good at manipulating emotions. Now, confronted with something real, I was gutted.

There were several things I could've done next. I could've repented everything. I could've gotten on my knees and prayed to God and Abraham Lincoln to wash away my lies and let me start all over again. I could've pulled aside the woman reverend, unburdened myself of everything I'd done since losing Polly, and asked her how to lead a true and righteous life. I could've stolen a moment to introduce myself to James, shake his hand, and congratulate him on being the better man. I could've found Polly's parents, thanked them for their kindness to me, and hugged them for raising such a wonderful daughter. I could've turned to red-cheeked Lucy, told her she was the sweetest and kindest person I'd ever met, and asked her to marry me.

Instead, I dashed out of the chapel, forced myself, on the pretext of a "medical emergency," into the rented Daewoo of one of Polly's cousins whom I'd met years before at a clambake, rode silently back to the Radisson, stopped at the front desk and had them sell me a package of cold medicine, consumed all eight pills, made for the ballroom, told the bartender that I was "with the family" and it was okay to start serving me early, and encouraged him to be generous in his pouring.

THINGS I DID, OR AM ALLEGED TO HAVE DONE, AT POLLY'S WEDDING RECEPTION

- Stopped the hors d'oeuvres lady, took ten shrimp, put them in a plastic cup, and told her to "scurry along and reload."
- Asked one of Polly's bridesmaids, who was a high school English teacher, which of Hemingway, Shakespeare, and Mark Twain was "the worst liar." Suggested that if any of them were alive today, they'd be writing car commercials.
- Confronted the reverend and asked her how long they've been ordaining ladies.
- Challenged James's brother George to a shrimp-throwing contest in the parking lot. Defeated him by hitting five windshields in six throws to his three.
- Gave Polly's mom a hug, holding said hug for well over a full minute, long after she had grown visibly uncomfortable.
- Told the story of Derek and the Mount Holyoke girl to the Buddhist monks, with added ribald detail of my own invention, at one point inviting the Mount Holyoke girl over and suggesting she provide some illuminative physical demonstrations.
- Told Derek I didn't want to fight him but would if necessary.
- Summoned a group of Australians and delivered a lecture on the theme "Honest Abe Lincoln: The Bearded Hero."

- Informed my tablemates at dinner that I probably could've slept with Polly's mom.
- Told Lucy that her attempts to quiet me were "crypto-fascist."
- Declared myself to be a skilled amateur chef. By way of demonstration, poured vodka all over Lucy's sea bass. When she protested, proclaimed that her palate was "unrefined."
- Told the reluctant bartender that he was a "cur" and I would fight him.
- Asked the teacher bridesmaid if she thought I could beat Josh Holt Cready in a fight.
- After unwrapping several false leads, found the Oenophile Select Temperature-Controlled Dual-Zone 28-Bottle Wine Refrigerator. Carried it outside. Smashed it against a Dumpster.
- Returned inside. Threw up discreetly into a napkin. Decided to deliver a few brief remarks and convinced the DJ to hand me the microphone.

I'm told my speech ended with the DJ turning up "The Chicken Dance" really loud to muffle my protesting screeches as Derek and Lucy led me out to the hallway. There I escaped their grasp and ran out the door. I gained control of a hotel shuttle bus and drove it in jerking loops around the parking lot until bumping into a curb.

The next day I woke up in the hotel bathtub.

Fish sometimes get a condition called pop eye, where gas built up inside them causes their eyes to bulge out and eventually burst. I had that. My arms were as weak and trembling as those of a veiny wheelchair-bound centenarian, and it took the greatest efforts of will and strength to extricate myself from the soilings that covered my clothes. My brain squirmed and writhed as though trying to undo itself from an intricate knot. I felt as though my innards had been reduced to a sickly chum, and my interior muscles at spastic intervals tried to heave them up and out. My best defense was to try and pass out before each new assault of nausea hit its violent apex.

All of this was but one level of my punishment. The endless ride back to Boston was punctuated from time to time as Lucy, in the dispassionate tones of the traumatized, recalled and related some new disgrace I'd committed. I could barely keep my consciousness threaded together for long enough spells to listen.

For my part, I had only two very clear memories, chance snatches of footage that somehow preserved themselves, Zapruder films from the drunken mind.

One was this: slouched in a corner of the ballroom, against the wall, sucking on a lime, I watched Lucy and Polly talking on the dance floor. Polly walked over. Focusing on my lime I pretended not to notice her pulling up her wedding dress so she could kneel beside me and touch my cheek.

"Pete," she said, "please go to bed."

"Happy wedding," I said.

"Please. Let them take you back."

Then she walked away.

The other memory was this: walking through the hall, Derek holding my arm like a gruff prison guard as I performed a half-remembered version of the sentimental Irish tune "The

Foggy Dew," we passed two middle-aged women sneaking cigarettes.

"Is that the guy who wrote the book?" one of them said to the other, trusting that I was too addled to overhear.

"Yeah," the other said. "Drunken writers, I guess."

"Well let me tell you," said the first. "I read it. And it wasn't good enough for him to get away with behaving like *that*."

18

"Some folks say eighty-five is too old to be a rodeo clown. They say a fella that old ought to hang up his striped-orange jacket and give up the game of entertaining kids and luring bulls off fallen cowboys. Well, some folks haven't met Earl Teacup, who says that at eighty-five . . . he's just getting started."

"Leonardo da Vinci, Claude Monet, Paul Cézanne. It used to be that if you wanted to be a painter, you had to have two hands. But when an accident changed Betsy Billinger's life, she didn't give up on her dream of expressing herself through art. In fact, she decided to pursue her goal twice as hard. And the results? To say the least, . . . they're colorful."

"They don't talk much. They eat a thousand pounds of shrimp every day. They live at depths as great as half a mile, and they won't fit into any swimsuit you'd find at the mall. But when it comes to dating, it turns out they've got some good ideas. Blue whales weren't always known for their love lives. But one group of researchers has been studying the way that whales mate. They've discovered that single whales . . . have a few things to teach single people."

"Roses, vanilla, and fresh-baked cookies: there are some smells that all of us know. But what about red alder, Mayhaw, or burnt plantains? Those are just a few of the odors that competitors have to identify at the World Smelling Championships. If you're looking for this year's event . . . just follow your nose."

—introductions to Tinsley Honig pieces on the ABC
newsmagazine *Dispatch* as recorded by the author
(ellipses indicate dramatic pauses)

Here begin the events that you, the reader may have followed. I'm sorry it took so long to catch up, as these parts are the real fireworks and doubtless the reason you bought this book in the first place. But after the backstory, I'm hoping I won't seem like quite as much of a bastard.

When I got the news that Tinsley Honig wanted to interview me, I was sitting in a lukewarm bath, thoroughly pruned, with more pubes and soap chunks floating around than anyone should be comfortable with.

This image—my pruned flesh, numb expression on my face, phone balanced precariously on the rim of the tub—can stand for the whole of the postwedding period.

But then David Borer and Lucy called with the wonderful news.

"You don't understand how big of a deal this is," Borer said. "You're *nothing* as a writer until you get on TV."

TV! And with Tinsley Honig no less! I was going to be a profile on *Dispatch*. With any luck, they'd tuck me in between a segment on old-fashioned pedophiles who lured children over their ham radios and a piece about Afghani land-mine kids who were learning to play soccer again.

"Your book is going to start selling all over again," said Borer. "They're already talking about printing a special *Dispatch* edition, which will include a DVD of the piece. Whatever, they've got a lot of bad ideas over here, the point is, this is very, very good news."

Lucy deserved the credit. Some girl who was in her pottery class was roommates with one of Tinsley's assistants. The book had thus wormed its way into the hands of that auburn-tressed and porcelain-faced angel of TV newsmagazine journalism. It made sense. I was a natural story: young guy writes a sensitive novel, can maybe save literary culture for the text-message generation. And my publicity photo made me look telegenic.

The whole "my life has collapsed on me" thing disappeared. It was hard, in fact, to imagine I'd ever thought that. My performance at Polly's wedding seemed like boyish hijinks from the distant past.

I looked around the bathroom, with its color-streaked towels from Target and the shave-scummed sink. Tinsley couldn't tape me here. That wouldn't work at all. What if Hobart came in, with his crazy hair, and started making potatoes just as Tinsley was about to ask me, on camera, how I'd learned to feel so deeply?

Luckily I had a backup plan. We'd do the interview up at Aunt Evelyn's. The sugar shack, the maple trees, the house made of local stone—*that* was an author's house. That was where I should pretend to live.

Something you may not realize when you watch these segments on TV is how fast they come together. I didn't have any time to prepare.

I wasted my time on the bus up to Aunt Evelyn's. That was time I could've used to plot out the whole interview, to come up with anecdotes and quips and facial expressions. But I spent the whole ride thinking about how my sales would go up after the interview, if I should buy an apartment in New York or skip right to the house on the ocean.

I got to Aunt Evelyn's in time for dinner. She made these intense fennel sausages—she was going through this whole serious-meats craze—and those were distracting, too.

The next morning, a Tuesday, the segment producer and the camera guy for *Dispatch* showed up at seven. They rolled up in a van, apparently having driven through the darkness from New York. It was hard to imagine what they'd talked about.

The camera guy, whose name was Skee or perhaps Skeet, was vampire-y thin. He looked ageless in a way hard-living dudes who've past a certain benchmark are ageless, but he also looked like he'd been pissed off about stuff since at least the mid-1970s. His skin was ashen, the kind of skin you'd imagine on a Dickensian undertaker.

The producer, whose name was Michelle, was maybe thirty and wearing—and this sounds hard to believe in retrospect but I double-checked at the time—two different scarves at the same time. But her most distinctive trait was a nervous and terrifying laugh, the sound of which could easily be mistaken for hysterical weeping.

Skee and Michelle helped themselves to the cantaloupe and maple-smoked bacon Aunt Evelyn had laid out. Michelle explained the day's procedure, punctuating her sentences with spurts of weep-laughter. She would "pre-interview me," she said. Tinsley didn't like to do the prep work herself, preferring to capture the spontaneity of first meeting me for the camera.

"Don't ask Tinsley about her hair," Skee said, his mouth full of cantaloupe and bacon. "She's a real testy bitch about it."

Michelle loudly wept-laughed and gripped him on the shoulder.

"And she won't really look at ya? Not right in the eyes anyway? So don't worry about that," he continued. "Just look kinda to just above her left ear. It'll look the same on camera." He worked a tricky piece of bacon out of his teeth with his left pinkie.

"Okay!" said Michelle, with a big doped-up grin.

"She's gonna insist on ringing the doorbell," Skee said. "So let's go frame that. By the time she gets here the trees are gonna be soaking up the light. It's gonna be like shooting inside a freakin' funhouse."

We walked around, looking for places to shoot, as Michelle asked me practice questions.

"Was it challenging writing a novel?"

I was baffled as to how to answer.

"I'm sorry, but that's honestly something she might ask." Nervous weep-laughter.

Out in the back woods there was a piece of a steel plow, rusting and half buried, left by some farmer a century ago. Maybe I could lean on that, say something profound about the passage of time?

"Nope," said Skee. "She won't come out here. She won't want to get the mud on her boots."

"But she walked around that pond with Preston Brooks!" I said.

Skee gave me a bent smile. "Well he's him, and you're you. And she's Tinsley. And I'm telling you, she ain't coming back here, and getting her boots all covered in this shit, and if she did I'd probably be the one hearing about it."

Michelle looked back and forth between us, then wept-laughed, to show it was all in good fun, but which also conveyed that she was as terrified as I was of this lanky madman.

"Why do you think we're so afraid of tornadoes?" Michelle asked as a practice question as we walked around to the sugar shack. "I'm sorry. I'm just trying to prepare you."

"No, that's okay, that's okay." I put on my best writer face.

"Tornadoes are a kind of chaos," I said, in my best writer voice. "A kind of churning and disorder we're all afraid of. I think my novel, really, is an attempt to bring some sense to that. To draw some order, some poetry out of the swirling madness we call life."

Michelle clenched my arm. "Good!"

"Listen, when you're about to say some shit like that, scoot in close to Tinsley so I can frame it with her hair," Skee said. "'Cause that kind of thing, they'll want to use it, but if her hair and part of her face isn't in it, she's gonna bitch me out, she's gonna bitch the editors out. It's gonna make *my* life real fucking miserable, and *they're* gonna be there till fucking two in the morning trying to splice it together, and *that's* gonna come down on me, and everybody's gonna be fucking pissed off all because you blew your best stuff and her hair wasn't in it! So don't fire off any of that shit on some shot where I'm getting you from behind, okay? Wait, and we'll get it when I'm shooting you straight on, or with one of these walls in the background. Okay?"

I nodded.

"Here, we'll practice. Say that again," he said, and he hoisted his camera to his shoulder.

"Uh, tornadoes are a kind of chaos—"

"Nope. See there, all I got behind you is that car, okay? And Michelle, she's playing Tinsley, she's not even in the shot yet. So, wait, here, I'll put my hand up like this when you should start talkin', and that'll mean I got it all framed."

We ran it through again, with Michelle standing in.

"Tornadoes are a kind of chaos, a kind of churning and disorder we're all afraid of—"

"Get up in her face, okay? Just so you're almost rubbing up against her boobs."

I slid closer to Michelle. "I think my novel, really, is an attempt—"

"Get really up in there, don't be shy."

"An attempt to bring some sense to that," I continued, almost rubbing up against Michelle's boobs. It all seemed much sillier at that distance. I could feel my voice getting weaker. "To draw some order, some poetry out of the swirling madness we call life."

"Good, all right, see, that's a shot I got, and won't have to fuckin' hear it from the guys in the editing bay that their wives were screaming at 'em for not getting home until fucking four-thirty." Weep-laughter from Michelle.

The last shot we rehearsed was up in the guest room, as I sat on the bed and Michelle pretended to be Tinsley, and I sat on a wicker chair with Aunt Evelyn's copy of *Hearts of Ice and Blubber* propped beside me.

"Novels may not seem sexy," I practiced saying, in a way that suggested novels were *totally* sexy. "But they may just save us."

"Good!" said Michelle. Skee smiled, showing yellowed teeth.

"Dude, I've heard a lot of this shit, but that was some of the best. Some of these guys, they try and explain like actually every little thing that they're doing. They get all tripped up trying to find like the right word or whatever. And you want to tell them, 'Listen, just say some shit, make my life easy, let's get this done.' That's what you're doing. That shit, 'novels are saving us' and whatever? That's making the editors' lives easy."

"All right!" said Michelle, checking her watch. "We need to hook up with the rest of the crew, and we'll be back—shooting in two hours!" She patted me on the knee. "You're gonna be great!"

Skee waited for her to leave.

"Listen," he said, as he packed up his camera. "She won't tell you this, but another thing—Tinsley hasn't read your book. No knock on you, she doesn't read any of 'em. But just don't trip her up with talking about some specific thing that happened in it. I've seen guys do that, it slows the whole fucking thing down, and she gets real pissed about it. Just say your shit about novels and stuff. And keep her hair in the shot."

There wasn't any time to think things through. In the kitchen the hair and makeup lady dolled me up. I could see Tinsley through the curtains, tinier than I'd expected. Then they checked the light and spotted me by the door. Through the cracks I could see the camera lights come on.

"Speed," I heard Skee say, and I heard footsteps scuffle into position on the doorstep.

"Good, are we good?" I heard Tinsley say.

"Yes, go on you. Doorbell's on the right," I heard Michelle say.

The doorbell rang. And as scripted, I opened it for what would be the first shot.

At that distance, with full makeup, in that light, Tinsley's face didn't look porcelain at all. Her features seemed huge, distorted, like in the ritual masks of the Haida people of the Pacific Northwest. So that threw me off.

And behind her was a small phalanx of people—a boom mic guy, and a kid holding a plastic rectangle thing designed to reflect light, and Michelle in the back with a clipboard.

And right in front of me, almost wedged between us, was Skee, his eyes obscured by the camera, his mouth gnarled with strain.

You don't think in a situation like that. It's beyond consciousness. Time washes you along before you can grab on to a thought.

That's why at first I just went through the motions. I shook Tinsley's hand, and she asked me questions I can't even remember. I spouted answers without knowing what I was saying. Words left my mouth before I had a chance to run them through the scanner, but bullshit being my default mode, they were at least semicogent bullshit.

That's how it went at first, anyway, and Tinsley and I were filmed walking down the driveway. All I remember hearing is the sound of the crunching gravel.

But in the second shot, a shot we'd rehearsed, I was supposed to sit at my desk in the sugar shack, with my computer in front of me, and pretend to be writing. A sort of *Unsolved Mysteries*–style dramatization of writing my novel. When we practiced I'd been fine with it.

But as we were doing it—I was sitting there, and Skee was crouched right next to me, filming up on my furrowed brow— I knew I couldn't keep it going. The Xpo, Pamela McLaughlin's fingers tracing a murder on a napkin, Miller Westly's two-pooled house, the audience in Montana, Marianne, the frozen fire-watcher, *Leaves of Grass*, the wedding, Polly touching my cheek, Margaret watching from an upstairs window, it was all part of it, I'm sure, all chips on the foundation. Until suddenly, sitting at the desk, fake-writing, I felt the whole structure collapse inside me.

People have asked me if I went crazy, or if something Tinsley did made me snap, or if I was just angry that day. But it was the opposite. Suddenly I felt a kind of dreary, resigned calm.

No one noticed at first. Skee got his footage, and Tinsley and the crew moved out, and Michelle led me out to the sugar-woods, and stood me by one of the maple trees that we'd picked out earlier. We'd had Aunt Evelyn set it up with the tubes and the pipes and all. It was a good metaphor, we'd all agreed at the time. I stood there waiting while they checked the light and Tinsley had her face touched up.

And then the camera was on.

"Speed."

"Okay, on Tinsley."

She leaned in close to keep her hair in the shot. I could feel Skee, just over my shoulder, breathing through his yellow teeth.

"Does writing flow from you, Pete, like the sap from these trees?" Tinsley asked.

"What?"

"Is creating a novel really a matter of tapping in, and drawing the words out?"

I didn't say anything at first. Tinsley tried again.

"When you're writing, do you feel it flow, like maple sap?"

I looked at Tinsley. Maybe she really did want to know if writing flowed like tree sap. Maybe she didn't. It didn't matter. Whatever it was, I decided not to lie to her.

"No. I mean, look."

My posture relaxed. My muscles eased. Relief washed over me.

"Look, I wanted to write a book that would be popular. And, you know, I made kind of a study of these things, and I'd read one of Preston Brooks's books, the one with the cancer kid and that guy wandering all over Ireland and all that, and I just decided, *Okay, fine. If that's what they want, great. I'm gonna fill it with mushy prose, and, you know, promises, and faintly heard songs, and lost loves.* All that stuff.

"And, yeah, I mean, once I decided that, that I was gonna write, you know, the baldest, most sentimental book ever, yeah, I guess it did come pretty easily. If I was stuck, you know, I'd just put in a dying Frenchman or an immigrant carrying a baby in a shopping bag, whatever. A dying dog on the road. It's easy enough to come up with that kind of crap, once you've decided to do it.

"So, yeah, I guess it did flow like syrup. It's not like I was James Joyce up here, slaving over every word. Give people what they want. If they want this crap, fine. You got it. It's a bunch of bullshit anyway. So, yes. Syrup, or whatever you said."

The only reason I know that's exactly what I said is because I saw it on TV a week later.

19

TINSLEY HONIG: Was it challenging, writing a novel?

PETE TARSLAW: Challenging? Not really. I mean, it's a titanic pain in the ass to actually type out all the words. And it has to more or less make sense, which is tricky. But the big part is just figuring out what readers want to hear. And that's easy; you just look at the best-seller list. Readers—or people who buy books, anyway—are really straightforward. Kind of dumb, even, in what they like. They like World War II, disasters, lost love. It's not hard to come up with stuff. Shooting fish in a barrel, really.

TINSLEY HONIG: Shooting fish in a barrel?

PETE TARSLAW: Well, I mean, not that easy. I did have to write the whole thing.

TINSLEY HONIG: So the actual writing was the most challenging part.

PETE TARSLAW: Well . . . yeah. Sitting there and doing it.

TINSLEY HONIG: How did you keep yourself sitting there?

PETE TARSLAW: Uh, well, you know, I thought about the money I was gonna make. The prestige.

TINSLEY HONIG: Mmm.

PETE TARSLAW: I wish somebody had told me how little money there was in books!

TINSLEY HONIG: [light laughter]

TINSLEY HONIG: Who would you say are your biggest literary inspirations?

PETE TARSLAW: Preston Brooks. You know that guy? Right, you interviewed him. Yeah—I mean that guy is such an obvious charlatan, his books are so cheesy in such stupid ways. Reading that guy,

seeing him, I figured, yeah, I can definitely pull this off. I guess
that's not so much 'inspiration.' But—you get it. He's just so terrible, I was like, if that guy can do it, I can do it.

TINSLEY HONIG: [indicating maple trees] The countryside here is
so beautiful. Did you try and include this place in your work?
PETE TARSLAW: No. I mean—
TINSLEY HONIG: The trees, the streams—
PETE TARSLAW: No. I mean—I could've, I guess. But I figured, Ver-
mont has so few people in it, not that many people buying books.
And the countryside up here, it's kind of complicated, you know?
There's rocks and stuff everywhere. But like a plain, or a field, that's
much easier to describe. You just say, you know, "It's lush and
golden and sweeping" and people get it. It seems like a bigger deal.

—excerpts from the transcript of episode 217
of *Dispatch,* aired 05/06/08 on ABC

How these things snowball is an interesting puzzle—Internet phenomena? Cultural controversies?—requiring a better sociologist than me, because not only am I not impartial, I observed the whole thing unfolding at the local FedEx/Kinko's.

To read the blog posts, the articles in Slate and Salon and the *Weekly Standard*—even the *Huffington Post,* where the fucking guy from *Wings* had an opinion—at my local FedEx/Kinko's, I'd have to put my credit card in that little machine, and get issued a Kinko's AccessKey or whatever it's called, and sit in a comfortless chair and watch my 25-cent minutes tick away as I tracked the rhetorical combat about whether I was evil or just misunderstood.

I couldn't use my own computer because some state police guys had come to my apartment door for it on the very morning before my *Dispatch* segment aired.

I hadn't even been there; I'd been so nervous that morning I'd woken up early and gone for pancakes. They'd dealt with Hobart. The agents had flashed a warrant and explained to him that I was a "person of interest" in the "ongoing Jonathan Sturges investigation." Then they seized my computer and took it away.

He was panicking when I got back. He kept choking on his own spit as he tried to explain it to me. But I shut him up and told him to calm down. He didn't know Sturges so the whole thing shocked him more than it did me.

When state police guys seizing your computer is only the second-worst thing to happen to you in a given week, that's a bad week. But I didn't have any spare mental energy to devote to possible criminal charges because I was about to become a full-fledged pop-culture controversy.

In retrospect it all makes sense: a young author goes on TV and issues sweeping derisions of literature. Of course it was a big deal. The only reason it wasn't a bigger deal is that I wasn't more famous. But it caught me by surprise.

Like all controversies, it evolved in clear stages.

1. The Inciting Incident

My interview on *Dispatch* aired. Tinsley introduced me thus:

"*The Tornado Ashes Club,* a best-selling novel about a grandmother, an unlikely fugitive, and a long-lost love, has touched the hearts of readers across the country. It's a tale full of tenderness and well-turned phrases."

Good so far.

"But the book's author, a young man named Peter Tarslaw, has some views on writing that are . . . far from traditional. I visited Peter at his family's maple sugar farm in Vermont, where he spoke about truth, fiction . . . and his literary rivals."

If you watched the segment on the oft-linked YouTube clips, then you know what followed: the opening bit of me lacing into Preston Brooks, the shots of Tinsley nodding, the series of set pieces as I spout out my various theories.

My quibbles, when I first watched the piece, were mainly aesthetic: my voice sounded much whinier than I believe it to be, my pants looked much too short even though they're not.

Hobart had been watching with me.

"What'd you think?"

"You were great, definitely," he said. He sounded nervous, which made me believe I really had been great. "Listen, about those state police guys—"

"Hobart, seriously, don't worry about that. It's my stupid boss. It's fine. I just got interviewed by Tinsley Honig!"

"Yeah, yeah. That's . . . it's incredible," he said.

Then my phone rang. It was Mom, as purely and naïvely proud as any mom, and I soaked it up and assumed that was how the rest of the world would take it as well.

If TV was still a one-shot deal, where you either saw something when it aired or you missed it forever, the signals zooming off unrecoverable into distant galaxies, then that would've been the end of it.

2. Outrage

Tracing it back in retrospect is like following the origins of some ghastly tropical disease—there are early cases, and threads and connection, and patches where it flares up especially strongly, but the very start is lost.

But it went something like this. Some literary-blogger types saw my interview. In their garrets full of dog-eared copies of *Emerson's Essays* and *Barthes on Barthes,* they cleaned their hands against their Powell's Bookstore T-shirts and started weighing in on what I'd said to Tinsley.

Somehow a clip of the interview got posted on YouTube. Now the blogger types had something to link to. More of these self-righteous vultures sat down at their stained desks and weighed in on the "Tarslaw Controversy."

What bothered most of them was how jarringly frank I'd

been—how I'd admitted baldly that I thought writing was just a con game.

But then other bloggers started suggesting that maybe everything I'd said was sarcastic. And then that argument kept the whole thing going.

The Controversy, really, was: What it did mean for fiction, what I'd said? Had I meant it? Did it matter? Very quickly people got lost in postmodern mazes of their own invention, and suddenly my simple frankness became a puzzle.

3. Response

Next time a Controversy arises, watch for this phase. It's the easiest to identify: the stage at which enough people are arguing and making noise about something that self-important journalists decide they better stake out some ground on the issue.

This stage got going the next morning, while I was still asleep. At nine I heard my phone ring and saw it was David Borer, but I assumed he was calling to congratulate me and rolled over. He kept calling, and I figured, *Dude, I get it, you think I'm terrific.* It wasn't until about two that I heard his message about "damage control strategies."

By the time I got to Kinko's, the Tarslaw Controversy had been kicking around long enough for distinct schools of thought to coalesce.

SCHOOLS OF THOUGHT ON
MY TINSLEY INTERVIEW

- **The Tarslaw-Is-a-Total-Bastard School,** epitomized by a 2000-word rant on The Pathetic Fallacy: *During his interview on the "news" show* Dispatch *last night,*

HOW I BECAME A FAMOUS NOVELIST

author Pete Tarslaw revealed the truth about publishing. Tarslaw's comments showed him to be the epitome of snark, admitting to manipulating reader trust as casually as Dick Cheney manipulated prewar intelligence. Like the child molesters featured in the show's first segment, Tarslaw coolly described his deplorable methods, as the manicured (?) hostess blithely nodded. It was the latest sign of how far we've fallen.

- **The It's-All-Tinsley's-Fault School,** which cropped up on the message boards at BetterReadThanDead .com: *Here we had a guy who was finally prepared to say what we've all been thinking about popular fiction, ready to blow the cover best-selling authors have been hiding under for years, and Tinzy (sic) starts asking him about how to make maple syrup!*

  This school didn't let me off the hook, though. There was in fact a conspiracy-minded subset that suggested the only reason I was on TV instead of, say, Alice Munro, was that the corporate types knew I wouldn't say anything too "smart" that would seem condescending to loyal TV viewers.

- **The Tarslaw-Is-a-Postmodern-Imp School,** expressed on Slate by "Book Girl" Meg Bierst: *Pete Tarslaw's interview on last night's episode of the ABC newsmagazine* Dispatch *is already becoming literary legend. Critics have leapt over themselves to denounce Tarslaw's supposed "cynicism."*

  They're wrong. It's true, Tarslaw's honesty—about his writing methods, his disdain for readers, his fellow authors —was shocking. But that was exactly the point. Tarslaw

is what the literary world has been waiting for: a genu-
ine prankster. His responses were exactly what inane
questions deserve: subtle jokes that pierce the ludicrous
bubble of hype that surrounds young authors. Tarslaw is
nothing less than the Borat of popular fiction.

She had to undercut it at the end by saying *It's a pity*
Tarslaw isn't as interesting as a writer as he is as an in-
terview subject. But still.

Unfortunately the first school seemed to be winning.
Controversy Stage Four commenced.

4. Press contact

Seven hours or so, that's how long it must take for a reporter to
have coffee, eat a bagel, cruise the Internet, come across a story,
decide to pursue it, and get someone's cell phone number,
because around four I got the first of a barrage of calls.

Back home by then, cooling off, I answered, and a woman
identified herself as a reporter for Fox News. That's who was
first, and they deserve the credit. The reporter was also smart
enough to play it off like she was on my side.

"This whole thing is crazy, huh? How do you feel about
all these writers attacking you?" She said *writers* like a fifteen-
year-old says *parents.*

Instinctively, I deployed the Pawson Method.

"Uh . . . [cough] . . . you know . . . [breathing sound, rising to a high pitch veering on sob, then dropping down, as
though I'm courageously keeping together] . . . before I talk
about this . . . I think I have to go home for a while."

It didn't work as well on reporters as it did on professors. She kept at me, so I mumbled, "I'm so sorry," and hung up.

After a series of UNKNOWN NUMBERs, I answered one of David Borer's calls.

"Dude, this is not good. Not good. I'm getting calls—it's like a sinking submarine here! Damage control, dude, damage control."

"Really? I mean, it was just an interview."

"Dude, they're talking lawyers over here. Okay? Lawyers! They're drafting you an apology."

"Apology for what? Everything I said was true."

"This is coming from the top down. I have no control over this. This is beyond me—we're on like a *corporate* level now. They're making calls. You might have to apologize to Oprah."

"What'd I do to her?"

"She's just—that's who you apologize to."

Why were people so angry at me? Just because of a TV interview where I told the truth? So I'd written a bullshit novel and fessed up to Tinsley Honig—who cares?

Jealousy was part of it. Would-be writers who in their private fantasies imagined themselves issuing real, meaningful, *literary* pronouncements to Tinsley Honig were furious that *I'd* gotten the chance and blown it.

If this had played out like a standard controversy, we would've entered stage five, Apology, followed by the sixth and final stage, Editorial Closure, where the opinionated weigh in on what the whole business tells us about contemporary mores.

But there's a way to complicate a controversy—to knock it off course and send it into more unpredictable terrain. It's this: start making money for somebody.

The next morning, back at Kinko's, I followed a whim and checked out a different Web site—the only Web site that really matters.

Amazon. And there I was taking off.

A few days before, sales of *The Tornado Ashes Club* had been ranked in the 16,000s. But now, suddenly, I was hovering around number 63.

Borer called again. But I heard no more talk of *damage control*. I heard about *containment strategies*.

By that afternoon, there was no more talk of *apologies*. There was talk of *statements*.

It wasn't that people had stopped piling on. Back at Kinko's, I read a post on Josh Holt Cready's own blog, where he said, "Peter [sic] Tarslaw may have written. But he is not a writer. He knows nothing of writing. Of what that means. Of what that demands."

That night, on NPR, they were doing a story about the whole thing. They'd been one of the calls I'd dodged, but they managed to get a quote from Preston Brooks himself. "I don't watch much television. And I don't know this Tars-loo fellow. I suspect he's a young man and like most young men he's got more mouth than sense. That's forgivable. But writers are a kind of monk. We ought to treat each other like monks. This fellow didn't treat me very well, it sounds like. And that's no way for an honest writer to treat anyone."

Of course! I couldn't believe I hadn't thought of it sooner! I'd started a literary feud!

I would be back on the best-seller list. Tenure was guaranteed! And someplace great, too! What university wouldn't want a genuine Controversial Literary Figure striding around their campus? And women! Women would love me for the same reason they send marriage proposals to serial killers! I'd been misunderstood! But without killing anybody!

Borer and the lawyers and publicists down at Ortolan must've got it, too.

"Dude, we figured out the response. First move: Malta Book Festival. Not a big-deal thing, but Preston Brooks is gonna be there. You and him, on a panel, answering questions, exchanging ideas, squaring off."

"Preston Brooks."

"The man himself. Just the two of you. Honestly, right now what we're thinking, just between us? Egg this thing on. Keep it going. I don't understand it, you don't understand it, Lucy—Lucy, do you understand it?"

She got on the line: "No."

"Nobody understands these things. But it's moving books. Moving books is good. Go down there. And, honestly, we had an apology, we had a statement, but we talked about it. You should just cut loose."

"Go to Malta and cut loose."

"Yup—no, wait. Marfa. Marfa, Texas. It's a town in Texas."

Marfa, Texas. I looked at a map. Way out there, West Texas. Me and Preston Brooks. An Old West literary showdown.

20

Egg-strewn plates clattered across the countertops. The jingle song of ice in glasses and the cascade of coffee into mugs, the "Good morning, Ida!"s and "See the game?"s and "Charles, don't play with that!" all melding together into a symphony of the ordinary. A diner. America. Ordinary morning. A place called Al's, just a mile from a cemetery, a tree-lined mile down Archer Avenue. And up above it all, the moon, where mankind had just planted its feet.

And at one table, a group of women. Looked like just back from church, dressed in their finest.

Perhaps, if the waitress had taken the time to guess, she would've known what they were. Where they were coming from. A funeral. A flag. Twenty years of funerals. Hugs. Tearstained letters. Private joys. Phone calls in the night. A waitress can always guess.

But if she did, she said nothing. She set the plates down. Said, "Enjoy, ladies."

Myra looked at hers. Watched the saffron current from the eggs that ran beneath the bridge of bacon.

And at the side of the plate, an apple slice. When Myra looked at it, danced it about her plate with a fork, it resembled another slice, a slice of map and jungle and shore that clung to the edge of Asia.

Eat, said Helena, leaning in. Eat, Myra. You have to.

I will, said Myra. I will.

I like this place, said Nellie, its a good, quiet place. She spoke with gratitude from beneath the brow of her church hat, her crown, the gleam illuminating her mahogany skin.

Food is a comfort, said Ruth, in that way Ruth had of saying what you felt, saying what was most true. Food is a comfort, she said, and bless God for that. If only for that.

Myra looked up at them. Friends, too, she said. Friends, too. They looked back at her, one to the other. One to the other. They looked back at the newest widow. And said nothing. There was no need.

Myra turned back to her plate, back to the runny eggs, the bridge of bacon. And that apple slice. The thin slice that looked so much like the place she'd never seen. The slice of earth and sorrow and bravery where her husband had fallen to the earth. And gone back to the earth.

The slice called Vietnam.

—excerpt from *The Widows' Breakfast* by Preston Brooks (Copyright © 2008 Penguin Press, reprinted with permission)

The Frito Chili Cheese Crunch Hungr-Buster is a cheese-burger covered with a thick lump of chili speckled with Fritos. It is a slop of beef, all of it ground and slick, many stages of processing away from actual steers. It is a French joke of what Americans eat and an American joke of what Texans eat.

That's what I ordered at the Dairy Queen in Marfa at four in the afternoon. I corralled the whole mess in my hands as orange, unnatural oils pressed out against my fingers.

This was warrior food. Combat food. Ass-kicking food.

Marfa is an interesting place. To get there, you fly to El Paso, which at first appears joyless—brown and dismal like a discarded cardboard box. But then you look across the river at the Mexican city of Juarez. A distant glimpse of *that* place is enough to make you want to plant grateful roses on the graves of El Paso's civic leaders.

Then you drive south for three hours across West Texas. Out in the open country, you pass a number of interesting things. Gullies and ravines and mesas and buttes. Rusted ranch gates and sunken houses with the roofs caved in. Cisterns set against the sage. Shadows moving along ridges. Moonish pock-marked landscapes. All that western stuff.

You may see, as I did, an eighteen-wheeler with a bumper sticker that reads GOD MADE TEXAS TO GIVE TRUCKERS SOME-THING TO DO, which is clever if theologically unsound.

On that road south, flanked by dry and empty ranches, you'll start to pass Border Patrol vans, with cheery green-and-white stripes that can lull you out of thinking about the ominous practicalities and complex geopolitics at work.

Then there's Marfa itself, which looks like "Friday Night Lights"-ville. I feel comfortable deploying the word *windswept* to describe it. There's a deserted quality; it looks the way towns probably will after the apocalypse, the way towns in movies look right before people realize there are zombies there.

The sign for the abandoned fifties Holiday Inn is faded into such perfectly retro elegance that you wonder if some hipster didn't invent it for an album cover. Above the wide streets there's a big water tower with MARFA written in block letters. An ornate courthouse presides over an empty square. Every few hours a freight train rattles through with its whistle set on maximum loneliness.

Marfa is famous for its Mystery Lights, dancing sky orbs that appear at night. It turns out these are just reflections of car headlights, but everyone treats them like they're the visions of Lourdes.

But the place has also become an artistic oasis. There's an old cavalry barracks where they kept German POWs during World War II. A conceptual artist bought and turned it into an art museum called the Chinati Foundation. He was the kind of guy who left the original signs in German on the wall. This museum lures a certain smileless European crowd, as well as feature writers for *The New York Times*. Nearby, bleak storefronts are being converted to minimalist galleries at an alarming rate. Marfa has the twin pillars of an artistic oasis: a good bookstore and a public radio station. The town has a bona fide, probably made-up, literary origin story, too. Marfa was named by the wife of a railroad baron in the 1880s, when railroad barons and their wives filled in maps on whims. She'd just finished reading the newly published *The Brothers Karamazov,* and she named this particular dot on the map after the servant character.

I've never read *The Brothers Karamazov.* I hear good things. It's a testament to the higher values of the 1880s that that's what a railroad baron's wife would read back then. These days, railroad barons' wives probably read Preston Brooks. But the point is, it's a perfect town for a literary festival.

More important, it was perfect ground for me.

In Marfa furrow-faced ranchers share space with exiled intellectuals. Texas cattlemen, the most no-bullshit people in the world, find common ground with hipsters so fed up with popular culture that they've moved to the desert.

Both those crowds should've agreed with me over Preston Brooks. Rancher types know bullshit when they see it. And intellectual types could enjoy the postmodern stunt of my writing a bullshit popular book.

I ate at Dairy Queen, because Dairy Queen is the people's food. And (in my admittedly confused logic) I was about to become the people's champion.

When my career as a novelist began, my ambitions were simple: to learn the con, make money, impress women, and get out. I'd sought to emulate Preston. But now the bizarre turns and strange travels of my past few months, and the electrifying controversy of the past week, had sped me into a new and grander role. Like it or not, what I'd done had come to stand for something grander—people were still sorting out exactly what. But this much was clear: no longer was I just another writer.

Tomorrow I'd destroy Preston.

I'd reveal him for what he was. With his prepackaged folkisms and his plaid shirt and his silver beard, he'd try to hoodwink readers as he had so many times before. But I'd be there! I'd call him on his bullshit! He'd sit there, quivering and exposed. It was going to be awesome.

To prep, I'd bought a copy of *The Widows' Breakfast,* and I flipped through it as I ate. It was as ridiculous as I'd hoped: brave children at funerals, tender female friendships, snow falling on proud brows: *A lustrous yearning from across the years . . . The bugler's adagio sounded above the grave. . . . The seasoned hands danced across her shoulders . . . Memory shifted and slid away like snow settling on the side of a sun-cooked mountain.*

I felt ready.

Now, I don't want to start any legal trouble with Dairy Queen. So let me stress here that correlation does not equal causation. It could've been the travel, it could've been something else I ate that day. I'm not accusing Dairy Queen or any of its subsidiaries of anything untoward. The girl behind the counter was wearing those clear plastic gloves, so I know basic sanitary practice was observed.

But the fact is that about an hour after I finished my Hungr-Buster, I began to feel very unpleasant.

Back at the Thunderbird Hotel I rolled around on the bed for a while. Then I lay on the calfskin rug on the floor and tried to massage my cramping stomach muscles into some kind of calm. I put a wet washcloth on my guts. It didn't work.

There were people in town for the book festival, reporters, too, I suspected. I'd planned on spending the evening winning a few of them over with personal-charm offensives over Shiner Bocks and Lucinda Williams, things on which all strata could agree.

But that was out of the question now. I knocked myself out with some Nyquil.

It was about ten when his voice woke me up. I knew it from the cadence, the crackle, though it was too faint to make out any words. He must've been out across the black gravel parking lot, by the fire pit. His curt laugh carried in the night air, and I could picture him as he must've been: arms crossed in a sweater, dispensing aphorisms for a semicircle of fawning admirers.

Preston Brooks, through the door, yards away. And though I fell back asleep, my sleep was bothered by alarming half dreams that appeared and vanished: Preston in a tank driving over a doghouse. A tiny me lost in his beard like a hiker in a forest. Preston eating Hungr-Buster after Hungr-Buster through a mouth in his forehead. Unsettling stuff, such that in the morning I was kind of a wreck.

But I'm not trying to make excuses.

The Arena

At the Marfa Book Company, the shelves were parted to the sides and the gap was filled by rows of folding chairs. A simple wooden table with two microphones, two glasses, and a single pitcher of water was set at the front.

The Audience

They were settling in by the time I got there. And they were from both categories. There were the pale and small-armed. But there were also broad-shouldered women with arms that looked like they'd been used for lifting grain sacks. Real Texans and exiled smarts. And combinations: in the front row a muscular older man, the kind of guy who maybe writes poetry but is still proud of his ability to drywall a house, leaned over to his thick-calved lady companion and said, "This should be interesting." There were several people typing on laptops.

To calm myself I scanned the audience and picked my target. She had sort of off-blonde hair, and in a tan skirt she was overdressed for the morning, which I liked. She was young but she wore on her face a semitired expression, as though she'd been exhausted by complicated and passionate love affairs, and she tossed back water from a plastic bottle she held with a sexy limpness.

Pregame

Preston wasn't there when I arrived. I cursed myself for showing up too early. Good power move on his part to make me arrive first.

The moderator, Ted, some kind of local radio guy, knew me by sight. He was a younger guy who looked like he ate a lot of crap that he knew he shouldn't. He came over, shook my hand. He thanked me for coming down.

"I really think this is going to be a fruitful discussion," he said. Then, excited, he said, "and feel free to cut loose as much as you want. I told Preston the same thing—I'm not gonna step in. We'll see where the conversation takes us."

He led me to the table and sat me down. I saw that in the back of the room they were setting up a camera.

"I'm sure you don't mind—we're taping this, show it on the community station."

The Arrival of My Opponent

Preston Brooks knew how to walk into a room.

He stood there, in the doorway for a solid minute. Completely still.

Then he began looking around. Slowly, like an alligator.

This was all an act, of course. He was waiting for people to see him. And after a few seconds, they did.

A guy in the audience jumped up—literally leaped out of his chair—and pointed to the stage. Preston Brooks nodded thanks, as though this guy was doing him a great favor by pointing out the stage.

Preston strode up. I tried to look relaxed. The radio guy said a few things to him that I couldn't hear over the sound of the filling-in audience.

Preston's presence, as he took his seat, was both scary and silly all at once. He gripped the chair with his hands as though it were a snake he was trying to strangle, then he lowered himself down.

Part of me wanted to lean over and explain everything to him. All this, how I'd gotten here. He looked weaker than he

had on TV, smaller. I could see his shoulders heave as he
breathed. I felt I could almost smell his breath, hints of leather
and apples.

Not knowing what else to do, I poured myself a glass of
water. From his shirt pocket Preston took out a leather notebook and jotted a note. He underlined it emphatically, three
times. Then he folded his arms and stared forward. I did, too.
I looked right into the camera and wished it wasn't there.

Nerves made the whole rest of the preliminaries zip by. I
glanced at Tan Skirt and saw her look back at me. Suddenly Ted
was introducing us. He didn't set it up as a debate or anything,
just sort of talked about how we were "two very different authors
with two very different views," and thanked us both for coming.

Kickoff

Ted turned to me.

"Pete, we'll kick things off with you. You had some interesting, and indeed controversial, things to say about Preston
Brooks in a recent TV interview—some of you may have seen
it. So let me ask you this—how do you think his novels are different from yours?"

Watch the video, if you haven't. I'm sure it's still on there somewhere.

On the video, my response sounds confident. I ramble a
little bit, and wave my left hand too much. My voice is, weirdly,
an octave too high. But basically I say what I meant to:

I say that I have a lot of respect for Mr. Brooks—I called
him this on purpose to make him sound like a boring teacher.

Obviously, I say, you have to give him credit for writing all those best sellers.

Then I say he's brilliant at what he does. He's absolutely brilliant at writing popular, you know, over-the-top books that, you know, women, old people, whoever, really love.

That he's great, truly great, at writing sentences that sound sort of grand and epic. That he's a genius, really, at coming up with plots that make readers cry and feel moved. I compare him to the guys who write greeting cards and commercials for detergent, and say they're all really brilliant at manipulating people.

And that, you know, who can blame him? I don't. That's what people want, and he's the best at it.

I say that he really inspired me, his whole, you know, schtick. I say I studied him, really, to try and write *The Tornado Ashes Club.*

But I say that obviously, I mean, his books are a little ridiculous. I mean, leprechauns? And cancer dads? And Katrina? And all those funerals? I mean, c'mon. It's all a bit much.

I was watching my target now, the woman in the tan skirt. She seemed to smile here. So I maybe got ahead of myself.

You can spot the exact moment, right on the video, where I half-smile back at her.

I decide to close out positive. So I say that, all in all, Preston deserves "a certain kind of respect" for what he does. After all, he's "a brilliant, top-of-his-game con artist."

The audio on the tape isn't good enough to hear this. But when I said that you could hear air going out of the room. You could feel the crowd almost recoil.

Then one by one they spring back forward. Because they realize Preston is about to unload on me. Ted fumbled with his mic, but couldn't interject himself in time to stop Preston with a question.

Here's a weird fact: looking back on it now, putting myself back in that chair as I drank water and let the words *con artist* sit in the air, I can't sort out whether or not I really believed what I'd just said.

Certainly I thought I did. But did I *really*? Or was I coasting by on some shell of self-deceit that I was just too cowardly to look through?

If you'd drugged me right then, given me some truth serum or something, would I have said the same thing?

I honestly have no idea. I can't remember.

Preston Unloads

He coughed. He took his time. He kept his arms folded.

"Until a week ago," he said—and he said this, and everything that followed, very precisely. Very clearly. Like a distinguished Latin teacher. But he wasn't directing it at the crowd. He was looking right at me, talking just to me, his crinkle-paper voice cutting the air.

"Until a week ago, I'd never heard of you. Pete Tarslaw. I hadn't heard of you or read your book.

"But then some friends told me about you. They said you'd written a book. Then you'd gone on television and pulled some kind of *stunt*.

"So I watched your television program. My daughter showed it to me. She seemed to think the whole thing was very funny. A young man poking fun at the old fart.

"Well, I like to be a good sport. Like to be in on the fun. But I didn't like this joke very much at all. It seemed to me, Pete Tarslaw, that you were a young man going around saying stupid things about writing. Something you didn't know a damn thing about."

His words, or at least the sound of them, had a grip on me. To try and wrestle out I offered a snarky smile to the audience.

No one returned it.

"You think I'm a con artist. You think I'm some Typewriter Johnson who puts pen to paper to sell armadillo soap. Well, I think that's a shame, a real shame. But I'm not surprised."

Here Preston looked away from me for the first time. He studied his shoes for a moment, then looked at the crowd. He knew how to stretch the time. Ted certainly wasn't moving.

"You know, my daughters tell me there's a drug now called Ecstasy. Imagine that. Ecstasy. The feeling I learned from a Shenandoah sunrise, or from gazing at Giorgione's *La Tempesta,* the feeling I had when I looked at my young bride, people get that feeling now from a drug."

He let that linger. I thought I saw an opportunity here. So I leaned into my microphone and made my **First Joke**:

"I don't really see how that's relevant," I said.

Nobody laughed.

Preston Brooks let the room not-laugh for a while.

"I'll tell you," he said. "I'll tell you why that's relevant.

"You seem to me like a lot of young men. And that's no crime. I was young and dumb once, too.

"So maybe you're young, and dumb. Maybe you've never done anything hard. Maybe you've never sweated. Or seen a wasted life at the other end of a bar. Or seen worry in a father's eye in a hospital hallway.

"Maybe you've never put your hand on the feet, the cold toes, put your fingers through the cold toes of your wife, who's died, alone, before you could get there. And now you touch the metal on the gurney, and now you touch her toes, and they're both cold now.

"Maybe you've never heard the shots—clickclick . . . BOOM, clickclick . . . BOOM—when they fire over a coffin with a flag draped on it.

"Maybe you've never seen an old man in Louisiana, sitting on a patch-tar roof. And he's weeping, a grown man weeping, a man who's seen a bushelful of bad things in his day, they're written on his face, but he's weeping like a little boy over a dog that's gone drowned.

"Maybe you've never felt the squeeze of a child's palm on your pinkie and your ring finger, as she tries to squeeze an extra bit of something, love maybe, right out of you.

"Maybe you've never lived in a place where you can hear the whine of oil derricks, and the people in town depend on each other, in relationships as deep and necessary as the animals on a reef.

"Maybe you've never felt that worry, that absolute sick, churning worry, when the bills come in and sit on the kitchen table until you're afraid to open envelopes, and your damn car won't work, and you'll have to take the bus three and a half hours, the prison bus, the shame of the prison bus, to visit your son who's locked up, just so you can sit and watch him lie to you, watch him tell you lies about how it's 'not so bad' inside, lie to you while you can see in his eyes that every day is killing your boy a cruel slow death. A death like Jesus himself died. And you just don't know what to do but beat your hands bloody against the cracked wall."

He took a breath.

"Maybe you've never sat at a bar, four whiskeys in, your whole life undone, but you sit there, tears streaming down your face, trying to write one true sentence ON A NAPKIN!"

That part rose into a crescendo. When he was done he slumped back into his chair for a minute, his eyes wet. He waited for a moment, as though refilling with indignation.

"Well I've felt that. Or something like it. I've felt that. I've listened to that. And my readers have, too.

"But you think I'm a con artist."

He unfolded his arms and let them lie upturned on the table.

"Truth is, I'm not surprised. Sad. Not surprised. Your generation is like that." Then he turned to the audience and smiled.

"You'll forgive me for saying that—*your generation*. I know I sound like an old man on a bus bench eating half a tuna sandwich. Well hell, I am an old man. Maybe not on a bus bench. Maybe no tuna sandwich."

He let the audience laugh for a minute. Then he snapped back at me.

"I've known clever young men like you, in love with no God save for your own cleverness. You're always looking for the falseness in everything. You're used to falseness. You grew up with that lie machine, the television. It's no wonder then that you look for liars everywhere. You make a sport of it. You chase priests and poets and policemen, writers, too. And when you find one, and catch him, you rub his face in the mud and dance about.

"The truth is, you have been cheated. You've had it too easy. You've never done anything hard. You've coasted by on sacrifices bought and borrowed."

Here I don't know what I was thinking. But I leaned forward again and interjected my **Second Joke**. And I'm embarrassed to report it, but it's on the video so I may as well.

"Our generation has, too, had it hard," I said. "What about the tech bubble?"

No one laughed.

After a solid eight seconds, Preston smiled a little.

"Jokes. Well all right. Young people should make jokes."

I thought maybe he was going to let me off with that. He did not. He pointed at me.

"Maybe you think anything earnest must be a joke. But you are wrong, damn wrong. Maybe you think I take things too seriously. But you're wrong there, too.

"You wrote your little book, *Tornado Ashes Club,* as some kind of joke. And my God, books are no jokes. Books save lives. We lose lives for books. So you better damn well think twice before you make a joke of them.

"You put something down on paper that you knew was a lie. That you knew was bad.

"That's the worst crime there is. That's a crime against readers. That's a crime against literature. That's a crime against anyone with a heart and a mind and a sense of compassion.

"You wrote your book to have a joke. To fool people. To impress a few girls and make a buck. You're like a naughty boy who apes the principal so he can get a few laughs.

"All right. Well let me tell you why I wrote my books.

"In 1653, England was falling apart. Young men like you were running about, smashing churches, tearing down altars. Laughing. Throwing mud.

"But in that year, in a place called Stanton Harold, a man built a church. There's a plaque in that church. I've seen it. And here's what it says."

Preston Brooks closed his eyes and declaimed. If you haven't seen the video, and you want to know what it sounded like, then read this next paragraph slowly and precisely, in a booming preacher voice:

"In the year 1653, when across the nation all things sacred were being demolished and profaned, this church was built by Sir Robert Shirley. It is his special praise to have done the best of things in the worst of times. And to have hoped in the most calamitous.

"To do the best of things in the worst of times," said Preston. "To hope in the most calamitous. That's why I write, young man.

"Are my efforts adequate? Are my books good enough? True enough? Do they capture what it feels like to be a widow who lost her husband in a foolish war? Or a teacher who sees her classroom flooded with swamp water? No. Hell no.

"But every day I sit down at my typewriter. Every day. And I make an honest try. Can you say that?"

He paused here.

My **Third Joke**: "Well, no, I don't use a typewriter."

No one laughed.

Preston breathed in through his nose.

"I make an honest try. Because I'm a writer. And that's

what a writer does. That's what a human being does. To try and capture this folly we call the world. This joy and this sorrow we call life. I write, sir.

"And if you think all my work is some trick, or some folly, well then let me say this so you can understand: if you think I'm a silly old man who still believes in silly nonsense like truth and love and beauty and honor and pride and sorrow and joy—*you're damn right I do.*"

So, okay. Given a few seconds, given an interjection from Ted or a station break or something, I could've thought of a response. I could've hit back. I bet I could've even made a fourth, and this time, good, joke.

I could've won the crowd back. I know it.

But there wasn't time.

Before I could think, before I could move, before I could figure out an appropriate expression and shift my face into it, I heard it.

It started snapping out from the back of the room. Patches of noise expanded and came together and grew stronger.

It's not that I couldn't believe it at first. But it took a few key seconds of neurons firing before I realized what it meant. My body figured it out first, actually, because suddenly my skin got blasted with sweat.

The crowd was erupting. Thundering, exhilarated, rapturous applause.

I looked up at the faces that blinded me like flashes. Through them, somehow, I made out the tan skirt girl, beating her hands, applauding as fast and as forcefully as she could.

They were with him. All of them. The ranchers, the intellectuals, everybody.

Something occurred to me then: *maybe there wasn't some-thing wrong with Preston Brooks. Or with the people who loved him. Maybe there was something wrong with me.*

I felt a terrible, wrenching feeling in my stomach.

It wasn't from the Dairy Queen.

21

Do you remember when we went to the old Presbyterian church? Grandmother said. The church up in Gethsemene? Up in that notch in the mountains that they called a village?

Yes, said Silas. I remember. I played in the rhododendrons. Pretended they were a cave. Pretended they were a pirate's cave and I was burying treasure.

That's right, said Grandmother, and she smiled. That's right. Do you remember why we went up there?

For the funeral, Silas said. He remembered.

Remembered the touch of old sorrowful hands, pressing against his scalp. Remembered the sight of somber nods, passing one another in the pews and the aisles. Remembered the taste of maple syrup, poured over pancakes at a mournful breakfast.

For the funeral of my cousin, he said.

That's right, said Grandmother. Poor girl. Poor girl burned to death, in a fire. Closed casket, shame to think. Pretty face like hers. "Amazing Grace" never sounded quite the same, not after she was gone. That voice of hers. That face.

But the choir sang it anyway, said Silas.

So they did, said Grandmother. So they did. And do you remember what you said to me, when they were finished singing?

I said it made my heart shake, Silas said.

That's right. That's right. It made your heart shake. And do you remember, Silas, what I told you when you said that?

You said—and Silas trembled, to think of the memory coming back. You said that's how you know something's true. You said that's how you know something's really true. When it makes your heart move inside you. That's when you know it's true.

—excerpt from *The Tornado Ashes Club* by Pete Tarslaw

An interesting fact about the US Attorney's Office in Boston is that they serve good coffee, Bay State Bean or something. Aunt Evelyn was there with me, and she seemed indifferent to it, but she has a very refined palate.

They had us sitting on blue plush chairs in a little lobby, which made the proceedings seem not too serious. There were even magazines, albeit boring ones: *Massachusetts Lawyer* and so forth. After about fifteen minutes of waiting I reached for one, but Aunt Evelyn looked over at me and shook her head. And certainly it wouldn't have helped if I'd been casually reading *Massachusetts Lawyer* when the prosecutors came in. The coffee was comfort enough.

Luckily for me, Aunt Evelyn was back to being kick-ass. She'd shown up for our meeting in an ageless gray wool lawyer suit. The frilly white-collar thing didn't soften her at all—she looked like an East German torturess.

You may wonder why the engines of federal justice were turning in such a way that it required my aunt to drive down from Vermont wearing a suit. And even now all the details have not been explained to my satisfaction. But Aunt Evelyn had made some calls and learned that the situation was indeed suit-wearing serious.

HOW WE'D ENDED UP HERE

An elderly Italian woman in an assisted living facility in Chelmsford received in the mail a packet of information about a mutual fund company called Via Appia.

She'd heard of mutual funds, and this one cited some intelligent-sounding ancient Roman analogies that warmed her heart and inspired confidence.

So she sent them all her money, which wasn't much. Via Appia had invested all of it in a brine shrimp company, without bothering about the necessary regulations or paperwork. The money never came back.

The misfortune would've been this poor woman's to bear alone, except that her son happened to be a Massachusetts state senator and the chairman of the Transportation Committee.

So the chairman called the attorney general, only to learn to his great indignation that defrauding old people in this particular way wasn't really a crime, at least not a state crime, so then he called the governor and made some irresponsible threats about highway funding. Then the governor called the US attorney.

This chain of phone calls ended with state troopers tracking down Jon Sturges. They did so in a cloddish enough fashion that Jon Sturges moved to the Cayman Islands. He didn't, however, allot much time to pack.

So the troopers found some pay stubs and such, which led them to my computer, which contained the very letter this elderly woman in Chelmsford had received. It had gone to some 200,000 nursing home residents, making it almost certainly the piece of my writing with the widest readership.

To be honest, after what had happened to me in Texas, I was numb to all this. I can't really remember feeling much passion either way about it.

Maybe a part of me was almost happy about it, happy the way you are when you get the punishment you know you deserve.

Maybe that's what made the coffee taste so good.

Finally the prosecutor came out and led us in. She wasn't even slightly intimidating—she introduced herself as Carolyn and she couldn't have been over thirty. She led us into a perfectly bland conference room. There was another prosecutor there, Mike, who was huge and buff, but in a going-to-the-gym-too-much way not in a busting-heads way.

There was a tape recorder, too. Aunt Evelyn took out her own tape recorder and put it next to theirs. "I trust no one objects?" This seemed to intimidate Mike and Carolyn, but they didn't object.

Then there was a round of legal discussion between Mike and Carolyn and Aunt Evelyn. I'd been firmly instructed to stay out of it, so I did. If they included all that preliminary stuff in *Law & Order,* each episode would have to be nine hours long.

Then Mike was allowed to talk to me.

"Mr. Tarslaw, we don't want to make a bigger deal out of this than it has to be. I can tell you quite explicitly that our goal is to bring charges against Mr. Sturges. Not against you or Mr. Mausbaumer."

"Mr. Mausbaumer?"

"Hobart Mausbaumer. He's your roommate, is he not?"

"Yeah, Hobart. He doesn't have anything to do with this."

Carolyn opened a folder and handed a paper to Mike, who looked it over.

"On 5/06/08, when our agents visited 1815 Lindsay Street, Apartment Five, to execute a warrant on your computer, Mr. Mausbaumer informed them unprompted that he had provided you with an unscheduled pharmaceutical, Reutical. At that point he was advised of his legal rights and declined counsel."

Mike looked up. "He's described here as being *very agitated and upset.*"

"Goddamn it Hobart!"

Aunt Evelyn didn't break. "I'd like to state clearly that this is new information. We're here to discuss a proffer for a charge of mail fraud—"

"Look," Carolyn said, "we're not the FDA. Reutical—it's not our business. You know the pressure we're under. We just want to get this concluded so we can pursue Mr. Sturges."

Then there was another round of legal discussion. Seriously, if *Law & Order* were even slightly accurate it would be crushingly dull.

The end result of all this is that I had to answer a few questions. Did I know Mr. Jonathan Sturges. Had I been in the employ of Via Appia Funds. Had I written documents on behalf of Via Appia Mutual Funds. So forth. There was only one that threw me.

"Do you know Mr. Hoshi Tanaka?"

"Wait—who?"

"Mr. Hoshi Tanaka. He's Mr. Sturges's partner."

"Is he a Japanese guy who goes to Wharton?"

"I have an address here of 65 North 34th Street, Apartment Six, Philadelphia, Pennsylvania."

"Christ."

"Do you know him?"

"No . . . I mean, no, I've never met him. I wrote his business school application essay."

More legal discussion. Carolyn handed Aunt Evelyn a document. She read it over. I signed it.

The end of all this was I was sentenced to six months of house arrest. But—thank God for Aunt Evelyn—I wouldn't have to wear one of those ankle bracelet things.

The house in which I was under house arrest was actually a condo. A move away from Hobart seemed like a good idea.

So I bought a one-bedroom place on Revere Beach. I had a view of the Atlantic after all. But if you've ever been to Revere Beach, you'll realize this was not quite a home from the back of the *New York Times Magazine*. It's one of those faded resort towns where framed pictures from century-old postcards are now unrecognizable. On the beach, chunky, grease-fattened seagulls pick their way through the waste of used condoms and torn-up lottery tickets, and Ziploc bags flap from the crevices in the wooden benches. Down the road is the dog track, Wonderland, the most ironically named place in the world, a hangout for degenerates who can't afford a bus ticket to the Indian casino.

Still, I paid for my one-bedroom up front, in cash, because *The Tornado Ashes Club* kept selling.

"Any press is good press," and there was plenty. Preston's tirade against me was replayed on *Fresh Air,* and, I'm told—although I couldn't watch—that the old bastard went on *Charlie Rose.* Once the criminal element was revealed, it was like a whole new basting and everybody went back for more. My name became a touchstone for pundits arguing about the vapidness of my generation and the demolition of standards.

The whole business raged on the Internet as well. I stopped Googling myself, out of sheer exhaustion, when somebody discovered I'd plagiarized passages from *Hearts of Ice and Blubber*. They had to fire David Borer for lousy editing after that came out, and what became of him I don't know. Lucy got his job. She also hooked up with Josh Holt Cready at a party.

My royalty checks got even bigger after the *Vanity Fair* article came out. I can't blame them for doing the piece—young literary prodigy turned mutual fund con artist and plagiarist is kind of a home-run story. But I wasn't thrilled with whom they chose to write it. Obviously, I'm no expert on ethics, but if Pamela McLaughlin's going to do an "in-depth investigation" of me, she should at least mention our night of passion at the W.

But whatever—it sold books. Things weren't so bad, really. I'd sit around and watch TV. Kelly's Roast Beef was within my 2,000-foot restriction, so I ate a lot of clam strips.

Aunt Evelyn still believed in me. So much so, in fact, that she worked an "educational exceptions" provision into my plea bargain. If I wanted to leave my home for "legitimate educational purposes," I just had to send a petition to Carolyn.

I only did this once, and it was to visit my alma mater.

Granby College had, at great expense and with enormous fanfare, hired away from Oxford this British professor of English Literature named Michael Mintz.

You maybe have seen this guy on *Fox News*. They love him there. He's got long hair and he always wears a scarf, and he's very pretty. His big idea, the idea that got him so much attention, is *free market criticism*.

Basically, he doesn't believe in literary merit or anything like that. According to him, the only way to judge a book, or any work of art, is by how popular it is. "Any other method," he says, "is nothing more than elitism."

When he got to Granby he sent me a very kind note. He said he was impressed by my "eye for the marketplace," and he invited me out to join him for lunch.

MY LUNCH WITH MICHAEL MINTZ

I had him meet me at Stackers, for nostalgia's sake. We both ordered Meaty Meat Combos, and he dove into his with manic English energy.

He told me he taught English 10B now, a class I myself had taken. I asked if they were up to *Middlemarch* yet.

"Oh no," he said, "that's been completely cut out. We're reading *The Diary of Penelope Smoot*. Marvelous book—in the 1870s it outsold *Middlemarch* threefold. It's a servant's narrative of her cruel mistress, sort of a *Devil Wears Prada* of its day."

He put his sandwich down and clasped his hands together. "What I ask students is—why? Why is a book so popular? What does it touch? Because people are the judge of books. Not academics. Not reviewers. People."

This point got him very agitated. He started to go off on how stupid academics were.

"Why should we trust the ethereal ever-changing whims of a self-appointed elite?" he said. "A hundred years ago, the 'learned professors' would've had us all bogged down in Latin verse and racialist studies of man. I say throw out the theory. Let's look at what's quantifiable. What can be measured. What the People want. There's no such thing as an 'underappreciated' novelist. Books are inexpensive to produce, inexpensive to buy—

they're an almost perfect free market, perfectly efficient, and they resolve themselves."

He went on in this vein for a while.

"But this is an idea that academics simply can't grasp. Try telling this to Harold Bloom at that lunatic asylum they run down in New Haven. Did you know," he said, "there was outrage—outrage—among a certain set of the Granby campus over signing me? Why? Because I was expensive! Well, absolutely! I'm good at what I do, and this is a free market! That's why I came to the United States at all—I'm not coming for free, am I? But academics, of course, are simply not used to competing in a market like that.

"See, you, I think, grasp this." The reason he'd invited me out here, it turned out, was that he wanted me to donate my papers to Granby. "We're going to start a new archive on all this. This is the future of literary studies. Market motive. The long tail. Profit-taking."

Then he started talking about Melville. "Think of Melville," he said. "Why did he write? *For money.* One reason only. Money."

"But wasn't *Moby-Dick* a failure, moneywise?" I asked.

"Of course. We don't read *Moby-Dick* in my class," he said. "We read *Typee*. Huge best seller in its day. Full of cannibals. Look," he said, "the novel was once a populist form, but these days it's like opera, kept alive by foundations and a few wealthy patrons. It can't sustain itself. If it wasn't for the Guggenheims and the MacArthurs, Thomas Pynchon would have to write for *CSI: Miami* and Cormac McCarthy would be a blackjack dealer."

Mintz went on—he was really worked up. "But what isn't dead is *story*. Please! Tell me a story! Everyone is begging! Look at the tabloids—Britney, Hazel Hollis, whatnot—they tell a story!

"What you should do now, of course," he said, "is write a memoir. Far and away the most popular genre of our time. Nothing compares. The novel's in the ash heap."

So that's what I decided to do. I decided to write a memoir.

But I resolved to make it as true as possible. I'd tell it the way it had happened. I'd get to the meat as efficiently as possible, cutting out the middle parts I'd learned to fill with lies and spackle. To tell my story, I'd need to include some examples of bullshit, but I'd leave those clearly cordoned off.

Here it is. I even managed to include a story about a murder.

Apologies to those who don't come off so well. But I get it as badly as anyone.

Michael Mintz was right—people do want memoirs. If I told you the advance I got for this thing you'd vomit with disgust.

I wrote most of it down at Sree's, after my house arrest was over. I'd drive down 93 and chat with Sree for a while. We'd talk about *Ghostbusters*. He told me the old man in the Patriots jacket had died. I'd order a fish fry and type.

During the time it took me to write this, I only read two books.

The first I found one day at the Stop & Shop. It was called *The Many Passions of the Bloodsweeps*. On the cover are the two impressively bosomed Bloodsweep sisters, Xenia and

Eustacia, in the respective embraces of Captain Topwater and Fermenteen Adanock. How this book compares to others in its genre I'm not sure, but there are some exquisite lines, like: *It was there, out in the poorly roofed bothy, between pitchforks and heaps of peat moss, pushed up against cracking oak boards, that Lady Xenia had first found the flower of her ladyhood blossoming, first felt the ache of woman, and first found its one effective salve—the arms of a boy, coiled with formations of muscle hewn from his labor.*

But the important thing is that this book was written by my former coworker Alice Dwyer, and I'd like to make up for some childish pranking on my part by recommending it here.

The second book I read was the one Lucy had given me a long time ago: *Peking* by Bill Lattimore.

Peking follows two characters. The first is a hunter-gatherer who's traveling across a valley 300,000 years ago. The second is an American paleontologist, Charles Naughton, working in China, who discovers the first man's skull in 1937. It's the story of the fossil known as Peking Man.

I'd heard of Peking Man, in passing, in some class or another. But when I was finished reading *Peking,* I felt I had to fling the book across the room, to get it away from me, like it was radioactive.

That's how powerful it was. It might be my special curse that I could tell just how good it was.

The book follows the story of the nameless man, who became a fossil. But it's not all *Clan of the Cave Bear* stuff—the language has this unbelievable resonance, it's like reading your own dream. The novel also tells the story of Naughton, who digs up this fossil, millennia later, just before the Japanese invade. It's two tiny stories, really, but somehow, together they slice a cross section of the whole of human experience.

It's a book about searching, and losing things. It's about human connections, how tangled we are with each other. How we struggle and grapple and claw our way across the earth. There are scenes in it, sentences even, that seem realer to me than my own memory—the man feeling a burning in his throat that his child has, too. Naughton turning the dust on his hands into mud as he pours a trickle of water down his arms. It's about fear and seizing. The way you have to settle. The way we're all cursed with an idea of perfect when the world is so messy. How there's never enough of anything. Mostly it's simple, tiny scenes—there's the Japanese invasion, but it comes in a broken-down truck, the skinny officer trying to hide how bad he has it. There's a tiger, but he's seen in snatches and glimpses and a quiver on the skin and when they finally kill him, his flesh hangs in the sun and gets pecked away by birds and flies, viscus drying into dust. You can feel thumbs pressing against rocks, and you're made to feel this stress, this weight we all shoulder, and you can feel the desperation to keep digging, to break through, to transcend the earth. As if there might be something other than the earth.

You get lost in the language of it, but not because it's trying too hard. It's not. What it's really about—and I thought about this for a whole day, sitting at the bar at Wonderland— is how the cruelties we inflict on each other start out so small but become inevitable. It's about what kind of creatures we are and how we came to be this way. These fictional characters that only exist as words on a page somehow seem to know better than I do how to live your life. That the only way to live is to lose yourself.

I can't even describe it right. And I won't bother excerpting it here. Go find it.

I wish I'd written something that good.